PENGUIN CRIME FICTION

RUMPOLE FOR THE DEFENCE

John Mortimer is a playwright, a novelist and a lawyer. During the war he worked with the Crown Film Unit and published a number of novels before turning to the theatre. He has written many film scripts, television and radio plays, including six plays on the life of Shakespeare, the Rumpole plays, which won him the British Academy Writer of the Year Award, "Unity," and the adaptation of Evelyn Waugh's *Brideshead Revisited*. His translations of Feydeau have been performed at the National Theatre. Penguin publishes his novels *Rumpole of the Bailey, The Trials of Rumpole, Rumpole's Return*, and *Rumpole and the Golden Thread* in single volumes and *The First Rumpole Omnibus*, containing *Rumpole of the Bailey, The Trials of Rumpole* and *Rumpole's Return*. A volume of John Mortimer's plays containing *A Voyage Round My Father, The Dock Brief* and *What Shall We Tell Caroline?*, his acclaimed autobiography, *Clinging to the Wreckage*, and *In Character* are also published by Penguin. John Mortimer lives with his wife and young daughter in what was once his father's house in the Chilterns.

John Mortimer

Rumpole for the Defence

Penguin Books

Penguin Books Ltd, Harmondsworth,
Middlesex, England
Penguin Books, 40 West 23rd Street,
New York, New York 10010, U.S.A.
Penguin Books Australia Ltd, Ringwood,
Victoria, Australia
Penguin Books Canada Limited, 2801 John Street,
Markham, Ontario, Canada L3R 1B4
Penguin Books (N.Z.) Ltd, 182–190 Wairau Road,
Auckland 10, New Zealand

First published in Great Britain by
Allen Lane in *Regina v. Rumpole* 1981
Published in Penguin Books in Great Britain 1982
Reprinted 1983, 1984
First published in the United States of America by
Penguin Books 1984
Reprinted 1984, 1985

Printed in the United States of America by
George Banta Co., Harrisonburg, Virginia
Set in Monotype Plantin

Contents

Rumpole for the Defence

Rumpole and the Confession of Guilt

This morning a postcard, decorated with an American stamp and a fine view of the Florida freeways, put me in mind of the long-distant day when my son Nick first left these shores, leaving his mother and father staring at each other in wild surmise alone in our 'mansion' flat in Froxbury Court, Gloucester Road. Nick had finished with Oxford and was about to take up the offer of a postgraduate course at the University of Baltimore, which would lead to his teaching sociology and eventually becoming the head of his department in Miami. Today's postcard was yet another invitation from our daughter-in-law, Erica, to hang up the wig, burn the *Archbold on Criminal Law* and retire to join Nick and his wife in the sunshine state, where Senior Citizens loll on beaches and never is heard a discouraging word from the likes of his Honour Judge Bullingham. If the time for such an uprooting were ever to arrive, it had not come yet. I still have enough strength and health to totter to my feet to address the jury. Pommeroy's claret still keeps me astonishingly regular and I am still more or less profitably engaged on the sort of work which I was doing in that far-off day when my son Nick first set off to seek a newer world and found a swimming bath, an outdoor cooking device, a 'car port' for two motors and my daughter-in-law, Erica.

I also remember the day Nick left for America because I was then defending a customer called Mr Gladstone in an attempted murder case which depended, in the main, on his own confession of guilt. Mr Gladstone was black. He lived in Brixton, and he was just sixteen years of age. I was reading his brief at breakfast with my wife Hilda (known to me as 'She Who Must Be Obeyed'), and something in the youth and boyishness of Mr Oswald Gladstone put me irresistibly in mind of Wordsworth. Picture me then, dressed for battle in black jacket, winged collar and striped trousers, champing toast, and quoting the old sheep of the Lake District.

> ' "There was a boy; ye knew him well ye cliffs
> And islands of Winander! – Many a time,
> At evening, when the earliest stars began
> To move along the edges of the hills,
> Rising or setting, would he stand alone."

More toast, please, Hilda.

> "Beneath the trees or by the glimmering lake;
> And there . . .
> Blew mimic hootings to the silent owls
> That they might answer him –"

Refill of coffee, please, Hilda!'

'Rumpole, I do wish you'd stop doing your legal work at breakfast. You're getting butter all over that brief. Now about Nick, about your son . . .'

'My client today is a boy, younger than Nick and engaged on rather less harmless pursuits than sociology. A brilliant client! I mean, he only took out a flick-knife and stabbed a young man in a bus queue. Outside Lord's Cricket Ground. At four o'clock in the afternoon! Well, I mean, if you have to do that sort of thing, at least do it during the hours of darkness and, if possible, not in St John's Wood Road.'

'Rumpole! I'm trying to have a serious conversation!' She gave me one of her severest looks.

'Well, I think the fellow who got stabbed took it seriously,' I told her. 'He was a total stranger, of course. Just someone my juvenile client felt like stabbing. Absolutely brilliant!'

'When are you going to say goodbye to your son, Rumpole, before he goes away to the other side of the world?'

There was a sinister charge lurking in Hilda's remark, but I had enough evidence to rebut her innuendo.

'I'm meeting Nick at twelve,' I told her complacently. 'In the Army and Navy Stores. I'll buy him a top coat for America, then we'll have a good lunch, steak and kidney pud, I imagine, something of that nature. I've got to get back to Chambers for a four-thirty conference, so you give him tea, and then he's off to the airport!'

'How can you meet Nick at twelve o'clock? You'll be in the Old Bailey at twelve o'clock.' She launched into her cross-examination. Again I had my answer ready.

'My case'll be over in half an hour. It's just a shortie. The young hopeful will have to plead guilty. Mr Gladstone signed a full confession of guilt to Detective Inspector Arthur, who is a most reliable officer. He grows prize chrysanthemums.' Hilda was momentarily floored by this answer, but She came back fighting.

'I don't know why you have to go down to the Old Bailey at all, on Nick's last day.'

'They say crime doesn't pay, but it's a living, you know. That nice breakfast egg of yours is probably a tiny part of the proceeds of an unlawful carnal knowledge.'

It wasn't an answer that pleased Hilda, and She came back with a sharp one below the belt.

'You're an Old Bailey hack, that's what you are, Rumpole,' She said. 'I heard your Head of Chambers, Guthrie Featherstone, say that at the garden party. "Dear old Rumpole," he said, "is a bit of an Old Bailey hack!"'

Hilda, I thought, had gone too far. I'm not exactly a hack. I've been at the work for longer than I can remember and, as is generally recognized down at the Old Bailey, there are no flies on Rumpole. After all I cut my teeth on the Penge Bungalow Murders. I could win most of my cases if it weren't for the clients. Clients have no tact, poor old darlings. No bloody sensitivity! They *will* waltz into the witness-box and blurt out things which are far better left unblurted. I suppose, when I was young, I used to suffer with my clients. I used to cringe when I heard their sentences and go down to the cells full of anger. Now I never watch their faces when sentence is passed. I hardly listen to the years pronounced and I never look back at the dock.

These thoughts were occurring to me as I put on the wig and gown, and tied a moderately clean pair of bands round my neck in the robing room. My old friend, George Frobisher, was standing beside me, dressing up for some crime, and we found ourselves chatting about our work for the day.

'My man decided to rob a dance hall on the night of the Police Ball!' George and I appeared to have no luck with our clients.

'We only get the stupid villains, George.' I tried to cheer him up.

'Why's that?'

'The bright ones are all on holiday in Majorca. My little attempted murder's bound to be a plea, of course.'

'Bates isn't too bad on a plea.' George confirmed my own ‾iew of my Judge. 'It's when you fight he gets so sarcastic.'

'All over in half an hour! I'm meeting my son Nick, you know. He's off to America.'

'You're proud of him, aren't you, Rumpole?'

'Three years doing politics and sociology. Postgraduate? Of course! Nick's got the brains of the family.'

'You're proud of that boy, Rumpole!'

Of course George was perfectly right. I thanked my lucky stars for Nick, and not for the first time I wondered what on earth I'd do if I'd given birth to one of the Oswald Gladstones of this world, a boy who apparently stabbed cricket fans simply because they were there. He even failed as a murderer and would have no doubt to plead guilty to an attempt only. Try as I might, I couldn't find a satisfactory explanation for Oswald Gladstone. I mean, I believe in Mutual Aid, Universal Tolerance, and the Supreme Individual. At heart, I've long suspected I'm an anarchist. Man is born free and is everywhere in chains. But my darling Count Leo Tolstoy, or jolly Jean-Jacques Rousseau, or even that old sweetheart, Prince Peter Kropotkin, would have drawn the line at shoving a flick-knife into a complete stranger, in broad daylight, waiting outside Lords for a number thirteen bus. For a whim!

I was still troubled by these difficult matters when I met my eager Welsh solicitor, Mr Winter, an ardent reader of *New Society* and a pillar of the Islington Labour Party, who was accompanied by his articled clerk, Jo (who was in turn accompanied, as always, by a well-thumbed copy of *Time Out*). We had arranged to fortify ourselves with cups of coffee (scarcely distinguishable from tea) in the canteen at the Old Bailey.

'What surprises me,' Jo said with deep suspicion, 'is how the other boys got away – including Ginger Robertson.'

'Surprise, surprise! Everyone got away. Except one little black boy.' Winter smiled in a meaningful way. 'Mr Rumpole'll crucify the police on this one.'

'Crucify them? What for exactly, Mr Winter?' I asked.

'Racialism. You'll roast them alive. Like you did in the Penge Bungalow Murders.'

'What was that, Mr Winter?' Young Jo is surprisingly ignorant of the great moments of legal history.

'Before you were born, Jo. Before ever you were born, Mr Rumpole was crucifying the police!' Winter told him proudly.

Poor old Winter! The gullible old sweetheart believes that the customer's always right. He can't tell a dodgy car salesman from the unknown political prisoner. It was a sign of Winter's incorrigible optimism on behalf of his clients that he went on to say, 'You'll have a bit of fun with this one, Mr Rumpole.'

'Fun, Mr Winter? You call standing on your hind legs to plead guilty for a Jamaican teenager who pushes a knife into anyone who crosses his path – fun? What do I say to the Judge? "Do understand, my Lord. He'd just seen the West Indies drop a catch. Can I have a 50p fine, and time to pay?" '

'Did you say, "plead guilty?" ' Mr Winter sounded deeply hurt.

'Have you got any other ideas?' I asked him.

'They pick on these boys.' Winter gave me his usual speech. 'That's what we've got to hammer home to the jury. The police victimize them, Mr Rumpole.'

'You mean the dear old British bobby has a blind, unreasoning prejudice against boys who stab people in bus queues?' I asked, purely for information.

'Anyway, can they prove it? No one identified him.' Winter, the optimist, turned his attention to the facts.

'That's true. He was just another boy with a flick-knife. A common sight, apparently, at the St John's Wood roundabout.'

'Fingerprints were all smeared. There were no bloodstains on his clothing,' Winter remembered.

'I really wonder why they dragged us out of bed to come here at all,' I murmured.

'So where's the prosecution case?' My instructing solicitor concluded his well-reasoned address.

'Gone! Vanished into thin air, Mr Winter!' I encouraged him. 'We'd get our costs against the police, a gold watch donated from the poor box, and have every Inspector in court demoted to the rank of P.C. If it wasn't for one tiny triviality.'

'What's that, Mr Rumpole?' Winter frowned.

'Our brilliant client made a full, frank, free confession to the police – signed and witnessed.'

'A confession to the police!' Jo repeated with contempt.

'He confessed to Inspector Arthur of E Division, a gentle, fatherly officer with a green finger for chrysanthemums,' I reminded them both as Mr Winter searched among his papers, and found a much-used photostat.

'Here's an article that might help from the *New Society*, Mr Rumpole. It gives you figures on the arrests of black teenagers in one square mile of London. There's an analysis in depth of racialism in the police. Obviously it's based on strong feelings of sexual jealousy.'

At which point Inspector Arthur, a grey-haired and bene-volent-looking man in plain clothes, passed with his side-kick Sergeant Shaw. They were carrying cups of coffee. I wished the Old Bill a cheery goodmorning.

'Nice to see you, Inspector,' I said. 'Chrysanths all right, are they?'

'Managed a First at the Division Flower Show, anyway,' the Inspector said modestly. 'See you in Court, Mr Rumpole.'

'In Court. Yes. What do you want me to do?' I asked Mr Winter as the officers passed by. 'Get Arthur to admit he forged the confession in a blue fit of penis envy? That'd give the old sweetie on the bench a fit of the vapours.' I lit a small cigar and Winter sounded disappointed as he said, 'Well you know best, Mr Rumpole.'

'Yes,' I agreed. Winter was still looking through his file hope-fully.

'We've got one character witness,' he said. 'The vicar. A Rev-erend Eldred Pickersgill. From the Sandringham Road Boys' Club.' Winter seemed proud of his coup and I hated to dis-illusion him.

'The reckless use of an offensive weapon will be far out-weighed by some clerk in holy orders who says the lad's ping-pong shows promise!' I said unkindly. 'We must face facts, Mr Winter. Oswald Gladstone'll have to plead guilty.'

I thought it might help us, calling a vicar.'

'You, Mr Winter, a founder member of the Islington Humanist Association?' I looked at him sadly. 'You fall back on a dog-collar?'

'Wouldn't the Judge like it?'

'Nothing inflames a sentence so much as an over-eager cleric. That's my experience. We'd better go down.' I stood up and the soliciting gentlemen followed me with Mr Winter still protesting weakly. 'There's a lot to be said for our client,' he said.

'Always,' I agreed, and then Jo reminded me. 'His mother put him in care when he was four. Can you imagine? Taking a little kid to the Brixton magistrates and handing him over as a menace to society. Can you imagine doing that?' As a matter of fact I couldn't.

It's part of the life of an Old Bailey hack to spend a good deal of his time down the cells. You walk in past the old door of Newgate, kicked and scarred, through which generations of villains were sent to the gallows or the treadmill. There's a perpetual smell of cooking down the Old Bailey cells, and the screws are often to be found snatching odd snacks of six-inch-thick jam butty and gallons of tea. When I asked the officer in charge of the gate if Mr Gladstone was at home, he said, 'I don't think he's gone out to lunch with the Lord Mayor.' He called down the passage, 'Counsel to see the piccaninny!'

You know what life at the Old Bailey blunts? It blunts the sensitivity. When you've been round the place as long as I have the sensitivity comes out like hair on the comb. Mr Gladstone was brought to us in the interview room. He was wearing a sharp suit and had a small trilby hat perched on his head. His smile was wide and he looked determinedly brave. He greeted me with, 'Who are you, dad?'

'This is Mr Rumpole, your counsel; he's defending you,' Mr Winter explained and Oswald Gladstone said proudly, 'I don't need no brief. I'll just tell the Judge, Ginger done it, didn't he?'

'Ginger Robertson,' Winter explained to me, 'is one of the boys that went missing. That's our defence. If you can destroy the police evidence.' I looked at my watch, we hadn't got all the time in the world, if I was to meet Nick in the Army and Navy and keep our appointment for lunch.

'How do you know Ginger did it?' I asked. 'Did you see him with the knife?'

'After. I see him with the cutter after. Ginger throwed it away, didn't he?'

'You tell us, old dear. Did you know he was going to use it?'

'Use it? What you mean?'

'Did you know Ginger might use the cutter?'

'I tell you, dad. I know nothing about that.' Young Oswald Gladstone looked round at us, three men all there because of him, and said proudly, 'Got me in a big Court, haven't they? Number One Court.'

'Oh yes, Mr Gladstone. You're a star,' I assured him. 'Why did Ginger do it?'

'Why?'

'Yes. Why stab a man whom none of you apparently knew?'

'I guess Ginger didn't like them M.C.C. supporters.'

I stared at Oswald then, and Mr Winter supplied his usual explanation. 'There was anti-coloured feeling on the ground. I told you, Mr Rumpole. This case has political undertones.'

'But this old darling at the bus queue. He hadn't even *been* on the ground!' Oswald smiled and blew out smoke from the cigarette Jo had given him. 'Guess Ginger couldn't find any M.C.C. supporters, and this fellow was there like. So Ginger said, "I might as well cut him." '

'Oh, dear me. How would jolly Jean-Jacques Rousseau explain all that?' I heard myself saying it aloud, and Oswald looked at Mr Winter. 'What's he on about,' he asked.

'Mr Rumpole is a very experienced counsel. If we can destroy the police here, sir . . .' Mr Winter turned to me.

' "If", "if". And if the Judge turns out to be a Jamaican teenager with form we might have a chance. Speaking for myself,' – I looked at the diminutive client, and said – 'I don't believe Mr Gladstone meant to kill him.'

'Ginger carried the knife! That's what he says.' Jo was still fighting.

'Ginger formed the intention, quite clearly,' Mr Winter argued.

'See, dad,' Ossie told me. 'Ginger don't take all the trouble to carry no knife unless he use it sometimes.'

'They carry these knives,' Jo gave his favourite explanation, 'to prove their virility.'

'I'll tell the Judge that. In his day it was conkers.' I had to think of a way of saving Mr Gladstone a long stretch and I had Nick's farewell to consider. So I asked, 'Who's prosecuting?' At which Mr Winter went through his papers again and said, 'Mr . . . Piecan.'

'Magnus Piecan? What a bit of luck! I might just get him to swallow A.B.H.?'

'Actual Bodily Harm,' Winter explained to Oswald, and I asked our client, 'You'd plead to that, of course?'

'What they give me for that?' Mr Gladstone sounded interested.

'Nine months – a year. That suit you?'

'You want me to do a year? For something I never done?'

'You'd rather fight, and do four years for what you say you never done? The Judge'll give you full credit for admitting . . .'

'Admitting? What I didn't do.'

'Look at it this way. What's the credit in admitting something you *did* do. Not much credit in that, is there?'

'Are you taking the mick out of me?' Mr Gladstone was right of course. It was a joke in poor taste, and I apologized. 'I'm sorry. It's a bad habit.'

'I tell you truth, dad. I never done this cutting.'

For an answer I dived into my brief (always a rash thing to do) and brought out a single, but most unfortunate, sheet of paper, and started to read from it aloud.

'My name is Oswald Montgomery Gladstone, though in our gang they calls me "Blades",' I read, and then asked Ossie, 'Is that what they call you?'

'Blades,' Mr Gladstone answered proudly. 'That's right. That's my name, with the others like!'

' "I mean," ' I went on reading, sure that Oswald's denials

wouldn't survive in the face of his confession, ' "I know you found the dagger so I better come clean, guv'nor. Anyway if you nabs Ginger he'll grass on me. We was mad at the M.C.C. supporters what annoyed us. So when I left the ground I had my knife ready but the M.C.C. blokes all scarpered. 'Cos I had the weapon I felt a bit of a fool not using it. And there was this bloke standing. So I just let him have it in the Auntie Nellie. I'm very sorry for all the trouble I caused." Signed O. Gladstone and witnessed D.I. Arthur and D.S. Shaw.'

'I told them.' Mr Gladstone shook his head. 'Ginger done all that.'

'Did you read this written confession, when you were in the police station?'

' 'Course I did.' Now Oswald seemed vaguely annoyed at my questions.

'Did you understand it?' I asked.

'I read it through, didn't I?' Oswald was becoming belligerent.

'I wasn't there. You've got to tell me.'

'Yes. I read it through.'

'Why did you sign it. If it wasn't true?'

'I got bored. They was going on so long. You ever had questioning in the nick?'

'Not . . . as far as I remember.'

'It gets boring. You'd do like anything to get it over with.'

'To get back to reading a comic in the cell?' I wondered, and again my question had a curious result. Oswald seemed delighted by it. 'Reading!' Ossie said proudly. 'That's it. I was doing reading. Tell you what. If I signed that, they promised me a smoke.'

'Didn't it strike you as a rather expensive cigarette?'

I looked sadly at Oswald, and decided that my only course was an approach to my learned friend, Mr Magnus Piecan. My worst suspicions about sport had been confirmed, it brings out the very worst in people. Football leads to violence and cricket to murder. God knows what ludo would do to a man.

Magnus Piecan spends his life trying to be a Judge. I believe that he thinks that a Judge is the only person in Court whose hands don't sweat and whose mouth isn't dry with panic, which may not be entirely true. Dear old Magnus is so afraid of doing the wrong thing that he makes notes with ten different coloured pencils, and never gets to his feet without checking his fly buttons.

'You for the black teenager, Rumpole?' he asked me, when we tracked him down, pacing nervously in front of old Bates's Court, waiting for the case in front of us to finish.

'Yes, I am, as it so happens,' and I tried an old gambit calculated to increase his nervous tension. 'As a matter of fact I heard from the Judge's clerk, Bates, J., wants to get away early today.'

'Tickets for Glyndebourne?' Piecan made the assumption.

'Glyndebourne? Probably all-in wrestling at the Wembley public baths. His clerk hopes very much the Judge isn't going to be kept late.'

'Well, this isn't going to take long, is it?' Piecan asked nervously.

'Long?'

'I mean, I can't really see where the defence . . .'

'Give it a couple of weeks,' I interrupted him airily. 'Three possibly. It's not a long point, but I'll have to go into it in a *little* detail. You appreciate the point, of course?'

'The point?' Poor old Piecan looked totally confused.

'The point of law,' I said, mysteriously. 'It's rather a nice one, isn't it? You spotted it, of course.'

'The point of law, Rumpole?'

'I knew you would, you clever old sweetheart, you dear old brain box. I made sure the point would not have eluded you. So we may get a pretty rough ride from the Judge, and you'll have to bear the brunt, of course, opening a two-week case before an impatient chap like Bates. Well, good luck to you.'

'Is it really going to take two weeks?' Piecan's voice was tremulous.

'Up to you, old fellow. Entirely up to you, if you want to shorten it.'

'I mean, I told my clerk it might be a plea.' Piecan sounded hopeful.

'That's what I told my client as well,' I chimed in gleefully. 'This is a case, I told him, where the prosecution will almost certainly make us an offer. Now, old love, what *are* you offering us?'

'I don't quite see what I *can* offer.' Piecan was puzzled and not happy.

'Don't you? Use your imagination, Piecan. Consider the mind of a boy! You see they were only playing games!' I made a few sword passes with my Pentel, to demonstrate. 'Rapier and dagger, that's two of your weapons! Have at you! Cardinal's lackey! Take that! From Rupert of Hentzau! You know how boys play games, don't you?'

'I suppose so,' said the mystified Piecan. Of course he didn't know; he was born aged forty with a thorough knowledge of the law of torts. 'What you're saying is, no criminal intent?' Piecan put it in the legal language he understood.

'They were fooling about,' I told him. 'My boy lunged at an imaginary musketeer, and winged a real live accountant from Muswell Hill.' I put my arm through his and walked him out of my instructing solicitors' hearing.

'As we lawyers say, Magnus, no bloody criminal intent whatsoever. What does that make it? You were at the crammers last.'

'Actual Bodily Harm.'

'I thought you might accept "Possessing an Offensive Weapon".' I tried to look gloomy.

'It'll have to be A.B.H.' Piecan was determined to be tough with me.

'Hard-hearted Magnus! Ah well, you've got your job to do.'

'I'll have to take instructions.'

'Take them, then, quickly.'

'By the way, Rumpole,' Piecan paused with a sudden doubt. 'Why's your chap called "Blades"? Because he's the one that carries the knife?'

'Of course not. The old dear's a snappy dresser. A masher. A dandy. A *blade*! Don't you know the expression?'

Anyway Piecan filtered off to consult his prosecution masters. I was lighting a small cigar as Mr Winter came up to me, and again showed his ignorance of the perilous nature of our position.

'What're they up to, Mr Rumpole? Got cold feet, have they?'

I looked at my watch. It was nearly ten. By eleven, it should all be over. 'I'm meeting my son, you know, Nick,' I told Mr Winter. 'He's off to the United States, to study social sciences, which are a mystery you probably understand. Yes. I think it'll turn out to be a plea.'

'You mean they'll want us to accept Actual Bodily Harm?' Mr Winter looked less than pleased that an agreement was in sight.

'Given a following wind, we might edge them into it.'

'I don't think Gladstone's the type who'll want to play ball, Mr Rumpole.' Mr Winter shook his head gloomily.

'Play ball? He's being offered a remarkably easy way out. He'd be a lunatic not to take it.'

One thing you can never guarantee about clients is that they *won't* behave like lunatics. Piecan came back and offered us a nice quick and easy plea to Actual Bodily Harm. Lunch with Nick now seemed a certainty. But when we put the deal and all its advantages to Mr Oswald Gladstone, he simply said, 'I can't do it.'

'Look, Ossie. Blades. Mind if I call you Oswald?' I started.

'Call me what you like, dad.'

'If only you had someone you trusted. I wish your family were here to advise you. Perhaps your mother?'

'She gave him to the Brixton magistrates,' Mr Winter reminded me.

'That's right. Yes. Well, your father.'

'My baby father?'

'The man his mother was living with at that time,' Winter translated. 'He's back in Jamaica, and his mother is living with Oswald's social worker, a Mr Hammurabi.'

'Well, get Hammurabi here.'

I wanted someone to advise Oswald for his own good, but Mr Winter opened his file again and gave us another jewel. 'Mr Hammurabi wrote us a report. He thinks Oswald should never have been let out of the detention centre.'

'Isn't there *anyone* in your family to advise you?' I asked Oswald, almost desperately.

'You my brief, ain't you? You tell me what to do.'

He was absolutely right of course. I took a deep breath and said. 'All right, Mr Gladstone, I'll advise you, to the best of my poor ability, as your counsel. Plead guilty to Actual Bodily Harm! You're risking four years, maybe five if you fight the attempted murder. It's a hell of a great bloody risk, my dear old thing.'

'You mean I don't have no chance?' Oswald asked the question, and I answered it as well as I could. 'As much chance as I have of leaving these marble halls and spending the evening of my days in a little villa in the South of France, being poured out long pink drinks by expensive secretaries. No chance. No.'

'You got another case you want to do, you want to go work for some of them rich villains?' Oswald looked at me, he seemed very angry. 'What's the matter with my case? Too much like hard work?' I didn't answer him and he sat down, suddenly deflated. 'All right. I'll plead guilty then! If that's what you want, I'll plead bloody guilty! My Mum – she wants me put away. All right. I'll plead guilty to something what I never done!' I lit a small cigar, and then I asked him, quietly. 'Are you still telling me – you didn't stab anyone?'

'Look, dad. I never had the knife!'

'Are you still telling me that?'

'You don't believe me?' Oswald looked deeply hurt.

'What I believe isn't of the slightest importance. Is that what you're still telling me?'

'I'm still telling you that. Yeah.'

The most common question I'm asked by such non-legal characters as cross my path, or get talking to me over a glass in Pommeroy's Wine Bar, is how you can defend a customer when you know he's guilty. Well, the answer is, of course, that you don't. Once the old darling tells you that he did the deed, you've got to advise him to plead guilty, admit all and take the consequences. If he refuses to agree, then you must leave him to his own devices. This is not so much a code of morality as a reflex action, an admission of guilt in conference means the end of the road for Rumpole. But the converse is also true. If a client insists that he's innocent, and maintains this attitude against all odds, you can't finally lead him into Court and force him to plead guilty. I may have been, at this moment, just Mr Oswald Gladstone's humble servant, but if My Master's Voice still insisted that he was innocent there was no possible manner in which I could pretend to the Judge that he was ready to surrender. These were the simple rules I had to obey in the end, even if they put paid to luncheon with my son Nick.

'If you still tell me you didn't stab anyone,' I told Oswald, 'we've got to fight the case, and that's all there is to it.'

It was then, of course, that Mr Winter began to get cold feet. 'Listen, Ossie,' he said, 'perhaps it would be more sensible . . .'

'If he goes on telling us he's innocent we've got to fight,' I repeated. 'Just give me five minutes to ring up the Army and Navy Stores.'

'Oh, is that Coats and Macintoshes? It's about my son Nick. He'll probably walk into your department at approximately midday. Well, I imagine you're pretty empty, aren't you, now we've lost the Empire?'

I was standing in the telephone box outside No. 1 Court, chattering to the Army and Navy. Oswald's instructions had meant a radical change in my plans. As I spoke, I happened to notice a worried-looking person in clerical garb loitering outside the window. However, I carried on my conversation with Coats and Macintoshes.

'Nick? Well, he's about twenty-three. Hair brown. Eyes blue. No visible distinguishing marks, that sort of thing. Please tell him, his father's stuck down at the Old Bailey. Thank you.'

I didn't have enormous hope in my message getting through, but there was nothing else I could do in the time available. As I emerged from the confined space, the cleric called my name.

'Mr Rumpole!'

'Yes.'

'I did so want to meet you. I'm Ossie's father.' I looked at the undoubtedly white padre in some confusion. 'His father in God you understand,' the man of the cloth explained. 'Eldred Pickersgill. I'm priest at St Barnabas Without. There's good in that lad, Mr Rumpole, real good in him, deep down somewhere!'

'Pity he doesn't bring it up and give it an airing occasionally,' I said on my way to the Court door.

'He's a hard worker. He works hard at his classes. No result as yet. Absolutely no result. But Oswald is not discouraged. He is, in my view, a natural optimist.'

'That's why we are fighting this case.'

I was about to go through the swing door and on to the battlefield when the vicar had an afterthought.

'Oh, Mr Rumpole,' he said. 'If you do call me as a witness, I prefer not to swear on the Bible.'

'What's the matter, Vicar,' I said severely. 'Have you no religion?' And I left him to attend to my secular affairs.

When I was a young man, just starting at the bar, the old Judges used to scare the living daylights out of me. Terrible old darlings they were, who went back to their Clubs and ordered double muffins after death sentences. They used to be bright purple with rage, or white as paper with voices like ice cracking as they put the boot in. All the same, you could work on those old Judges. You could divert their rage on to the opposition, or move them to tears about an old lag's army record. 'I agree, he has his faults, my Lord, but he did extremely well on the Somme.' Mr Justice Bates was a newer type of Judge, a civil servant, with not a tear in him. I could never get on terms with Bates. There he was, at the start of R. *v*. Gladstone, giving me a look of vague disgust, as if he were Queen Victoria with a bad period. There was nothing for it, however, but to join battle, and at first R. *v*. Gladstone proceeded uneventfully.

Detective Inspector Arthur had just finished giving evidence at the end of the prosecution case when I rose to cross-examine, and I was aware that the judicial atmosphere was somewhat chilly. Perhaps the old darling on the bench was a member of the M.C.C. All the same, I launched cheerfully into the first question.

'Mr Arthur. You would agree the only real evidence against my client is this statement he is alleged to have signed at the police station?'

'Isn't that evidence *real* enough for you, Mr Rumpole?' said the learned Judge. You see what I mean by the judicial atmosphere.

'We shall see, shan't we?' I could see Bates, J., looking displeased as I said that. 'Have you the alleged statement there, Inspector?'

'I have, my Lord.' Mr Arthur addressed the Judge respectfully, and the Judge looked respectfully back. I intruded on this mutual respect with another question.

'Did you read that document through to my client, Mr Gladstone, before he signed it?'

'As I remember, he read it himself.'

'You're sure of that?' I challenged him. A memory of something young Oswald had said in the interview room had given me an idea.

'Yes. Quite sure. As a matter of fact he read it aloud to me.'

'He read it all through out loud?' I thought that was unusual, and decided to pin the Inspector to his story.

'Yes, he did, my Lord.' Mr Arthur again got a glance of approval from the bench.

'And you didn't read it back to him?'

'No. I don't believe so.'

'You swear you did not?' The Judge looked as if he didn't care for my doubting the words of a police officer, but the Inspector gave me his answer.

'I swear I didn't read it to him. Mr Gladstone read it to himself.' I picked up the document in question and looked at it with mild distaste.

'And this is a statement alleged to have been made by a West Indian teenager?'

'It was made by your client.'

'Every word his?'

'Every word.'

'Oh dear me, Inspector, don't you think you officers ought to brush up on your Jamaican?' There was a slight stir of laughter in Court in which the Judge didn't participate. After the usher had called, 'Silence,' the Inspector looked vaguely hurt and said, 'I don't know what you mean sir.'

'Neither do I, Mr Rumpole,' the Judge grumbled. I continued to address the witness. 'Just that you've composed this piece of sparkling prose in the dead language of dear old Edgar Wallace.'

'Mr Rumpole,' the Judge answered for the witness. 'Are you suggesting that your client's statement was *composed* by this officer?' So then I had to explain to the judicial old darling, as to a child, 'I am simply suggesting, my Lord, that the whole shooting match comes out of the old police book of verbals. No self-respecting young criminal talks like that nowadays, does he?'

It was then that my son Nick walked into Court, as he had done in his schooldays to listen to my old murders. Although this was only an 'attempt', I was determined to put on a good show for Nick. I beckoned to him to come and sit beside Mr Winter and Jo in the seat behind me. I whispered my apologies for not turning up in the Army and Navy, and he whispered that he'd telephoned my Chambers and discovered where I was to be found. And then His Lordship asked if he could have a few moments of my valuable time.

'My Lord, by all means.' I gave Mr Justice Bates my full attention.

'You were suggesting to the Detective Inspector that this statement was not couched in the language of "a self-respecting young criminal".'

'Of course it isn't. It's the language of a middle-aged Detective Inspector.'

'Mr Rumpole, the jury may not be as expert as you are on the way "self-respecting" criminals talk.' I ignored the somewhat snide innuendo and said with a smile, 'Then let me demonstrate, my Lord. Let's read it together, Detective Inspector.'

'Very well, sir.' He was always cooperative, the dear old chrysanthemum grower. I started to read from Oswald's statement. ' "I know you found the dagger so I better come clean, guv'nor." You left something out, didn't you? What about "it's a fair cop" and "you've got me bang to rights"?'

There was a louder laugh. The usher called, 'Silence,' again, and the Judge's voice was icy. 'Mr Rumpole, is this cross-examination meant to be taken seriously?'

'Only if this bit of paper is meant to be taken seriously, my Lord,' I said, and went on reading before he had time to interrupt again. ' "If you nab Ginger he'll grass on me." Do you know, Inspector? Had Mr Gladstone been going to evening classes in old-time cockney? Had he written a thesis on the argot of the Artful Dodger?'

'Not that I know of, sir.'

'Mr Rumpole!' It was the Judge again, sounding a warning note which I ignored. I kept on at the Inspector. 'Or did these quaint phrases drift up from your memories of happier times when all confession statements taken by the police started "It's a fair cop" just as a formality?'

'Mr Rumpole!' The Judge took the words out of Mr Arthur's mouth. 'I sincerely hope there'll be some evidence to support this attack on the officer's integrity.'

'At the moment, my Lord, I'm simply attacking his prose style.' Not bad, I hope you'll agree; and I wanted Nick to see me at my best.

'You're suggesting the Inspector is lying?' The Judge seemed slow to follow my drift.

'Oh, my Lord, certainly. No doubt the same suggestion will be made to my client. The compliments are mutual.'

'Mr Rumpole, you have some experience in these Courts.' Now the Judge was trying the effect of being menacingly polite.

'A little, my Lord. Just a little.'

'Over a long period of years?'

'You might say, my Lord, from time immemorial.'

'And you know perfectly well the limits to which defending counsel may go?'

'I've often been reminded of them, my Lord.'

'I imagine you have. If the cross-examination we have just heard is typical of you, Mr Rumpole, I imagine you have had to be reminded often. One does not expect to have to repeat such reminders to counsel of your advanced age and seniority. Now have you any other questions to ask this officer? I mean, *proper* questions.'

'Oh, a great many. I was anxious not to interrupt the flow of Your Lordship's rebuke.' I was delighted Nick was hearing this, and I turned to attack the Inspector with renewed strength.

'Wouldn't you agree, Inspector Arthur? This is really a Golden Oldie of a confession statement?' There was more laughter, another call for 'silence' and a long sigh from the

Judge who said, wearily, 'The jury may have some idea what the question means. I have none.'

Inspector Arthur, I knew, understood the question perfectly well.

'What's the answer, Inspector?'

'As your client knows full well, that is his own confession, Mr Rumpole. His own confession of guilt.'

This clearly appealed to the Judge as a curtain line. He turned apologetically to the jury. 'This case is obviously going to detain us a considerable time. We have yet to learn the nature of the defence. Shall we say, two o'clock, members of the jury?'

The Judge had risen and vanished before I could say certainly not two o'clock, what about half past two, which would give me a decent chance of a farewell lunch with Nick? As it was, Simpsons in the Strand was out of the question, there were no tables to be had in the Newgate Street Wine Bar, and we ended up in a pub round the corner, where the cold beef was off, and all they had left was a cheese sandwich, which was no particular good even as a cheese sandwich, and no pickle! Nick had a half of lager, and I took refuge in a large rum, washed down with a pint of Guinness.

'What time's your plane, Nick?'

'Six o'clock. It's one of those charters.'

'You're having tea with your mother?'

'She wants me to.'

'Then don't try and cut it, eh?' I gave my son a conspiratorial wink. 'Watch out for She Who Must Be Obeyed.'

Nick didn't laugh at that, as he used to in the old days. Perhaps he was hungry and missing the roast at Simpsons. After the disappointments of the morning, I thought a little financial support might be in order, and I pulled out the cheque book accordingly. 'Got all you need in the way of money, Nick?'

'I've got enough. I worked all last August.'

'Oh yes, of course.' He seemed to mean it so I put the cheque book away.

'Dirty sort of work, wasn't it? I take my hat off to you. I could never dig up the Underground!' I saw Nick look at me then, and somehow it wasn't the look of unqualified admiration which I had been used to when he came home from school and dropped in on my murders. 'I don't think I could do your job either,' he said.

'Oh, come on Nick. The Old Bailey's not so bad. You can have quite a lot of good, clean fun down the Bailey.'

'Is that what you were having this morning?' I'd had enough of the cheese sandwich and felt for the box of small cigars.

'I forget. Do you smoke these things?'

'No.'

'No. Of course not.' I prodded one between my lips, lit it and gave a resounding cough. 'Filthy habit.'

'No, but *were* you having fun?' For once I saw my son looking genuinely puzzled.

'Well, now. Yes! Yes, perhaps I was. In my own quiet way.'

'That Judge!' Nick seemed appalled by what he had seen in Court. 'That Judge,' I told Nick, 'was defending bad cases of non-renewed dog licence when I was doing the Penge Bungalow Murders – alone and without a leader!' I was not, as you may have gathered, over-impressed by Mr Justice Bates.

'I don't know how you could go on when that Judge said those things to you, Dad.'

'Bless you, Nick. I'll tell you how you deal with judicial insults. You smile a sweet smile of Chinese inscrutability and say, "If your Lordship pleases". You take the rough with the smooth. In a dozen oysters there's always one that gives you the collywobbles. It's just bad luck that of all the Judges available I had to pick the one who looks as if he's got woman trouble.' I might have added, 'and of all the women available for matrimony I had to pick your mother,' but I looked at Nick and suspected that this thought might not, at that particular lunch-time, get an entirely sympathetic reception.

'I suppose the Judge thought you were wasting his time,' Nick went on.

'*His* time? How long should it take to rob a boy's life of five years?' I looked at my watch, I'd soon have to be back in Court. This is no proper farewell, I thought, to my son Nick. 'I had hoped the case might be a shortie.'

'And the Judge didn't like you pretending.'

'Pretending what, Nick?' For once I wasn't following my son's drift.

'Pretending your mugger's innocent. I mean Judges must get sick and tired of all those phoney defences. Looking at the policeman's notebook and all that sort of nonsense, when surely everyone *knows*.'

'What do they know?'

'Well. That boy actually admitted . . .'

'So they say. No one *knows* anything until it's proved. And even then you may have a nagging doubt.'

Nick was laughing then, imitating one of my stock court-room phrases, ' "Members of the jury, while there remains a particle of doubt." I remember you practising that speech in front of the bathroom mirror, while I put my rubber duck's head under the water, so he wouldn't be embarrassed. Doubt's your stock in trade, isn't it?'

'Better than being a cleric and dealing in improbable beliefs.' I swallowed about a quarter of a pint of Guinness and tried a final apology. 'Nick, I'm sorry I was busy . . .'

'I didn't mind. Not till I saw what you were busy at.'

'Do you find it so disreputable?' I looked at him, in some sorrow, and not much anger.

'If that boy's guilty, which he obviously is . . .'

'They're all guilty of something, my dear old thing. Everyone's guilty of *something*. If anyone gets off it's a plus.'

'A plus for who?'

'For them, of course. It's a strange quality of human nature, Nick.' I signalled for a refill of our glasses. 'People show an almost comic relief at not being locked up. They actually *enjoy* not having to share one chamber-pot through endless nights with vindictive, frightened and sexually frustrated strangers. Do you find that so very odd?' There was silence as the barmaid gave us our drinks. Nick didn't answer my unanswerable question. I raised my glass to him and said, 'My clients relish a good win as much as I do.'

'What about society?' Nick still looked worried. 'I mean, all that getting people off – is it much good to society at large?'

'Society can open a door at night and go to the lavatory.'

'Shouldn't you see it's protected occasionally?'

'Just at the moment I've got my hands full protecting young Ossie Gladstone.'

'By telling lies?'

'By telling his story for him, as well as I can. What do you think I am, Nick? I'm nothing but a ventriloquist's doll, perched on Mr Gladstone's knee.'

'You think that's a very dignified position?'

'Oh, Nick, you can't be born or die in a dignified position. How the hell can you live in one, my old darling?' I drank the Guinness, and remembered something about Mr Gladstone. 'You know about that boy. His mother sent him away, when he was four. Sent him away from home, I mean.'

Curiously enough, Nick didn't seem to be thinking about Oswald Gladstone. He was putting me, for some reason, in the dock.

'But today, when I saw you standing there, saying things you really didn't mean . . .'

'That's *not* what I was doing.'

'I suddenly knew why, well, why you've never said much you meant to me, have you?'

'Nick! I'm sorry we couldn't manage Simpsons. It'd've been so much pleasanter.'

'Yes. We'd've had steak and kidney pud and you'd've been in a good mood and told me a string of funny stories about your favourite murders. But you wouldn't have actually *said* anything. Not something of your own. I suppose it's all that ventriloquist business. You must forget your own voice sometimes.'

That, at last, was an allegation I could rebut. 'Now, my voice. It's a good voice. I do flatter myself.' I tried it out on a snatch of Wordsworth. ' "There was a boy; you knew him well ye cliffs And islands of Winander . . ." '

'I think that's what Mother finds so difficult,' Nick said, and now I was beginning to lose my patience. '*She* finds difficult? And *what* does the Leader of the Opposition find difficult exactly?'

'Knowing exactly who you are,' Nick said, and I felt little sympathy for She's problem. 'Well, we've been married thirty years,' I said. 'If She doesn't know *that* by now . . .'

'It's just that she's not very happy actually. I wanted to talk to you about it before I left,' Nick said.

'It's not easy to talk here.' Indeed the bar was full of noisy jurors and solicitors' clerks, villains and even noisier coppers. I felt helpless and apologized again. 'If only he'd pleaded.'

'No. But I knew what she means now. Now, I've seen you in action. Is that what you call it?'

'In action. Yes, I suppose it is.' I drained my glass and Nick went on. 'She says you're always arguing, but she doesn't know if it's an argument or just a game, like the game you were playing in Court this morning. She says you seem to hate her sometimes, but she can't tell if you mean it. In a way, she says, she'd rather you really hated her than pretended to.'

'But I say wonderful things to her. Very often! Wonderful, complimentary things.' I protested at a manifest injustice.

'Of course, she doesn't believe those either.'

'*She's* not very happy. *She's* not. What do you think *I* feel, Nick? What do you think?'

But he could give no answer to my question. 'I don't know. I don't know what you feel, Dad.'

And I don't know what else we might have said to each other if we hadn't been interrupted at that precise moment by my instructing solicitor, Mr Winter, and his side-kick, Jo. The un-welcome Winter announced that he had got a message, through the prison officer, that our client Mr Gladstone required our immediate presence down the cells. He had, it seemed, new instructions to give us. I reminded him that my son Nick was just off to America, but Mr Gladstone, it appeared, would brook no delay.

'My Master's Voice,' I said regretfully. 'Have a good trip then, Nick. I mean, it's not for ever, is it? You'll be back soon, I'm sure. On holidays.'

'I expect so.'

'I'm sorry about the lunch being so scrappy.'

'That's all right.' And Nick smiled.

'Damn it. We haven't had a talk yet even.'

'No. No, we haven't.'

Mr Oswald Gladstone, when we got to the interview room, had plenty of time to talk. He was another young man who seemed not altogether pleased with Rumpole.

'That Judge, dad,' he said in a tone of rebuke. 'He sure don't like you . . .'

'I'm not absolutely crazy about him,' I admitted.

'It's the jury that matters, Oswald.' Mr Winter tried to re-assure him. 'Mr Rumpole's getting through to the jury.'

'From what I seen, that Judge, he's pretty angry with you, dad.' Oswald frowned at me.

'It's part of the wear and tear of legal life.' I was prepared to be philosophical.

'So when I seen that, I decide to plead guilty.'

'But Mr Rumpole explained. If you tell us you didn't do it . . .' Mr Winter protested.

'I tell you now. I don't want this going on.'

'But if you *didn't* do it . . .'

'I made that statement, didn't I?' Oswald shook his head. 'That Judge. He's getting *really* angry.'

'But Oswald. I told you. It's the *jury* that matters, not the Judge.'

'It's gone all against us.' Mr Gladstone had lost his early ebullience. In vain, Winter continued, cheeringly, 'I've seen them all at work, and Mr Rumpole's cross-examination was top hole! I mean, he had D.I. Arthur right on the ropes.'

Oswald gave me a look of pity. 'I'm sorry, dad. I know you tried real hard.'

'Thank you.' Well, it hadn't been a day of kind words for Rumpole.

'Just wasn't working for you, was it? So I'm pleading guilty.'

'If you're quite sure.' I could have wished he'd made his decision in the morning.

'I'm sure.'

'We'd better take written instructions then.' It's always a wise precaution to get a client's signature to a change of plea, so I started to write, just as Inspector Arthur had started to write on a previous occasion.

'Cheer up the old Judge, anyway.' Oswald smiled.

'Well, I think you're doing the wrong thing, Oswald,' my instructing solicitor rambled on. 'I think it's a tragedy. I mean, give Mr Rumpole another half hour with that Inspector and he'll come out as what he is, a nigger hater.'

'He didn't call me no nigger.' Oswald shook his head. 'He never called me that.'

'Well, if you think you know what you're doing.' Winter was still grumbling, but Oswald was looking at me with, I thought, some apprehension.

'What you got there, Mr Rumpole?'

'Written instructions. For you to sign.' I finished writing and handed Mr Gladstone the sheet I had torn out of my notebook. 'You *can* sign that, can't you?'

'Yes. Yes, I can write my name.' Oswald sounded hurt.

'Read it through first. Just read it through. Before you sign it.' I went on playing the Inspector Arthur part. Oswald took the paper, glanced at it, and said confidently, 'O.K. I read it.'

'Are you sure?' I was watching him carefully.

'O.K.' Oswald began to sound irritable.

'Why don't you read it out loud? Come on, old dear. Just so we're sure you've got it perfectly clear. Out loud. Like you did down at the nick.'

There was a long, a very long pause, during which I knew the answer to the case of Mr Oswald Gladstone and his confession of guilt.

'You can't read, can you, Oswald?' I said quietly. 'Why didn't you tell us?'

Ossie was too ashamed of not reading to try to get off a little charge of attempted murder. He looked away from me, and said, 'What do you want me to do?'

'I think,' I told him, 'I want you to fight.'

On my way back to Court I ran into the Rev. Eldred Pickersgill still hanging about and waiting to give evidence. I was able to check a few facts with him before I pushed open the glass swing door and prepared myself to go a few more rounds with Detective Inspector Arthur and Mr Justice Bates.

'Detective Inspector. You remember saying before we adjourned for luncheon that you didn't read out his alleged statement to my client?' I got straight down, you see, to the pith of the argument.

'Yes, sir.' The officer in the witness-box now sounded bored.

'But, you said, the reverse was the case, and he read his statement out to you?'

'That's perfectly true.'

'Would it interest you to know, Inspector, that Oswald Gladstone can neither read nor write?'

'But . . .' The Judge, of course, had picked up the document and was looking at the scribbled signature. I interrupted to explain, and give him further details thanks to the Reverend Eldred Pickersgill.

'Oh, he can scrawl his signature – just, my Lord. But the whole realm of poetry is a closed book to him. Wordsworth is silent. Dickens and Thackeray might not have existed. He can't even look up and tell what street he's in or follow the simplest directions for assembling a model aeroplane!'

'Well, he either can read or he can't. Which is it?' the Judge asked, testily.

'He can't, can he, Inspector?'

For once, Inspector Arthur seemed lost for words. The Judge, bless his little ermine cuffs, repeated the question.

'Do you accept, Inspector, that this young man could not read?'

Another long pause, and then the Inspector made an admission. 'If counsel says so, I must accept that, my Lord.'

'So it follows from that that you never put his reading to the test?' I asked innocently.

'It must do.'

'And your evidence this morning was quite misleading?'

'Yes. But . . .'

'No "buts", Inspector. It was either true of false. Which?' Dear old Arthur spent a long while searching for a word and came up with, 'It was incorrect.'

'And if he couldn't read, my client wouldn't've known if you had written down his words, or *your* words, Inspector?'

'He . . . might not know.' The possibility was enough for me, I breathed a huge sigh of relief.

'He told you, didn't he, about a boy called Ginger Robertson?' I hoped I had prevented the proof of Oswald's guilt. Now I had to do something to suggest he might even be innocent.

'Yes, he did,' the Inspector agreed.

'Who was present at the scene of the crime?'

'Yes.'

'Who is not there in that dock?'

'No.'

'Because the combined power and brilliance of the detective force has not succeeded in catching that young gentleman, Ginger Robertson? Are the police still out looking for him?'

'No.'

'Why not?'

'Because we got Gladstone's confession?'

'And because of that worthless document, you didn't trouble to find the true criminal?'

I thought of how I would describe my triumph to Nick, and settle all his doubts about my profession. I would say, 'You see, Nick, sometimes it goes well. Sometimes it goes beautifully. Sweet and easy as cutting off a hunk of Stilton cheese or knock-ing back a glass of claret. You've got to lay the ground, though. You notice I tied old Arthur down before lunch. Got him committed to his story? Then I didn't really know why I was doing it. But it was the instinct, you see. That's why they use Rumpole, Nick. It's the dear old instinct. See how it's working for us? They're never going to believe his confession now. See how it's working for us, Nick?'

I looked behind me, but the seat beside Mr Winter was empty. My son had gone to start a new sort of life in another country.

At the end of the prosecution evidence, I made a speech to the jury, and didn't call Oswald. They took about an hour to acquit. When I said goodbye to my client he looked discontented, and asked me why I had to show him up for not being able to read.

All the same I was in a moderately satisfied mood as I stood in front of the porcelain of the Gents attached to the Old Bailey robing room and recited a particularly triumphant bit of Words-worth to myself.

> ' "She was an elfin pinnace; lustily
> I dipped my oars into the silent lake.
> And, as I rose upon the stroke, my boat
> Went heaving through the water like a swan . . ." '

36

'So you had to fight your case, Rumpole.' George came pottering up beside me.

'Yes, George. It was a pretty good day. Had a bit of fun with the Detective Inspector. He'll probably go home and kick the chrysanthemums.'

'So you never got away to see your son?' George asked.

'Sorry?'

'You had a fight on your hands. You never got away to meet your boy?'

'Well, Nick came up here. He came up to the Bailey. To watch the old man in action.'

'He'll have enjoyed that.'

'Oh yes! Nick's always liked the Bailey. Since he was a schoolboy. He used to come up to my murders and then I'd give him a rattling good tea!'

Back in mufti, I was on my way out of the Bailey when I ran into a gratified Mr Winter and his side-kick Jo.

'You crucified old D.I. Arthur, Mr Rumpole.' Winter beamed. 'You really did.'

At which moment, the Detective Inspector and his Sergeant passed us on their way out to a villainous world. The D.I. looked displeased and didn't answer when I gave him a cheery good night. I felt some sympathy for the officer, and said to Winter, 'Poor old sweetheart. You know, Ossie may have said all that to him. Every word. The only mistake the Inspector made was to ginger it up with a little lie.'

'His *only* mistake? Do you believe that?' Mr Winter gave me a tolerant smile.

'Who knows?' And I told him, 'It's not my job to believe anything.'

After dinner, I sat in the chilly living-room of the 'mansion' flat finishing a bottle of Château Fleet Street, and thumbing through the papers in a rather attractive little murder my clerk had landed for me. My wife, Hilda, was knitting some woollen garment intended as a substitute for a more efficient form of central heating.

'You saw Nick, then,' she said.

'Yes. Yes, I saw him. Well, we had a scrap lunch, but very pleasant. Very pleasant indeed.'

'He said you had a sandwich in the pub!' She Who Must Be Obeyed said accusingly. I looked up from the interesting description of another stab wound and apologized. 'Well, you know how it is in the Bailey. It's difficult to make plans.'

'Nick said he talked about you, about your work. He seemed to think it was a little, well, off-colour somehow.'

'Did he? Did he give you that impression?' I was genuinely surprised when She sounded indignant.

'I must say, I wasn't having that from Nick!' I looked at her questioningly, and Hilda went on. ' "Your father," I told him, "is a member of an Honourable Profession. Besides which, think of all he's done for you. Public school, Oxford, and a lot of help in going to America." '

'All paid for by the proceeds of crime.'

'I certainly did *not* say that! I said, "Nick. You should respect your father." That's what I said.'

'Thank you, Hilda.'

'Well he should.'

I got up and found a small cigar. I was more troubled, perhaps, than I had liked to admit about what Nick had said to me. 'Nick thinks we ask all the wrong questions. Just so we can get the wrong answers. That's what he thinks.'

'He really upset me, talking like that.' Hilda clicked her needles disapprovingly.

'He's perfectly right, of course.'

'Rumpole!'

I applied a torn-off page of the *Criminal Law Review* to the electric fire and lit the small cigar.

'I mean, "Why?" That's what we ought to be asking about Mr Oswald Gladstone. Not "Who did it?" "Who's guilty?" "Can you prove it?" "Yes I can." "No, you can't." "Bags I have the last word and the burden of the proof." But *why*? Why ever did that happen? Outside Lords, for no reason whatsoever. I mean, God knows I believe in freedom. But jolly Jean-Jacques Rousseau, I'd like to ask him a few pertinent questions.' Nothing was heard in the room but the click of Hilda's needles. Then she said, 'I have absolutely no idea what you're talking about. So far as I am concerned, you belong to an Honourable Profession. And you do it very well. I heard that at the garden party.

"Rumpole," Guthrie Featherstone told me, "is stubborn as a mule in cross-examination." '

'You know what else Nick said?' I asked her.

'So far as I can understand, Nick talked a lot of nonsense.' She went into a spurt of high-speed knitting.

'He said you didn't know exactly who I am.'

'Of course I do. You're Rumpole!' She stopped knitting then and looked at me, only a little puzzled. 'Aren't you?'

Well, yes. I'm Horace Rumpole. What *was* Nick talking about? Everyone down the Bailey knows me. I'm an amiable eccentric who drops ash down his waistcoat and tells the time with a gold hunter and calls Judges old sweethearts. Also I recite Wordsworth in the loo.

That's who I am, isn't it?

Rumpole and the Gentle Art of Blackmail

A certain amount of detachment, the learned Head of my Chambers, Guthrie Featherstone, Q.C., M.P., says, is essential to the life of a barrister. This means that you should be able to see your client sent down for a long stretch, wave him a cheery goodbye and potter off to the Sheridan Club for a touch of cold pheasant with nothing more than a mild 'Oops!' at having backed another loser.

Detachment, I suppose, comes easily to Guthrie. He plays golf with a number of Her Majesty's Judges and when he stands up to defend, he often gets a small smile from His Lordship which seems to indicate, 'Well, we know you've got to go through the motions, old chap. Better luck next time when you'll be appearing for the prosecution.' When I get up on my hind legs, the judicial attitude is to identify me more closely with the criminal classes. Indeed I sometimes think that as I stand in the robes and old horsehair wig I might as well be wearing a cloth cap, mask, striped jersey and carrying a bag marked 'swag', from the glassy-eyed stare of disapproval I get from the old sweetheart on the bench.

Quite frequently, of course, I can rise above it. Sometimes I can even manage a touch of the famous Featherstone detachment. When defending Bertie Timson on yet another charge of carrying housebreaking implements by night, for instance, I know what verdict the old darling expects, and any better result will be accepted with the utmost gratitude.

But when it comes to defending a young man with no previous convictions, about whom you have the horrible suspicion that he may be innocent, then proceedings may become extremely sticky, not to say, hair-raising, and detachment is extremely difficult. Adverse verdicts, in such circumstances, tend to be taken to heart and inflict wounds which can only be soothed by a prolonged dosage of Pommeroy's ordinary claret (Château Fleet Street 1979) and an influx of other briefs. The scars, however, remain.

It is not, happily, very often that you get a client cursed with the possibility of innocence, but it does happen, and such a client was young Vernon, gardener and handyman at St Joseph's College, Oxford, whose case caused me a number of sleepless nights under the dreaming spires. The situation wasn't made any easier by the fact that R. v. Vernon was a case concerned with an offence of the kind which draws a swift intake of breath from Her Majesty (who, of course, concerns herself in the prosecution of all potential villains), and usually involves a prolonged stay at one of the Royal Residences in Wandsworth, Pentonville or the Isle of Wight. The crime in question was blackmail, in this case of a 'distinguished public figure', and carried out in a particularly nasty manner.

Blackmail, technically speaking, the demanding of money with menaces, is, as I say, looked on with grave disapproval by the powers that be; but it's an essential part of family life. When it is used, however, it does require a certain amount of basic skill.

> I will do such things . . .
> What they are yet I know not – but they shall be
> The terrors of the earth.

That vague menace of King Lear, of course, was absolutely hopeless as a bit of blackmail. The good blackmailer utters a threat which is short, clear and perfectly possible. My wife had that lesson to learn, over the matter of the new loose covers for our drawing-room chairs.

Picture me, that morning, with She Who Must Be Obeyed (or Mrs Hilda Rumpole to give her the name under which she sometimes passes) at breakfast in our matrimonial home at 25B Froxbury Court, Gloucester Road. I was on my way to Oxford, not primarily for the purpose of visiting my old college, but to Her Majesty's Prison, in order to confer with my client, Vernon, and She, having been on a tour of inspection of our 'mansion' flat, looked vaguely discontented and narrowed her eyes in the manner of someone about to put the screws on.

'Rumpole!' she said. 'We need new chair covers.'

There is only one way to deal with such an unnecessary and generally unhelpful remark – pretend you haven't heard it.

'Got to hurry breakfast, I'm afraid,' I muttered. 'I'm catching a train to Oxford.'

Whatever else you may say about my wife Hilda, she gets top marks for persistence. She ignored my convenient deafness and carried on.

'When we went to the Featherstones' sherry party, I was admiring their chintz chair covers. So jolly and spring-like, I told Marigold Featherstone.'

'I'm going there to study a rather jolly and spring-like little case of blackmail.' I was consuming the tea and toast at breakneck speed.

'We can't invite the Featherstones to dinner here until we've got new chair covers, Rumpole.' Hilda reached a verdict: 'Our old chair covers would simply let us down.'

'I don't know. They've held me up for a good many years.' It is a mistake to attempt any sort of pleasantry with She, particularly at breakfast. My wife looked distinctly unamused and trumpeted a warning, 'Really, Rumpole!'

'The charge is blackmail,' I told her, hoping she might take the hint. 'Demanding money with menaces. Within the sacred precincts of St Joseph's, Oxford. My old college, Hilda.'

She was neither deterred by my hint of crime nor interested in my reminiscence. With a carefully sharpened voice she continued:

'Rumpole! Are you going to let me buy new chair covers or not? Marigold Featherstone only paid three hundred pounds to get hers done, and the sofa.'

The mention of this hideously round figure made me choke on my tea.

'Three hundred pounds! Hilda. Do you think I'm made of money? Besides, that represents, at a rough estimate, almost one hundred bottles of Pommeroy's claret-style plonk . . .'

But now the knives were definitely out. In a voice of cold steel Hilda came to the menace: 'Rumpole, I'm giving you fair warning! If you don't give me the money for new chair covers to brighten up our living-room, I'll . . .' But then there was a fatal moment of hesitation. I jumped in fearlessly with, 'What'll you do, Hilda?'

Her bluff was called. She Who Must Be Obeyed visibly faltered. 'I . . . I haven't thought yet. But I'll . . . I'll take a most serious view. I promise you that.'

You see what I mean? She and old King Lear had a lot to learn about the gentle art of blackmail. No doubt they could have profited by lessons from the client I was about to see, languishing in Oxford prison.

However, I wasn't taking any risks and I swallowed the last gulp of tea and bolted for Paddington station and on to a rather grimy diesel, bound in a westerly direction. How long was it since I had taken a train to go up to St Joseph's College, Oxford, for the study of law? Law is a subject which, I may say, never interested me greatly. People in trouble, yes. Bloodstains and handwriting, certainly. The art of cross-examination, of course. Winning over a jury, fascinating. But law! The only honourable way to pass a law exam is to make a few notes on the cuff and take a quick shufti at them during the occasional visit to the bog.

Oxford! They were romantic years I had spent at St Joseph's no doubt. Those were the first nights when I got tipsy on College claret in the company of my boon companion, P. J. Fosdyke. Fozzy Fosdyke was a thinnish and nervous-looking historian who had a devilish method of playing draughts, a cunning way with a limerick, and a tendency to become over-excited at the sniff of a small dry sherry. Fosdyke and Rumpole were as inseparable, in those distant days, as the three musketeers, with poor old Monty Simpson, whom I had an irresistible desire to call 'Shrimpson' because of his pop eyes and eyebrows like waving antennae, making up the trio. We three used to drink bitter in pubs by the station together, and, on endless Sunday afternoons, go for walks through the countryside.

As the train got into its stride, and we were granted a view of trees, the river and cows champing at sunlit grass, sizeable chunks of *The Oxford Book of English Verse* (Sir Arthur Quiller-Couch edition) came floating into my mind.

> Pale blue convolvulus in tendrils creep
> And air-swept lindens yield
> Their scent, and rustle down their perfumed showers

Of bloom on the bent grass where I am laid,
And bower me from the August sun with shade;
And the eye travels down to Oxford's towers ...

What a joy it was, I thought, to be getting away from London, far from the terrors of Judge Bullingham and my clerk Henry, and the V.A.T. man and She Who Must Be Obeyed! And then, at last, I got a splendid view of the coal heaps round the canal as the train rattled and gasped its way into Oxford station.

'Rumpole!'

Walking down the platform I was accosted by a stout person whom I didn't recognize. He was accompanied by an elderly grey-haired man whose sprouting eyebrows gave him the appearance of an anxious crustacean.

'It's never Horace Rumpole?' The stout man sounded positive.

'Well, it is sometimes.'

'You remember me, don't you, Rumpole? P. J. Fosdyke. We were up at St Joseph's together.'

'My God, Fozzy Fosdyke!'

'And you recollect old Simpson. Senior Classics Fellow now at St Joseph's.'

'Monty Simpson! Senior Fellow?'

It seemed incredible, until I remembered that standing in front of my two old friends I too must have seemed like some sort of antique or relic from the past. Simpson twitched his eyebrows and said in that high, slightly hysterical voice of his, which always sounded like a scream from the depths of the sea, 'We were all at St Joseph's together!'

'In the year dot,' I said, putting the record straight.

'We climbed in one evening. Over the wall and straight into the Principal's bedroom.' Simpson was becoming nostalgic.

'Which you mistook for the upstairs bog,' Fosdyke reminded me.

'And we were greeted by the sight of the Principal's wife sitting bolt upright in bed in a pink nightie.' Simpson was bubbling with long-remembered mirth.

'And hair curlers.' It was something that stuck in my mind.

'A sight to drive a man to life-long homosexuality,' Simpson thought. And then he asked me, 'What are you doing in Oxford?'

'Oh, a bit of legal business.' Compared to the work of a Senior Classical Fellow it sounded on the sordid side.

'Do you have to hurry back? Come for a drink at the old Coll. this evening. Or something to eat, we dine early.' Fosdyke issued the invitation, and Simpson backed it up by nodding, his eyebrows waving gently in the air.

Fosdyke explained that he was also on the academic staff of my old college, being a Tutor in Modern History. We had no more time for catching up on the news of our various careers as duty called in the shape of a good-looking young girl with nice eyes, clean jeans and a knapsack full of papers.

'Mr Rumpole?' she said. Someone must have described a crumpled sort of legal person in an old hat to her. 'I've come to take you to the prison.'

'Oh Rumpole! What have you done now?' P. J. Fosdyke was laughing like an undergraduate. 'Can it be that landlady's daughter in Longwall Street?'

'Do you want us to come with you and bail you out?' Simpson was signalling joke with his eyebrows. Very wry fellows, these academics.

'This is P. J. Fosdyke and Mr Shrimp ... I beg his pardon, Simpson. Both dons of a sort from St Joseph's, my old college.'

'St Joseph's!' The girl seemed to be looking at all of us with a new wariness, and my old friends with a kind of hostility.

'Yes, and you are ...'

'Sue Galton. I'm an articled clerk with Newby and Paramore, your instructing solicitor in the Vernon case.'

'Vernon!' This time Fozzy Fosdyke looked slightly uneasy, and the Shrimp gave out one of his piercing underwater laughs.

'Well, Rumpole. Do come and have a drink up at the Coll. For old times' sake.'

'Yes, of course. Of course I will. For the sake of old times.'

'Come on, Mr Rumpole. I've got a taxi outside. We can't keep Peter waiting.'

Peter? Who was Peter? And then I remembered, our client was Peter Vernon.

'Why?' He is not going anywhere, is he?' I said, and because of the hurt look in Sue Galton's eyes I immediately regretted having said it. She must be one of the new sort of instructing solicitor, the sensitive variety.

Peter Vernon, as I'd gathered from a glance through my brief on the way up in the train (always ask your client, at the start of any conference, to tell you his story in *his own words*, that saves a lot of preliminary reading), was a young man in his early twenties. His father was a shop steward in the Cowley works and Peter had a number of A-levels, but just couldn't find work that suited him, rebelling, in a way I found quite understandable, from the tedium of the assembly line. He finally landed a job as a gardener at St Joseph's, a pleasant enough existence, I should have imagined, mowing the croquet lawn and planting out snapdragons. He was all set, it seemed, for a gentle and rustic existence in the heart of Oxford. In fact, his statement had read, 'I was extremely happy at St Joseph's until this business with Sir Michael started.'

Sir Michael Tuffnell, Oxford Professor of Moral Philosophy, Principal of St Joseph's College for the past five years, was a popular guru known to millions. He was a grey-haired and distinguished-looking old party, with a twinkling eye and a considerable sense of humour, always ready to be wheeled on to the telly or 'Any Questions' when anyone wanted a snap answer on such troublesome points as 'What is the meaning of meaning?' Or 'Is God dead?'

Sir Michael was a person, certainly, of the utmost brilliance and respectability, whose grasp of the Nature of the Universe was such that God no doubt relied on him to tell him whether or not He existed, a question that Sir Michael answered with a respectful and tentative negative, meanwhile keeping his options open. Apart from his brilliance as a philosopher, he was known as a patron of the arts, an expert on Italian opera and the holder of progressive and even radical opinions. Perhaps he was rather self-consciously determined not to be thought of as a remote academic or an intellectual snob. He seemed to have gone out of his way to be kind to the new young gardener, to talk to him and to lend him books and records. There was no evidence from the prosecution that the relationship between the Philosopher and the Gardener had ever gone so far as what would be called, in any self-respecting social inquiry report, a deeply caring one-to-one single-sex situation. Indeed, my client, in his statement, denied that anything of the sort had ever occurred.

According to Sir Michael, this represented a change of story by Peter Vernon. The young gardener, he said, had threatened to tell the world, or at least the Senior Common Room, of passionate goings on in the Principal's lodge. For a while Sir Michael gave my client cheques, considerable sums in cash and a handsome gold engraved cigarette case to prevent this baseless accusation being made. Finally, and with considerable courage, the Principal went to the Oxford constabulary and denounced his gardening blackmailer.

It seemed a straightforward, sordid and averagely unpleasant case. But as we sat in the taxi on our way to the prison, Miss Sue Galton, leaned forward, fixed me with her sincere look (blue eyes and brown hair, I noticed, made an attractive combination) and added to my instructions.

'Mr Rumpole. Before we get to the prison, there's something I ought to tell you. You see, Peter's not in the least gay.'

'Well, I'm sure he isn't.' I sympathized entirely. 'Not stuck in Oxford gaol for the past six months awaiting the attentions of one of Her Majesty's Judges on a nasty charge of blackmail.'

'No. You don't understand.' Miss Galton sounded impatient.

'Tell me.'

'Peter's just not queer. He's not homosexual.' There was the smallest hesitation before she added, 'You see, I can guarantee that. Personally.'

'Can you, Miss Galton?'

'Oh yes. You see, Peter's my boyfriend. We're going to get married when you get him off.'

This, I must say, was an added complication. If I lost the case, as, after a brief glance at the papers, seemed highly probable, I should not only have an aggrieved client, but a broken-hearted solicitor on my hands. Moreover, I didn't see how I could question the fiancé without some embarrassment to his legal adviser. I don't think I had ever had a solicitor who'd been to bed with the client before, at least not in such complicated circumstances. I hadn't fully worked out all the implications of

Miss Sue Galton's evidence before our taxi reached the prison and she rang for admittance.

After the gate had opened, after the formalities were complete and the shades of the prison-house began to close upon the growing Rumpole, we were shown into the cupboard they grandly called an interview room, and Peter Vernon was brought to us. As he came in, Miss Sue Galton began to glow in a way which provided little evidence of Vernon's homosexuality. He gave her a smile, and then welcomed me with a mixture of modesty and gratitude.

'Hullo, Mr Rumpole. It's kind of you to come all this way. I know you're busy.'

'I got you some fags, Peter.' Miss Galton dived in her kit bag and came up with a packet of Gauloises.

'Oh, thanks, Sue.' He took one and lit it, the smoke mixed with the usual prison smell of urine and disinfectant to give us a genuine continental atmosphere.

'How are things in the Oxford nick?' I said politely, and he smiled at me.

'Well, it's not the Senior Common Room at St Joseph's. But it's not so bad, I suppose. There's one or two decent screws. Blokes you can talk to.' He was being perfectly fair. Then he looked at my solicitor, concerned. 'You haven't been worrying, have you, Sue?'

'What do *you* think?' Her smile was rueful.

'Well, you're not to worry,' he reassured her. 'We'll be all right. Now we've got Mr Rumpole. Sue told me, sir, you're marvellous at getting criminals off.'

'Really? She's too kind.' Something about all this politeness was worrying me. But they really were quite the nicest young couple I'd ever been banged up in a nick with.

'Well, you may have a bit more trouble with me.' Peter Vernon blew out smoke thoughtfully, he was still smiling.

'Oh yes? Why?' I asked him.

'Well, I suppose my problem is – I'm not a criminal.'

I looked at Peter Vernon. To say that he was a good-looking boy is an understatement. You can see faces like his on Greek statues and Florentine paintings. And, as I have said, the most disturbing thing, from the point of view of an old hack advocate about to undertake his defence, was that he looked innocent. I started a difficult interview cautiously, still embarrassed by the presence of the clearly devoted young girl, who gazed at our client as he talked, and took copious notes.

'Well now, Peter. How long did you work at St Joseph's?' I decided to begin at the beginning, as far as possible from the unfortunate heart of the matter.

'About ten months.'

'You met Sir Michael soon after you started there?'

'Oh yes. He came up to me in the garden one afternoon. He was very charming.'

'Do you remember what he said?'

'When he first spoke to me?'

'Yes.'

'Well, I do, as a matter of fact. He said ...' Peter Vernon closed his eyes and repeated the words as though he understood them.

> '"Such was that happy Garden State
> When man first walked without a mate."

And I said:

> "After a place so pure and sweet,
> What other help could yet be meet?"'

There was no reason why anyone should be surprised to hear Andrew Marvell repeated in the nick, but I was. I lit a small cigar and blew out smoke as Peter went on with his story.

'He used to come out and see me – if I was alone in the garden. Sometimes he'd bring me a glass of sherry or a packet of fags. We'd talk ...'

'What did you talk about?' Uneasily I realized I had asked the stock prosecution question in all homosexual cases. Young men and old men, prosecutors always seemed to assume, with their resolutely filthy minds, have absolutely nothing to talk about except sex. Peter Vernon answered quite calmly, and his answer seemed convincing.

'Oh, we talked about all sorts of things. Music ...'

'Peter's great on music.' Miss Sue Galton added her pennyworth eagerly.

'And opera,' Peter Vernon went on. 'He told me that opera was another world. I'd never seen one, but he told me I was like Siegfried, Wagner's Siegfried. Then one day he asked me if I'd like to come up to London, to go to Covent Garden with him. We had dinner at his Club.'

'Where?' Would Sir Michael have taken a young gardener he was having an affair with to his London Club? I supposed that might depend on the extent of the philosopher's sublime self-confidence.

'Somewhere in St James's. The food was terrible. You'd do better in a bistro in Oxford. Then we went off to Covent Garden.'

'And Wagner? Pretty hard going I imagine?'

What I know about Wagner's operas could be written on a postcard and still leave room for the stamp. Claude Erskine-Brown is the Wagnerian expert in our Chambers, and he tells me that Tristan and Isolde were in love with death, which seems to me, at my advanced age, a rum sort of thing to fancy. I mean, who wants to hop into bed with a terminal disease?

'I'd have liked to stop listening but I felt I had to. Out of politeness to Sir Michael at first. But then out of . . . I don't know why. It upset me. The music upset me terribly.'

Miss Galton looked at her lover with enormous sympathy.

'Did you come back to Oxford that night?'

'Sir Michael drove me back, yes.'

'And then?' I asked, and our instructing solicitor looked at our client; I was reminded of an eager fiancée watching a Wimbledon champion, her breath held, her fingernails stuck into the palms of her hands. What would he do with the question, lob it out of court or smash it into the net? In fact, Peter Vernon made a neat return, and his fan club breathed again.

'I've got a room near the station,' he said. 'He dropped me off there and then . . . I suppose he drove back to the College.'

'After that?' Miss Galton looked at me as though, Peter Vernon having won game and set, further play was surely no longer necessary.

'After that we went to dinner in London once or twice. Oh, and I had tea with him in his rooms a few times.'

My client was carefully squashing out his cigarette end in the top of an old tin provided.

'And that's all?'

'Yes, that's all.'

All, at any rate, that I was going to get for the moment. I pulled out my watch, looked at it with incredulous despair and said something about having to telephone my clerk immediately.

'You can do that from the office when we get back.' Miss Galton suggested.

'Henry'll be gone then, I'm afraid. You couldn't ask them if you can make a call at the gate, could you? Just ring my Chambers and say I will be back tonight. But not till much later. I'm having dinner with old friends in Oxford. But I'll be free for the breathalyser case at Chelmsford tomorrow. There's a good girl. Do you want 10p?'

She went reluctantly, almost as though she were leaving her lover alone with a rival.

When she had gone I spent a good deal of time looking at Peter Vernon in silence. Then I said, 'I can't get you off you know, unless you tell the truth.'

His looks betrayed nothing. He was still smiling charmingly, looking a little puzzled, but not in the least offended.

'Because if you don't tell the truth about you and Sir Michael, the jury will never believe you about the blackmail.'

We then went into another bout of silence. Although I had got rid of our solicitor, her presence, like her perfume, was still vaguely about us. I tried the approach direct.

'Look. What do you think? Would Miss Sue Galton rather marry a free man who's had a few strange experiences or wait for four years for a convicted blackmailer? Anyway, there's no defence unless you did it. You went to bed together and he gave you presents for it. Isn't that the story?'

Peter Vernon was no longer smiling. He took another cigarette and lit it carefully.

'How do you know?'

'Because that's always the story, in your sort of case.' There is no experience, I thought, like the experience of an Old Bailey hack.

'So you don't believe it?'

For the first time Peter Vernon looked put out. No one likes to be told that his defence is just Number Two, Standard Size.

'You tell me. And then I'll see if I believe it.'

So then, my client began to tell me the story.

'It happened that first night. After *Siegfried*. I suppose I did it out of politeness. You know. Like the way you're taught to say "thank you" after a children's party.'

'You didn't care for him?' For a moment I almost felt sorry for Sir Michael.

'I don't think it was him I liked, ever. It was his whole world. Oh, the way he talked, and the music he played me and even that freezing old Club with the Regency paintings and the rotten food. I was grateful to him for showing me all that. The rest didn't seem terribly important.'

'He gave you money?' I was anxious to return to the charge on the indictment.

'Yes. Cheques a few times. He must have been mad to do that, mustn't he?' Peter Vernon asked me.

'And you were mad to pay them into your bank account. Why did you keep the money? I mean if you were not a blackmailer?'

'I just kept it . . .' He smiled vaguely.

'And the cigarette case?'

'Yes. That was the last thing he gave me. I kept it all because . . . Well, you know Sue and I are going to get married. We've got a lot to save up for.'

It was, I suppose, an unusual way to furnish a bottom drawer. Oddly enough, he made it sound completely natural. At this point Miss Sue Galton returned to us and said that although she had telephoned my clerk, Henry, he seemed to know nothing about a breathalyser at Chelmsford the next day. I looked suitably puzzled and said I supposed my clerk was always the last to know.

I took my leave of the young engaged couple, having given Peter Vernon a piece of advice which would have been fatal to most of my clients. I counselled, if he wanted to have any prospect of an early marriage, to tell the truth. If there were any lies to be told, they were best left to the Professor of Moral Philosophy, who might even be better at it.

I had expected a quiet drink with Fosdyke and Simpson in one of their rooms, and felt distinctly embarrassed when, having given my name to the porter at St Joseph's (some spotty youth, clearly far too young for the job), I was sent over to the Senior Common Room where a whole flock of dons, looking, with tattered gowns drooping from their shoulders, like bedraggled birds were sniffing the sherry and pecking at the biscuits. I was well into the aperitifs before I realized that I was expected to dine at High Table, in embarrassing proximity to the principal witness for the prosecution in R. *v.* Vernon. It was really, I told Fozzy Fosdyke, not on.

'Of course it is,' Fosdyke filled my glass. 'The food's not bad at all. Ah. You'd like to meet Humphrey Grice, our Senior Law Tutor. This is my old friend, Horace Rumpole. It seems he's known as "Rumpole of the Old Bailey".'

The man to whom I was introduced was the most raven-like of all the dons. He had almost jet-black hair, hardly going grey, which also grew from his ears and on the back of his hands. He had strong yellow teeth.

' "Rumpole of the Old Bailey", eh? How very amusing,' said the law tutor Grice. 'What do you think of academic lawyers down at the Old Bailey?'

'Well to tell you the truth,' I had to admit, 'we hardly think of them at all.'

'But you'll have read my paper on "The Concept of Constructive Intent and Mens Rea in Murder and Manslaughter" in the *Harvard Law Review*?' Humphrey Grice looked puzzled and not a little hurt.

'Oh rather!' I lied to him. 'Your average East End jury finds it absolutely riveting.'

Further badinage along these lines was prevented by Simpson who came up with a distinguished-looking grey-haired man in a black velvet dinner jacket, to whom he introduced me.

'Rumpole, this is our Principal. Sir Michael Tuffnell. My friend, "Rumpole of the Old Bailey".'

'How are you, Rumpole? So glad you could join us.'

Sir Michael had the knack of making you feel that you were just the sort of valued companion he'd been hoping might drop in for dinner. Without switching off the charm for a second he turned to Humphrey Grice: 'Gulls' eggs, tonight, isn't it, Humphrey? We usually have gulls' eggs on the first Thursday in Lent, and we make ourselves stop at three . . .'

I couldn't let this extremely gracious old telly star feed me gulls' eggs on false pretences, so I muttered, 'Sir Michael, could I have a word?'

'Fasting is a state of mind. I do believe that,' the Principal said to the world at large, and then to me, 'Yes, what is it, Rumpole?'

'Fosdyke invited me to dinner, but I should tell you that I'm appearing for young Peter Vernon on the blackmail charge.' I let him into the secret. If the news caused Sir Michael the faintest distress, he didn't show it. In fact he didn't even bother to lower his voice as he said, 'Oh good. Do your best for him, won't you? I feel genuinely sorry for the lad.'

'But it's no doubt embarrassing for you, Sir Michael, having me here . . .' I felt rather awkward myself, carrying on a conversation in a whisper.

'Embarrassing? Why should it be? We shall be drinking some rather seductive Sancerre with the eggs.'

And as Sir Michael took my arm to lead me into dinner, he said: 'And of course, Rumpole, we won't talk "shop".'

So we went into hall, to High Table, where the oak and the old silver glowed in the candle light, and the Principal said grace standing in front of the paintings of former heads of St Joseph's, who had concealed in their gentler academic lives who knows what strange secrets without ever having to give evidence in a criminal Court.

For the first, and I hope the last, time I sat down to gulls' eggs and Sancerre, to be followed by saddle of lamb and Margaux, with a major prosecution witness a week or two before a criminal trial. But Sir Michael was consistently charming to everyone, although he did show, from time to time, an understandable impatience with the academic lawyer, Humphrey Grice. When we returned to the Senior Common Room (coffee, Romeo & Juliettas and vintage Cockburn) the talk was brought round by Grice to what I thought was an uncomfortable subject. He was talking to Fosdyke, but in a voice which carried across the room.

'Interesting piece on Sir Charles Dilke in the *Historical Review*, Fosdyke. Tell me, do you think Dilke might have made a great Liberal prime minister, if he hadn't been caught out by his sexual indiscretions?'

'Dilke was an extraordinary talent.' Fosdyke sniffed his port.

'You know Keir Hardie invited him to lead the Independent Labour Party?'

'Humphrey Grice probably finds that far more shocking than hopping into bed with a couple of ladies at once.' Sir Michael joined fearlessly in the discussion of an ancient scandal.

'If a man is a natural leader, I don't believe his private life makes the smallest difference,' Fosdyke insisted. 'So the answer to your question, Humphrey, is undoubtedly "Yes".'

This didn't seem to please Grice particularly, so he turned to me for support. 'If a man can't run his private life, it's quite obvious that he can't run his country. Wouldn't you agree, Rumpole?'

I looked at the Principal, took a gulp of strengthening port and tried to sound neutral.

'I suppose we've all got things we'd rather not have broadcast to the nation. It's probably just bad luck if you get found out.'

'Quite right. Dilke and Parnell had bad luck. Lloyd George had the luck of the devil.' Simpson's voice came with its muted scream, out of the depths of a chair in the corner of the room.

'It's not luck, in my opinion. It's the use of a little common sense.' Sir Michael was carefully cutting the end off a cigar.

'Yes, Principal. Let's hear your expert opinion.' Grice was stuffing a charred pipe with Old Holborn and giving a yellow smile. Sir Michael settled himself for an elegant oration.

'What is a scandal, if I may ask the rhetorical question? A scandal is a secret that gets found out. It's a subject for lies and cover-ups. If you don't lie, if you don't try and conceal, then there's no scandal. Take Watergate . . .'

'Oh really, Principal. Do we have to?' Simpson shrilled from his corner.

'A tragedy, in my opinion. Those two complacent little scribblers got rid of America's only competent President.' Grice's voice was like a rusty nail on a slate, but Sir Michael came melodiously in to agree with him entirely.

'Exactly! Who'd have given tuppence about Watergate if Nixon had told the truth about it? What was it, a trivial bit of housebreaking, almost a student prank? It became a scandal because of the lies. The moral is, if you want to kill a scandal, tell the truth.'

Sir Michael looked triumphantly round his colleagues. No one spoke, except of course Grice, who said:

'Is that what you intend to do, Principal?'

There was an awkward pause. The dons looked at Grice with varying degrees of antagonism, but Sir Michael said, unperturbed:

'Since you have the bad taste to ask the question, Humphrey, after dinner and in the presence of a guest, the answer is unquestionably "Yes".'

As he said this, the Principal gave me a glowing smile, and an invitation to put up for the night in a College guest room. I telephoned She Who Must Be Obeyed, who didn't seem unduly aggrieved, and walked with Fosdyke and Simpson across the moonlit quadrangle, past the fountain, towards the crumbling golden stone of Founder's Buildings.

'Sir Michael was very charming,' I said. 'I mean I must have been a bit of a spectre at the feast, in all the circumstances.'

'You know we all felt frightfully sorry for him,' Fosdyke told me. 'But he's been so bloody honest about the thing that I don't think it'll do him the slightest harm.'

I thought that on the whole, Sir Michael Tuffnell had handled the scandal which had broken over St Joseph's College with intelligence and skill.

'It'll be so much water off the back of a particularly fly old duck. Is that what you think, Fosdyke?' I asked.

'Much to the fury of Humphrey Grice,' Simpson squawked from the shadows.

'The academic lawyer?'

'He's been after the Principal's job for years.'

At the whiff of college politics, Simpson became audibly excited. 'Grice was the runner-up when Michael was elected. It was Grice who started the scandal really. Went round telling everyone about the Principal's jaunts to London with the gardening boy. All perfectly innocent, of course, but it laid poor Michael wide open to blackmail from two ruthless neurotics.'

'Two . . .?' I didn't follow.

'That's how I'd describe Humphrey Grice.' Simpson was positive. 'And your client too, I'm sorry to say, Rumpole.'

I ignored that. Peter Vernon had more on his plate than Simpson's ill will. Instead I asked, innocently enough, 'So you believe your Principal, when he says nothing happened?'

'The Professor of Moral Philosophy!' Fosdyke sounded shocked. 'Who wouldn't believe him?'

'Yes, I know, Fozzy,' I said, for P. J. Fosdyke had hit on the Achilles' heel of our defence. 'That's exactly what I'm afraid of.'

'And no one's going to believe Vernon, are they?' Monty Simpson turned the knife in the wound. 'No one can stand a blackmailer.'

The next morning I had a leisurely breakfast with Fosdyke and Simpson, and then wandered through the town to land up breathing in the dust and powdered leather of a secondhand bookshop in the Turl. There I propped myself up to read a tattered volume of memoirs by some long dead legal hack, recalling life on the old south-eastern circuit (when, in his experience, no case seemed to last more than a day, and most ended with the black cap at twilight). I was enjoying myself in a mild sort of way, postponing the evil hour of my return to my clerk, Henry, and She Who Must Be Obeyed when a voice like tearing metal pierced the calm of the bookshop.

'You do actually read books then? Your life isn't entirely practical?' Grice blew a sweet cloud of Old Holborn all over me. It was the academic lawyer, crept out of his lair on a shopping spree. He gave me a cunning and conspiratorial sort of smile as he said, 'I say, a bit of a cheek you turning up to dinner with the Principal. Fosdyke tells me you're defending young Vernon.'

'I'm afraid I got trapped. I apologized. It was most embarrassing.'

'Not at all. Tuffnell needs reminding,' said Grice. 'The case isn't far off.' At which he grinned in a way I can only describe as ghoulish. He seemed to relish the idea of my playing Banquo's Ghost at Sir Michael's dinner table. 'I don't think he realizes just how serious it is.'

'For my client?'

'Oh no. For the Principal's career. There's no possible doubt, you know, that he's guilty.'

'My client?' I asked again innocently, knowing quite well what the answer would be.

'Oh no, Sir Michael Tuffnell, "Star of Television". The relationship was definitely physical.'

Fortunately, apart from an antique and no doubt deaf cleric reading an illustrated Boccaccio in a corner, the shop was empty. Otherwise, the Senior Law Tutor might have been involved in a quite non-academic action for slander.

'Oh yes.' He piled on the defamation like a starving man filling his plate at a cafeteria. 'Jemms, the porter, distinctly saw the boy Vernon coming out of the Principal's lodge at dawn.'

'Well,' I tried to put the opposing view, 'I came out of Founder's Buildings, which houses P. J. Fosdyke, at dawn, but I hope no one thinks that the relationship is definitely physical.'

'And I have had a long talk with the Principal's cleaning lady . . .' Grice was clearly prepared to call evidence.

'Have you indeed . . .?'

'I just thought,' he ended triumphantly, 'that *someone* should see the truth come out at the trial. What do you think, Rumpole?'

As he stood in front of me, he looked less like a raven and more like an old vulture getting a far-off whiff of recently killed zebra. I said, 'I think, if I may say so, Grice, that your interest in the law doesn't appear to be entirely academic.'

In the weeks that intervened before the trial, my wife Hilda again tried to raise the subject of the loose covers for the drawing-room chairs.

'Rumpole,' she said, 'I wonder you're not ashamed to be sitting on those tattered remnants.'

'I went to Oxford,' I said hastily, 'and I met my two dear old friends, Monty Simpson and Fozzy Fosdyke. We were inseparable you know. We used to set off with a bottle of beer and a slice of cold Christmas pudding, and tramp to Woodstock.'

'If the Featherstones ever came here, they'd think the place was a tip.'

' "Two scholars whom at College, erst he knew" ' –

58

I did my best to drown her in Matthew Arnold –

' "Met him, and of his way of life inquired . . ." '

'They'd think you were down on your luck, Rumpole,' she persisted, but I gave her more of the 'Scholar Gypsy'.

' "Whereat he answered that the Gypsy crew,
His mates had arts to rule as they desired,
The workings of men's brains . . ." '

'Couldn't you give me a cheque, Rumpole?'

'Not that my mates are a Gypsy crew, you couldn't call Guthrie Featherstone a Gypsy crew, and we can't rule the workings of men's brains, although I might put certain things to a jury, entirely for their consideration of course.'

Under the cover of this nonsense, I had made it to the door, and was almost clear of Froxbury Court when Hilda uttered her final threat.

'If I don't have a cheque for new loose covers, Rumpole, the consequences will be serious.'

'What will the consequences be?'

'I told you. Serious.'

You see my wife had absolutely no understanding of the art of blackmail. For Sir Michael Tuffnell, it was alleged, the consequences of his failure to pay up had been spelled out with the utmost clarity.

I sat in chambers toying with the brief R. v. Vernon, and thought about St Joseph's. By my third year I had forsaken the company of Fozzy and Shrimpson. I no longer walked to the Cumnor Hills or Bablock-hithe. I had become engaged to the eldest daughter of Septimus Porter, my tutor in Roman law.

Unhappily my engagement to poor Cissie Porter had to be broken off by reason of her early death. But had she lived, had we married, how would history have been altered? I couldn't believe that Miss Porter, so docile and eager to agree, would have ended up by blackmailing me over a matter of loose covers.

'You were at St Joseph's too weren't you, Rumpole?'

I looked up and saw that Guthrie Featherstone, Q.C., M.P.,

our learned Head of Chambers, had manifested himself beside my desk.

'What do you mean, *too*?'

'Well, I was at St Joseph's, as you know, from 1952 to 1955.'

'After my time.'

'I know it was. The point is I was up the other night. Giving a talk to the Law Society on my famous cases.'

'Must have been a pretty short talk.'

'Horace! Of course I don't get the sort of sensational stuff you do. I don't hit the headlines, or the *News of the World*. I don't think I'd care to either. What I meant to say is, I had dinner with the Principal. What a perfectly charming fellow.'

'Oh charming. I agree.'

'The point is, of course he's being enormously brave about it, but Michael is most frightfully embarrassed about this case.'

'Not half as embarrassed as my client.'

'It really is an appalling thing to happen, to a man who has the Order of Merit.'

'Well, if he didn't want it to happen, Sir Michael Tuffnell, O.M., shouldn't have rushed round to the Old Bill to pour out his soul.'

'What could he do? He was being blackmailed.'

'Isn't that for the jury to decide?'

'Horace.' Guthrie Featherstone essayed the boyish smile which he puts on before he's going to attempt something unusually devious. 'How do you feel about defending blackmailers?'

'Much as I feel about defending anyone. Glad of the money.'

'But blackmail's such an extra loathsome crime.'

'Perhaps that's why Peter Vernon needs to be defended extra carefully. You wouldn't like him convicted out of prejudice?'

'I really think,' Guthrie was choosing his words carefully, as though he were a Judge at first instance and utterly scared of the Court of Appeal, 'I really do think that Michael is just a little *wee* bit upset at the fact that Vernon's being defended by an old St Joseph's man.'

'I can't think why. Peter Vernon's a St Joseph's man too, after all. He's a St Joseph's gardener.'

'Oh well, Horace, if that's the attitude.' And Guthrie Feather-stone started to beat a measured retreat.

'Don't come to dinner next week, Guthrie, will you?'

'Have you asked me?'

'No. So please don't come. If you do I'll simply have to spend a fortune on loose covers.' Guthrie then withdrew, feeling perhaps, that his mission on behalf of Sir Michael Tuffnell had not been a total success.

When our Head of Chambers had gone off to govern the country (or at least to sit in moody silence through an all-night sitting), I turned my attention back to the brief, and a thought, as yet no bigger than a very small man's hand, appeared on the horizon. I lifted the telephone and asked Harry to put me through to Miss Sue Galton of the Oxford solicitors. After we had exchanged pleasantries and I had inquired after her fiancé's health ('Bit worried now the trial's next week, actually.' *He* was worried – what on earth did she think I was?), I asked Miss Galton to remind me of the date when Sir Michael first went to the police and complained that he was being blackmailed.

'November the first last year.'

'And what are the dates on the cheques?' I heard the rustling as she consulted her file.

'August, September. One in October.'

'All before the Principal went to the police?'

'Before that, yes.'

'Listen. I want you to find out about the gold cigarette case. Get a photograph of it or something. Go round Oxford jewellers. Find out when Sir Michael bought it.'

'*When*?'

'Yes. The date's important. Find out *when*.'

'Do you think that's going to help us?' Miss Galton asked me.

'I really don't know. Something has to.'

I went back to Oxford the day before the trial for a final conference. Miss Sue Galton had, she told me, drawn a blank with the Oxford jewellers. I sent her up to London. I had an idea that Sir Michael might have bought the case when he stayed at his Club in St James, just across the road from Bond Street and the Burlington Arcade. It seemed a forlorn hope, and she hadn't returned the next morning when I sat gloomily in Court, listening to the opening of Her Majesty's case against Peter Vernon.

The Oxford Crown Court was full of students – perhaps they were all learning law and anxious to perfect their knowledge of 'demanding money with menaces'. Perhaps they merely wanted to see a distinguished academic in a spot of bother. The Red Judge in charge of the proceedings was Mr Justice Everglades, known to his few friends as 'Florrie', a highly educated old sweetheart with no affection for the criminal classes, who were mainly the sort of people he never bumped into at Glyndebourne. When Peter Vernon pleaded not guilty to the charge of blackmail, the Judge looked at him with a kind of bored disgust; he had not yet had occasion to acknowledge the presence of Rumpole. He listened to Bernard Crompton, Q.C., opening the case for the Crown, with obvious satisfaction.

'Members of the jury,' old Bernard started, after the usual formal introductions. 'We may be able to forgive some forms of criminal activity. The man who steals because his wife or his children are in need, the man who loses his self-control and commits an assault, may even deserve our sympathy. But blackmail, you may think is a truly unforgivable crime. Blackmail is a slow poison which feeds on its victims' fear and, of course, members of the jury, the higher position a man reaches in his public life, the further he has to fall, and the more he's got to lose. And no one, you may think, is in a more vulnerable position than the distinguished head of a great Oxford college, a man like Sir Michael Tuffnell, whom you probably all know well from your television screens.

'Sir Michael is, of course, Professor of Moral Philosophy and Principal of St Joseph's College in this ancient university.'

Bernard Crompton was my contemporary and a member of the old Oxford circuit. He was a dangerous prosecutor, covering his considerable intelligence with a bluff and common-sense manner, and being able to talk to the jury as though he were one of them, sitting not in counsel's benches, but beside them in their jury-box.

'But the mere fact that blackmail is a crime which we all hate and despise mustn't make you more ready to assume that this young man, Peter Vernon, is guilty. In all criminal trials, the prosecution bring the case and they have to prove it. If you're in any doubt about it, at the end of the day, say "not guilty".'

Bernard was the most dangerous sort of advocate because he was entirely fair. It was a deadly method of prosecuting and the way he got his convictions.

'And remember,' counsel for the Crown reached his peroration, 'these allegations of sexual misconduct are horribly easy to bring and terribly hard to refute. But if you are sure,' he fixed the jury with a frank and serious stare, 'when you've heard all our evidence, that young Vernon threatened to make these dreadful accusations and so extracted money from Sir Michael, and you will have evidence of the cheques actually paid into Vernon's bank account and the valuable gold cigarette case found in his possession, then your only verdict, according to your oath, must be one of guilty.'

The jury looked impressed and deeply conscious of their duty. They tried not to lick their lips as Bernard announced that he was about to call the evidence with the assistance of his learned junior. At which moment, there was a small stir in the bench behind me. Miss Sue Galton, had returned, not a moment too soon, from the jewellers' shops of London. I leant back and she whispered into my ear:

'I found the shop finally. In the Burlington Arcade. I'm going upstairs to get a witness summons.'

'Tell me the date he bought it, just the date.'

She told me while Sir Michael Tuffnell, having stepped modestly into the witness-box, held up the New Testament, and swore by Almighty God that the evidence he was about to give would be the truth, the whole truth and nothing but the truth. Florrie Everglades glared at us for whispering at this solemn moment, and then turned his attention to the distinguished witness. Having seen so many leather-jacketed tearaways, and polo-necked villains in witness-boxes, Florrie was clearly delighted with the appearance of a grey-haired and good-looking holder of the Order of Merit, wearing a double-breasted blue suit and a spotted bow tie, who could speak the Queen's English and didn't think *Rigoletto* was something you eat with tomato sauce. Although a Cambridge man, Mr Justice Everglades clearly had every sympathy with the embarrassing position in which the Principal of St Joseph's found himself. He gave the witness a welcoming smile and said, 'Sir Michael, you understand that in blackmail cases, the victim can remain anonymous, and merely be referred to as Mr X. I will direct the reporters in Court to refer to you in that way.'

'My Lord, I am extremely grateful.' Sir Michael gave the Judge a small but gracious bow. I was sure Everglades, J., was delighted and I saw no chance of poor old Peter Vernon being referred to as 'Mr X'. Bernard Crompton interrupted my reverie by launching into his examination in chief.

'Sir Michael, you are the Principal of St Joseph's College?'

'I am.'

'You are the Oxford Professor of Moral Philosophy, a Fellow of the Royal Society and hold the Order of Merit.'

'Yes, I do.' The admission couldn't have been made more modestly. Bernard went on to trickier matters.

'Sir Michael, when did you get to know the defendant, Vernon?'

'About eighteen months ago, my Lord.' Sir Michael Tuffnell turned respectfully to the Judge as a good witness should. 'When he came to us as an under-gardener and general handyman.'

'Did you have any relationship with him, other than as a college servant?'

There was a slight pause. The witness was clearly choosing his words, but he made an excellent choice. 'I think he became a friend. I hope all the college servants are my friends.'

'Did you offer him any particular form of friendship?'

'My Lord. May I explain?'

Florrie Everglades seemed almost flattered to be spoken to by the witness. The old sweetheart answered with more than usual unction.

'Please, Sir Michael. And do take your time. Would you care to sit down?'

I was only surprised he didn't offer him a glass of port and a nibble of biscuit.

'I got talking to Peter Vernon . . .' There was another slight hesitation, and Bernard helped out.

'In the garden was that?'

'In the garden, yes,' the witness agreed. 'I found that he was a very intelligent young man, with genuine, if unformed, musical tastes. He had done well at school, but his parents had opposed him going on to higher education. And he'd been unable to find a job which suited his very real talents. I thought that he might be feeling jealous of the young men of his age who were enjoying academic life at St Joseph's.'

'So?' Bernard nudged the evidence in gently.

'So I felt I should invite him to take some part, at least, in the intellectual life of our community.'

I looked at him; what a dear old philanthropist the great man was!

'I invited him to my rooms. We talked.'

'About?' Bernard was astute enough to ask my best question, and so anticipate my cross-examination.

'About music. And philosophy. I tried to have the sort of discussion with him I would normally have with an under-graduate.'

The Judge was nodding with approval and writing it all down. Dear old Bernard took another brave step forward.

'Did he ever stay the night in your lodge?'

I looked up, wondering if Sir Michael would be fool enough to deny it. Of course he wasn't.

'Once or twice. When we were talking late. I put him up in my spare bedroom.'

'And did you go to London together?'

'Again, I think it was once or twice. I took him to Covent Garden and dinner at my Club.'

'Did your friendship continue happily?'

Sir Michael, with a look of genuine distress at the Judge, said with deep regret, 'I'm afraid it didn't.'

'What happened?' Bernard nudged again.

'One day, Peter Vernon came to me in the garden and said that if I didn't give him money he would write round to all my colleagues at St Joseph's and tell them we had been sleeping together.'

'And *had* you?'

Sir Michael looked at the jury then, and became the perfect English gent making the perfectly frank denial.

'Certainly not.'

'How did you react?'

'I'm afraid foolishly. I knew I was innocent of what he was suggesting, my Lord, but I was afraid of the scandal.'

'Naturally.' Florrie looked at the jury and explained the obvious to them – 'A man in your very vulnerable position.' I should have chucked a glass of water at the old darling then, but I refrained.

'And I was afraid that one of my colleagues, at least, might say, "There's no smoke without a fire."' Sir Michael's explanation sounded perfectly reasonable, and I knew who he was talking about – Grice, the academic lawyer.

'So you gave him the cheques which we have seen?' Bernard was relaxed; his examination was a coast downhill all the way from then on.

'Yes. And sometimes cash.'

'Amounting to some six hundred pounds. And the gold cigarette case which was, how much?'

'I think that was five hundred, my Lord.'

'About five hundred . . .' Florrie was writing it all down.

'And then?' Bernard moved him on gently.

'Then I began to think about it and realized that if I went on paying Vernon, he would blackmail me for ever. I decided that I must face up to the possibility of scandal and go to the police.'

'I'm sure we all realize that required considerable courage, Sir Michael,' said the Judge, and I wondered if he was going to give him his V.C. then or after the trial.

'Yes. Thank you, Sir Michael. Just wait there, will you? In case my learned friend has any questions.'

Bernard Crompton subsided with an air of great satisfaction, and the Judge looked with distaste at counsel for the defence. He sighed and said: 'Have you any questions, Mr Rumpole?'

'A few, my Lord.' I was hoisting myself on to my hind legs, preparatory to going into my act. 'Just a few.'

The Judge looked at the distinguished witness in an apologetic sort of way, and the jury viewed me with the vague interest they always accord to a new character in the drama, as Sir Michael prepared himself with a smile of almost amused co-operation.

'In your book, *Morality and Modern Man*, you said something to this effect. "Modern man will do good, and tell the truth for its own sake, not out of fear or respect for a possibly non-existent deity." '

I had done my homework, but I didn't feel that the jury were immediately grabbed by the question.

'I did, yes.'

'And yet you began your evidence by swearing on the Bible?'

'Yes.'

'Why did you do that? Why didn't you affirm, if you don't believe in God?'

Sir Michael dealt with my ignorance with patience, as though I were a serious but not over-bright pupil at a seminar.

'I said God was possibly non-existent. That means I have to recognize that He possibly exists.'

'And on that outside chance, you took the oath as you did?' I was merely asking for information, but the Judge didn't like it.

'Mr Rumpole,' he asked in a markedly unfriendly manner. 'Are you criticizing Sir Michael for taking the oath in the usual fashion?'

'Oh no, my Lord.' This time *I* was giving the seminar. 'I am criticizing Sir Michael for trying to present himself to this jury as something other than he is.'

I turned to the witness and asked a brutally non-academic question. 'You're lying about yourself, aren't you?'

'Perhaps you could make clear what you mean, Mr Rumpole.'

'The truth is that you and this young man were lovers.'

'No. I have already told you . . .' I knew quite well what he had already told us. I battled on.

'And as a lover, you gave him presents from time to time.'

'Is *that* what they were . . .?' Sir Michael smiled, and the Judge pursed his lips as though he expected nothing better from the defence.

'Certainly that's what they were,' I suggested strongly. 'The sort of expensive presents another man might give his mistress.'

'I have no idea what a man might give his mistress.' Sir Michael smiled at the jury, but I noticed they didn't smile back.

'I expect you haven't! You never married, Sir Michael?'

'No. I have been denied that happiness.' I supposed some of us might say he'd been exceptionally lucky, but I let that pass.

'So you have no one else to give presents to?'

'It's true that I have no immediate family . . .'

'No one but young Peter Vernon?'

'I've already told the Court why I gave him that money.'

My Lord, the learned Judge, who had been listening to the exchange with growing impatience, nodded his agreement.

'Because you were afraid of being accused of something you hadn't done?' I asked with an almost genuine bewilderment.

'Exactly.'

'And you knew that Mr Humphrey Grice, your Senior Tutor in Academic Law, would use any scandal to have you dismissed as Principal, because he coveted your place?'

I followed Sir Michael's eye up to the public gallery, where the law don was leaning eagerly over the rail, waiting for the kill.

'That was something I did have in mind, yes,' the Principal admitted.

'And you were particularly fearful, because you knew the charge was true?'

'Mr Rumpole, this witness has already denied that unpleasant suggestion!' Florrie intervened, and I toyed with the notion of asking the old darling if he'd care to go in to the witness-box and give evidence himself. I rejected the idea and persisted with the material available.

'Sir Michael. We've heard my learned friend, in his opening speech, tell us the date when you went to the police to make this charge of alleged blackmail. It was November the first, was it not? Of last year.'

'I believe so. Yes.' For the first time Sir Michael Tuffnell sounded doubtful.

'You can take the date from me. The police did nothing for well over a month . . .'

'They were making inquiries, my Lord,' Bernard Crompton rose to his hind legs to protect the honour of the force. 'At Vernon's bank, for instance.'

'Yes, of course, Mr Crompton. I'm sure most of us in Court understand that perfectly well.' The Judge looked coldly at Rumpole, who didn't understand. I asked my next question undeterred.

'And it was during that month, but after the first of November, while the police were making their inquiries, that you gave young Peter Vernon this gold cigarette case? Might I just have it, usher. Exhibit twelve.'

The usher obliged, and I stood in Court holding the heavy gold object, weighing it in my hand. The jury paid me the compliment of looking intensely interested. Florrie gave a slight frown and Bernard Crompton lay back in his seat and studied the ceiling. Sir Michael Tuffnell looked as though he'd just stumbled on something which upset his whole theory of the Universe – proof of the existence of God for instance.

'No, I'm sure,' he said, 'I'm sure that can't be right.'

'It can't be right if you're telling the truth, can it? You wouldn't decide to put an end to the blackmailing by complaining to the police, and *then* spend five hundred pounds on a gold cigarette case for Peter Vernon?'

'No. Certainly not!'

Oh, Tuffnell, my dear old sweetheart, I breathed a sigh of relief, you have delivered yourself into my hands.

'But you see, that's exactly what you did, Sir Michael. I will be calling evidence to prove that you bought this case on the fifth of December last year at a jeweller's in Burlington Arcade, near your Club, and gave it to Peter Vernon as a Christmas present!'

'What date was that, Mr Rumpole?'

For the first time in the course of my cross-examination, the learned Judge was preparing to make a note.

'The fifth of *December*, my Lord.'

'Why should I do that, Mr Rumpole?' The witness was asking me the question.

'I'll tell you, Sir Michael. Because you wanted to frame Peter Vernon on a blackmail charge . . .'

'*Frame* him!'

Mr Justice Everglades was showing signs of genuine distress, but I addressed myself entirely to the witness. 'Oh, yes. You wanted to make sure that Peter Vernon wasn't going to be believed if he ever told the truth. You knew that Grice was on to your trail like an old bloodhound, and you also knew Peter was planning to get married to a young lady solicitor. You didn't know him very well, did you? You thought he'd start talking –

about your nights together. And if he was going to talk, you wanted him to talk from the dock, where no one would believe him.'

'But I'd already given him the cheques.' Sir Michael was now driven to try and argue the prosecution case.

'Presents. Presents that could be used to get Peter Vernon arrested and have him convicted as a criminal whom no one could believe. You might have got away with it, Sir Michael, if you hadn't wanted to add one final bit of evidence. The gold cigarette case that you bought him in London *after you'd gone to the police*!'

From then on, in spite of a bumpy ride from the Judge, it was really downhill all the way for Rumpole. We called the jeweller from the Burlington Arcade, who had his books in good order, and there could be no doubt about the date when Sir Michael bought the case that was designed to frame a black-mailer. Peter Vernon went into the witness-box, was greeted with a blast of hostility from the Judge, and left it with the jury looking as if they might all chip in for a set of Tupperware to give the happy couple. When it came to my turn to address the Court I was able to do a bit of a Bernard Crompton for the defence.

'Members of the jury. We may be able to forgive some forms of criminal activity, the man who steals because his wife or his children are in need, the man who loses his self-control and commits an assault. But blackmail, and here I agree with every word that my learned friend, Mr Bernard Crompton, said to you on behalf of the Crown, is really the meanest form of crime! Blackmail, when it means planting false evidence on an innocent young man so that you can have him convicted of an offence he had never committed, so that you can gain the advantage of being safe from scandal, must be the meanest crime of all. Who was the blackmailer in this case, members of the jury? Was it the young man in the dock, or the older man in the witness-box? Who is lying about whom? Ask yourselves that question. And remember that the answer is a gold cigarette case, bought to bolster up a false charge, and bought *after* Sir Michael had complained to the police.'

*

When the case was over, Peter Vernon came out blinking into the sunlight, surprised to be free, and Miss Sue Galton was surprised only that he had never told her everything. They went away, I suppose to flog the cigarette case and buy wallpaper, saucepan scourers, lino tiles, acres of Vim and other domestic articles.

After I had said goodbye to the young couple, I saw Sir Michael getting into a taxi. He smiled his own goodbye at me, I thought very charmingly. He resigned a little while later as Principal of St Joseph's College, a job Humphrey Grice, so Fozzy said in his letter to me, doesn't do as well, and the food at High Table has deteriorated. Sir Michael has just presented a hugely successful telly series on 'Man – the Moral Animal'.

As for me, I caught the train to London immediately after the trial, and like Matthew Arnold's old gypsy

... came, as most men deem'd, to little good
But came to Oxford and his friends, no more.

Seated at breakfast in the mansion flat some weeks later I opened an envelope which was lying beside my plate, and regretted having done so when a document fluttered out, marked with a huge sum of money.

'Hilda,' I put the question fearlessly to She Who Must Be Obeyed, 'what on earth's this?'

'It's an estimate, Rumpole. For redecorating the flat.'

'Why should we want the flat redecorated?' I didn't follow.

'To brighten it up, Rumpole.' Hilda then paused dramatically, and said, 'Of course, if you'd agreed to buy new chair covers, that wouldn't be necessary.'

Now that was a decent bit of blackmail, clear and open, and, of course, quite effective. I had absolutely no alternative but to say, 'All right then, Hilda. Chair covers it is.'

Rumpole and the Dear Departed

> Let's talk of graves, of worms, and epitaphs;
> Make dust our paper, and with rainy eyes
> Write sorrow on the bosom of the earth.
> Let's choose executors and talk of wills;
> And yet not so – for what can we bequeath
> Save our deposed bodies to the ground.

The only reason why I, Horace Rumpole, Rumpole of the Old Bailey, dedicated, from my days as a white-wig and my call to the bar, almost exclusively to a life of crime should talk of wills, was because of a nasty recession in felonies and misdemeanours. Criminals are, by and large, of an extraordinary Conservative disposition. They believe passionately in free enterprise and strict monetarist policies. They are against state interference of any kind. And yet they, like the owners of small businesses, seem to have felt the cold winds of the present recession. There just isn't the crime about that there used to be. So when Henry came into my room staggering under the weight of a heavy bundle of papers and said, 'Got something a bit more up-market than your usual, Mr Rumpole; Mowbray and Pontefract want to instruct you in a will case, sir,' I gave him a tentative welcome. Even our learned Head of Chambers, Guthrie Featherstone, Q.C., M.P., could scarce forbear to cheer. 'Hear you've got your foot in the door of the Chancery Division, Horace. That's the place to be, my dear old chap. That's where the money is. Besides it's so much better for the reputation of Chambers for you not to have dangerous criminals hanging about in the waiting-room.'

I said something about dangerous criminals at least being alive. The law of probate, so it seemed to me, is exclusively concerned with the dead.

' "Let's choose executors and talk of wills; and yet not so" –

for, besides having nothing to bequeath, Rumpole knows almost nothing about the law of probate.'

That is what I told Miss Beasley, the Matron of the Sunnyside Nursing Home on the peaceful Sussex coast, when she came to consult me about the testamentary affairs of the late Colonel Ollard. It was nothing less than the truth. I know very little indeed on the subject of wills.

Miss Beasley was a formidable-looking customer: a real heavyweight with iron-grey hair, a powerful chin and a nose similar in shape to that sported by the late Duke of Wellington. She was in mufti when she came to see me (brogues and a tweed suit), but I imagine that in full regimentals, with starched cap and collar, the lace bonnet and medals pinned on the mountainous chest, she must have been enough to put the wind up the bravest invalid.

She gave me the sort of slight tightening of the lips which must have passed, in the wards she presided over, as a smile. 'Never you mind, Mr Rumpole,' she said, 'the late Colonel wanted you to act in this case particularly. He has mentioned your name on several occasions.'

'Oh, really? But Miss Beasley, dear lady, the late Colonel Bollard . . .'

'Colonel Ollard, Mr Rumpole, Colonel Roderick Ollard, M.C., D.S.O., C.B.E., late of the Pines, Balaclava Road, Cheeveling-on-Sea, and the Sunnyside Nursing Home,' she corrected me firmly. 'The dear departed has come through with your name, perfectly clearly more than once.'

'Come through with it, Miss Beasley?' I must say the phrase struck me as a little odd at the time.

'That is what I said, Mr Rumpole.' Miss Beasley pursed her lips.

'We should be alleging fraud against the other side, Mr Rumpole.'

The person who had spoken was Mr Pontefract, of the highly respected firm of Mowbray and Pontefract, an elderly type of solicitor with a dusty black jacket, a high stiff collar and the reverent and deeply sympathetic tone of voice of a reputable undertaker. He was someone, I felt sure, who knew all about wills, not to mention graves and worms and epitaphs. And the word he had used had acted like a trumpet call to battle. I felt myself brighten considerably. I beamed on La Beasley and said with confidence,

'Fraud! Now, there is a subject I do know something about. And whom are we alleging fraud against?'

'Mr Percival Ollard, Mrs Percival Ollard . . .' Mr Pontefract supplied the information.

'That Marcia. She didn't give a toss for the Colonel!' Miss Beasley interrupted with a thrust of the chest and a swift intake of breath. 'And young Peter Ollard, their son, aged thirteen years, represented by his parents as guardians, *ad litem*.' Mr Pontefract completed the catalogue of shame.

'The Colonel thought Peter was a complete sissy, Mr Rumpole!' Miss Beasley hastened to give me the low-down on this shower. 'The boy didn't give a toss for military history, he was more interested in ballet dancing.'

'Young Peter, it appears, had ambitions to enter the West Sussex School of Dance.' Mr Pontefract made this announcement with deep regret.

'You should have heard Colonel Ollard on the subject!' Miss Beasley gave me another tight little smile.

'I can well imagine,' I said. 'Mr Pontefract . . . just remind me of the history of Colonel Ollard's testamentary affairs.'

I needed to be reminded because Pontefract's instructions, as set out in his voluminous brief, were on the dryish side. As a lawyer, Pontefract was no doubt admirable, as an author he lacked the knack, which many criminal solicitors possess, of grabbing the attention. In fact I had slumbered over his papers and a bottle of Pommeroy's plonk in front of the electric fire in Froxbury Court.

'Colonel and Percival Ollard were the only two sons of the late Reverend Hector Ollard, Rector of Cheeveling-on-Sea,' Pontefract started to recap. 'They inherited well and by wise investments both became wealthy men. Percival Ollard started a firm known as Ollard's Kitchen Utensils which prospered exceedingly. During the last six years the brothers never met; and Colonel Roderick Ollard, who was an invalid . . .'

'It was his heart let him down, Mr Rumpole. His poor old ticker.' Miss Beasley supplied the medical evidence.

'Colonel Ollard was nursed devotedly by Miss Beasley at her nursing home, Sunnyside,' Pontefract assured me, and was once again interrupted by Matron.

'He was a real old sport, was the Colonel! Often had my incurable ladies in a roar! Quite a schoolboy at heart, Mr Rumpole. And I'll take my dying oath on this, the Percival Ollards never visited him, not after the first fortnight. They never even wrote to him. Not so much as a little card for a Christmas or birthday.'

I was about to 'tut-tut' sympathetically, as I felt was expected, when Pontefract took up the narrative. 'When the Colonel died all we could find was a will he made in 1970, under which his estate would be inherited by his brother Percival, his sister-in-law Marcia, and his nephew, Peter . . .'

'The ballet dancer!' I remembered.

'Exactly! In equal shares, after a small legacy to an old batman.'

'Of course their will's a forgery.' Miss Beasley clearly had no doubt about it.

'I thought you said it was a fraud.' The allegations seemed to be coming thick and fast.

'A fraud *and* a forgery!'

It was all good, familiar stuff. In some relief I stood up, found and lit a small cigar.

'Concocted by the Percival Ollards,' I said gleefully. 'Yes, I see it all. You know, even though it's only a probate action, I do detect a comforting smell of crime about this case. Tell me, Miss Beasley. Where do you think the Colonel should have left, how much was it, did you say, Mr Pontefract?'

'With the value of The Pines, when we sell it. I would say, something over half a million pounds, Mr Rumpole.'

Half a million nicker! It was a crock of gold that might command a fee which would even tempt Rumpole into the dreaded precincts of the Chancery Division. I sat down and asked Matron the sixty-four-thousand-dollar question.

'Well, of course, he should have left his money to the person who looked after him in his declining years,' Miss Beasley said it in all modesty.

'To your good self?' I was beginning to get the drift of this consultation.

'Exactly!' Miss Beasley had no doubt about it. But Pontefract came in sadly, with a little legal difficulty.

'What I have told Miss Beasley is,' he said, 'that she has no *locus standi*.' I had no doubt he was right but I hoped that the learned Pontefract was about to make his meaning clear to a humble hack. Happily he did so. 'Miss Beasley is in no way related to the late Colonel.'

'In absolutely no way!' Matron was clearly not keen to be associated with the Percival Ollards.

'And she doesn't seem to have been named in any other will.'

'We haven't found any other will. Yet.' Matron looked more than ever like the Duke of Wellington about to meet her Waterloo.

'So she can't contest the February 1970 will in favour of Peter Ollard. If it fails, she stands to gain ... nothing.' Mr Pontefract broke the news gently but clearly to the assembled company.

Little as I know of the law of wills, some vague subconscious stirring, some remote memory of a glance at *Chancery in a Nutshell* before diving into the Bar Finals, made me feel that the sepulchral Pontefract had a point. I summed up the situation judicially by saying,

'Of course in law, Miss Beasley, your very experienced solicitor is perfectly right. I agree with what he has said and I have nothing to add.'

'There is another law, Mr Rumpole.' Miss Beasley spoke quietly, but very firmly. 'The higher law of God's justice.'

'I'm afraid you won't find they'll pay much attention to that in the Chancery Division.' I hated to disillusion her.

'Miss Beasley insisted we saw you, Mr Rumpole. But you have only confirmed my own views. Legally, we haven't got a leg to stand on.' Mr Pontefract was gathering up his papers, ready for the 'off'.

'Well, we'll jolly well have to find one, won't we?' Matron sounded unexpectedly cheerful, 'Mr Rumpole. I won't keep you any longer. I'll be in touch as soon as we find that leg you're looking for.'

And now Miss Beasley stood up in a business-like way. I felt as though I'd been ordered a couple of tranquillizers and a blanket bath and not to fuss because she'd be round with Doctor in the morning. Before she went, however, I had one question to ask:

'Just one thing, Miss Beasley. You say the late Colonel recommended me, as a sound legal adviser?'

'He did indeed! He was mentioning your name only last week,' Miss Beasley answered cheerfully.

'Last week? But, Miss Beasley, I understand that Colonel Ollard departed this life almost six months ago.'

'Oh yes, Mr Rumpole.' She explained, as though to a child, 'that's when he died. Not when he was speaking to me.'

At which point I sneezed, and Matron said, 'You want to watch that cold, Mr Rumpole. It could turn into something nasty.'

Miss Beasley, of course, was right. The reason I hadn't been able to concentrate with my usual merciless clarity on the law governing testamentary matters was that I had the dry throat and misty eyes of an old legal hack with a nasty cold coming on. A rare burst of duty took me down to the Old Bailey for a small matter of warehouse breaking, and four nights later saw me drinking, for medicinal reasons, a large brandy, sucking a clinical thermometer and shivering in front of my electric fire at Froxbury Court, dressed in pyjamas and a dressing-gown. She Who Must Be Obeyed looked at me without any particular sympathy. There has never been much of the Florence Nightingale about my wife Hilda.

'Rumpole! That's the third time you've taken your temperature this evening. What is it?'

'It's sunk down to normal, Hilda. I must be fading away.'

'Really! It's only a touch of flu. Doctor MacClintock says there's a lot of it about.'

'It's a touch of death, if you want my opinion. There's a lot of that about too.'

'Well, I hope you'll stay in the warm tomorrow.'

'I can't do that! Got to get down to the Bailey. The jury are coming back in my murder in the morning.' I sneezed and continued bravely, 'I'd better be in at the death.'

'That's what you will be in at. If you *must* go traipsing down to the Old Bailey, don't expect me to feel sorry for you.'

I was about to say, of course I never expected Hilda to feel sorry for me, when the telephone rang. She rushed to answer it (unlike me, she takes an unnatural delight in answering telephones), and announced that a Miss Rosemary Beasley was on the line and wished to communicate with her counsel as a matter of urgency. Cursing the fact that Miss Beasley, unlike my other clients, wasn't tucked up in the remand wing of the nick, safe from the telephone, I took the instrument and breathed into it a rheumy, 'Good evening.'

Matron came back, loud and clear, 'Mr Rumpole. I am sitting here at my planchette.'

'At your *what*?' Miss Beasley had me mystified.

'Sometimes I use the board, or the wine glass or the cards. Sometimes I have Direct Communication.'

'That must be nice for you. Miss Beasley, what *are* you talking about?'

'Tonight I am at the planchette. I have just had such a nice chat with Colonel Ollard.'

'With the *late* Colonel Ollard?'

I was, I had to confess, somewhat taken aback. When Matron answered, she sounded a little touchy. 'He wasn't late at all. He came through bang on time! It was just nine o'clock when we started chatting. He says the weather over there's absolutely beautiful! It's just not fair, I told him, when we're going through this dreary cold spell.'

'Miss Beasley.' I asked for clarification. 'Did Colonel Ollard come over from the dead, simply to chatter to you about the weather?'

'Oh no, Mr Rumpole. I shouldn't be telephoning you if that were all. He said something *far* more important.'

'Oh did he? And can you let me into the secret?' My temperature was clearly rising during this conversation. I longed for bed with both my feet on a hot water bottle.

'The Colonel said that Mr Pontefract had never looked in the tin box where he kept his dress uniform, in the loft at The Pines.'

'Well. Suppose Mr Pontefract never has . . .'

'If he looked there, the Colonel told me, Mr Pontefract would find, wrapped in tissue paper, between the sword and the ... trousers, a later will, signed by himself in the proper manner.'

I could see the way things were drifting and quite honestly I didn't like it at all. The day might not be far distant when Miss Beasley might in fact find herself tucked safely up in the nick.

'Is that what the Colonel said?' I asked, warily.

'His very words.'

'You're quite *sure* that's what he said . . .'

'How could I possibly be mistaken?'

'Well, I suppose you'd better ring Pontefract and get him to take a look. I just hope . . .'

'You hope *what*, Mr Rumpole?'

'I hope you're not considering anything *dangerous*, Miss Beasley.'

After all, what could all this planchette nonsense be but a rather obvious prelude to forgery?

'Of course not! I'm perfectly safe, Mr Rumpole. I've just been sitting here chatting.' Matron sounded her usual brisk self. I tried to remember if there'd ever been a woman forger, with a nursing qualification.

'Yes. Well, if you ring Mr Pontefract,' I suggested, but apparently all that had been taken care of.

'I've done that, Mr Rumpole. I just thought I'd ring you too, to tell you the joyful tidings. Oh, and Mr Rumpole. The Colonel sent you his best wishes, and he hopes he's been a help to you, giving you a leg to stand on. Cheerio for now! Oh, and he hopes your cold's better.'

As I put down the receiver, I felt, as I have said, a good deal worse.

'Who on earth's Miss Rosemary Beasley?' Hilda asked when I had finished sneezing.

'Oh her. She's just someone who seems to be on particularly good terms with the dead.'

The next day, still feeling in much the same condition as the late Colonel Ollard, but without the blue skies to cheer me up, I staggered off to the Old Bailey and heard my warehouse breaker get three years. When the formalities and the official good-byes were over I walked back to Chambers and there, awaiting me in my room, was the lugubrious Pontefract. He came straight out with the news.

'It was just as she told us, Mr Rumpole. There was a tin box under a pile of old blankets in the loft at The Pines, which we had overlooked. In it was the full dress uniform of a colonel of the Royal Dorsets.'

'And between the sword and trousers?'

'I found a will, apparently dated the first of March 1974. Over four years after the other will in favour of the Percival Ollards. It revokes all previous wills and leaves his entire estate to ...'

'Miss Rosemary Beasley?' I hazarded a guess.

'You've hit it, Mr Rumpole!'

'It didn't need great powers of divination.'

I couldn't help looking round nervously to see that we weren't in the presence of the mysterious matron.

'Mr Pontefract, as our client isn't with us today ...'

'I'm quite thankful for it, Mr Rumpole.'

'You are? So am I. You know that the late Colonel apparently spoke from the other side of the grave, to tip our client off about this will?'

'So I understand, Mr Rumpole.'

'Mr Pontefract. I know you are accustomed to polite civil law and my mind turns as naturally to crime as a vicar's daughter does to sex, but ...'

I didn't know how to make the suggestion which might wound the old gentleman; but he was out with the word before me.

'You suspect *this* will may be a forgery?'

'That thought had crossed your mind?'

'Of course, Mr Rumpole. There is no field of endeavour in which human nature sinks to a lower depth than in the matter of wills. Your average Old Bailey case, Mr Rumpole, must seem like a day out with the Church Brigade compared to the skul-duggery which surrounds the simplest last will and testament.'

As he spoke I began to warm to this man, Pontefract. He was expressing my own opinions fairly eloquently, and I listened with an increased respect as he went on.

'Naturally my first thought was that our client, Miss Beasley, had invented this supernatural conversation in order to direct our attention to a will which she had, shall we say, manu-factured?'

'A neutral term, Mr Pontefract.' But well put, I thought. 'That was my first thought, also.'

'So I took the precaution of having this new-found will ex-amined by a well-known handwriting expert.'

'Alfred Geary?'

There is only one handwriting expert Her Majesty's judges pay any attention to. Geary is now an old man peering at blown-up letters through thick pebble glasses, but he is still an irrefutable witness.

'I went, in this instance, and regardless of expense, to Mr Geary. You approve, sir?'

'You couldn't do better. The Courts listen in awe to this fellow's comparison between the Ms and the tails on the Ps. What did Geary find?'

'That the signature on the will we discovered . . .'

'Between the dress sword and the trousers?'

'Is undoubtedly the genuine signature of the late Colonel.

It was the one piece of evidence I hadn't expected. If the will was not a forgery, if it were a genuine document, could it pos-sibly follow that the message which led us to its hiding-place was also genuine? The mind, as they say, boggled. I was scarcely listening as Mr Pontefract told me that the Percival Ollards would be attacking our new will on the grounds of the deceased's insanity. It was my own sanity I began to fear for, as I won-dered if the deceased Colonel would be giving us any more instructions from beyond the grave.

When I got home I was feeling distinctly worse. I mentioned the matter to She Who Must Be Obeyed and she swiftly called my bluff by summoning in the local quack who was round, as he always is, like a shot, in the hope of a fee and a swig of my diminishing stock of sherry (a form of rot-gut I seem to keep entirely for the benefit of the medical profession).

'He's not looking in a particularly lively condition is he?' Doctor MacClintock remarked to Hilda on arrival. 'Well, we've got to remember, Rumpole's no chicken.'

I was unable to argue with the doctor's diagnosis, as it was undoubtedly true, and what's more, I had a clinical thermometer stuck between my jaws. I could only grunt a protest when Hilda, with quite unnecessary hospitality, said, 'You will take a glass of sherry, won't you, Doctor? So good of you to come.'

I mean to say, when I do my job of work, the Judge doesn't start proceedings with, 'So nice of you to drop in Rumpole, do help yourself to my personal store of St Émilion.' I was going to say something along these lines when the gloomy Scots medico removed the thermometer, but he interrupted me with, 'His temperature's up. I'm afraid it's a day or two in bed for the old warrior.'

'A day or two in bed? You'll have to tell him, Doctor, he's got to be sensible.'

'Oh I doubt very much if he'll feel like being anything else.'

I began to wish they'd stop talking as if I'd already passed on, and so I intruded into the conversation.

'Bed? I can't possibly stay in bed . . .'

'You're no chicken, Rumpole. Doctor MacClintock warned you.'

I noticed that the thirsty quack had downed one glass of Pommeroy's pale Spanish-style and was getting a generous refill from the family.

'You warned me? What did you warn me about?'

'You're not getting any younger, Rumpole.'

'Well, it hardly needs five years' ruthless training in the Edinburgh medical school and thirty years in general practice to diagnose that!'

'He's becoming crotchety.' Hilda said, with satisfaction. 'He's always crotchety when he's feeling ill.'

'Yes, but what are you warning me about? Pneumonia, botulism, Parkinson's disease?'

'There is an even more serious condition, Rumpole,' the doctor said. 'I mean there's no reason why you shouldn't go on for a good few years, provided you take proper precautions.'

'You're trying to warn me about death!'

'Well, death is rather a strong way of putting it.'

The representative of the medical profession looked distressed, as though he realized that if Rumpole dropped off the twig there might be no more free sherry.

'Odd thing about the dead, Doctor.' I decided to let him into a secret. 'You may not know this. They may not have lectured you on this at your teaching hospital, but I can tell you on the best possible authority, the dead are tremendously keen on litigation. Give me a drink, Hilda. No, not that jaundiced and medicated fluid. Give me a beaker full of the warm south, full of the true, the blushful Château Pommeroy's ordinary claret! Dr MacClintock, you can't scare me with death. I've got a far more gloomy experience ahead of me.'

'I doubt that, Rumpole,' said the Scot, sipping industriously. 'But what exactly do you mean?'

'I mean,' I said, 'I've got to appear in the Chancery Division.'

The Chancery Division is not to be found, as I must make clear to those who have no particular legal experience, in any of my ordinary stamping grounds like the Old Bailey or Snaresbrook. It is light years away from the Uxbridge Magistrates' Court. The Chancery Division is considered by many, my learned Head of Chambers in particular, to be an extremely up-market Court. There cases are pleaded by lawyers who spring from old county families in a leisurely and courteous manner. It is a tribunal, in fact, which bears the same sort of relation to Inner London Sessions as the restaurant at Claridges does to your average transport café.

The Chancery Division is in the Law Courts, and the Law Courts, which prefer to be known as the Royal Courts of Justice, occupy a stately position in the Strand, not a wig's throw from my Chambers at Equity Court in the Temple. The Victorian building looks like the monstrous and overgrown result of a misalliance between a French château and a Gothic cathedral. The vast central hall is floored with a mosaic which is constantly under repair. There are many church-shaped windows and the ancient urinals have a distinctly ecclesiastical appearance. I passed into this muted splendour and found myself temporary accommodation in a robing room where there was, such is the luxurious nature of five-star litigation, an attendant in uniform to help me on with the fancy dress. Once suitably attired, I asked the way to the Chancery Division.

I knew that Chancery was a rum sort of Division, full of dusty old men breaking trusts and elegant young men winding up companies. They speak a different language entirely from us Criminals, and their will cases are full of 'dependent relative revocation' and 'testamentary capacity', and the nice construction of the word 'money'. As I rose to my hind legs in the Court of Chancery, I felt like some rustic reveller who has blundered into a convocation of bishops engaged in silent prayer. Nevertheless, I had a duty to perform which was to open the case of 'In the Estate of Colonel Roderick Ollard, deceased. Beasley *v.* Ollard and ors'. The judge, I noticed, was a sort of pale and learned youth, probably twenty years my junior, who had looked middle-aged ever since he got his double first at Balliol, and who kept his lips tightly pursed when he wasn't uttering some thinly veiled criticism of the Rumpole case. This chilly character was known, as I discovered from the usher, as Mr Justice Venables.

'May it please you, my Lord,' I fished up a voice from the murky depths of my influenza and put it on display, 'in this case, I appear for the plaintiff, Miss Rosemary Beasley, who is putting forward the true last will of a fine old soldier, Colonel Roderick Ollard. The defendants, Mr and Mrs Percival Ollard and Master Peter Ollard, are represented by my learned friends, Mr Guthrie Featherstone, Q.C. . . .'

It was true. The smooth-talking and diplomatic Head of our Chambers had collared the brief against Rumpole. Never at home in the rough and tumble of a nice murder, the Chancery Division, as I have said, was just the place for Guthrie Feather-stone.

'. . . and Mr . . .' I made a whispered inquiry and said, 'Mr Loxley-Parish.'

Guthrie had got himself, as a Chancery Junior, an ancient who'd no doubt proved more wills than I'd had bottles of Pommeroy's plonk. I turned, as usual, to the jury-box and got in the meat of my oration.

'My client, Miss Beasley, is the matron and presiding angel of a small nursing home known as Sunnyside, on the Sussex coast. There she devotedly nursed this retired warrior, Colonel Ollard, and was the comfort and cheer of his declining years.'

Mr Justice Venables was giving a chill stare over the top of his half glasses, and clearing his throat in an unpleasant manner.

Here was a judge who appeared to be distinctly unmoved by the Rumpole oratory. I carried on, of course, regardless.

'Declining years, during which his only brother, Percival, and Percival's wife, Marcia, never troubled to cross the door of Sunnyside to give five minutes of cheer to the old gentleman, and Master Peter Ollard was far too busy cashing the postal orders the Colonel sent him to send a Christmas card to his elderly uncle.'

It was time I thought that the Chancery Court heard a little Shakespeare.

'Blow, blow thou winter wind
Thou art not so unkind . . .
As man's ingratitude.'

At which point the judicial throat-clearing took on the sound of words.

'Mr Rumpole,' the Judge said. 'I think perhaps you need reminding. That jury-box is empty.'

I looked at it. His Lordship was perfectly right. The twelve puzzled and honest citizens, picked off the street at random, were conspicuous by their absence. Juries are not welcome in the Chancery Division. This was one of the occasions, strange to Rumpole, of a trial by Judge alone . . .

'It is therefore, Mr Rumpole, not an occasion for emotional appeals.' The Judge continued his lesson. 'Perhaps it would be more useful if you gave me some relevant dates and a comparison of the two wills.'

'Certainly, my Lord,' I said, always anxious to oblige. 'By his true last will of the first of March 1974 the late Colonel recognized the care of a devoted Matron . . .'

'Just the facts, Mr Rumpole. Just give me the plain facts,' snapped the old spoil-sport.

'And the plain fact is, under the previous will of the fifteenth of February 1970 the Percival Ollards had managed to scoop the pool.'

'Scoop the pool' was, it seemed, not a phrase or saying in current use in the Chancery Division.

'You mean, I suppose,' the Judge corrected me, 'that Mr Percival Ollard, together with his wife and son were the sole beneficiaries of the deceased's residuary estate.'

Somehow I managed to finish giving the Judge the brief facts of the case without open warfare breaking out. But the atmosphere was about as convivial as a gathering of teetotal undertakers.

I then called Matron to give evidence. She filled the witness-box with authority, she was dressed in respectable and respectful black, she gave her answers in ringing and resonant tones, and yet I could tell that the Judge didn't like her. As she gave her touching description of her devoted care of the late Colonel, and her harrowing account of the Percival Ollards' neglect of their relative, Mr Justice Venables looked upon Matron as though she was a person who had come to his Court for one reason only, money. Well, it was a charge which might, with equal justice, be levelled against me, and Guthrie Featherstone and even, let it be said, the learned Judge.

'Finally, Matron,' I asked the last question with a solemnity which would have deeply moved the jury, if there had been a jury. 'What did you think of the deceased?'

'He had his little ways, of course, but he was always a perfect gentleman.' She looked at the Judge; he averted his eye.

'What did you call each other?' I asked.

'It was always "Matron" and "Colonel Ollard".'

'But you were friends?'

'It was always on a proper basis, Mr Rumpole. I don't know what you're suggesting.' Miss Beasley gave me an 'old-fashioned' look, whereat Featherstone, seeing a rift in our ranks, levered himself to his hind legs and addressed a sympathetic Judge.

'I hope my learned friend isn't suggesting anything, by way of a leading question . . .?'

'Certainly not, my Lord!' And I went on before His Lordship had time to answer. 'Miss Beasley, during the years that Colonel Ollard was with you, did Mr Percival Ollard visit him at all?'

'I think he came over once or twice in the first couple of weeks. Once he took the Colonel for a run on the Downs, I think, and a tea out.'

Featherstone had the grace to subside, and my questioning continued.

'But after that?'

'No. He never came at all.'

'And his family, his wife Marcia, and the young Nijinsky?'

'The *what*, Mr Rumpole?' Mr Justice Venables was not amused.

'Master Peter Ollard, my Lord. A lad with terpsichorean tastes.'

'Oh no. I never saw them at all.'

'Yes. Thank you. Just wait there a moment, will you, Miss Beasley?' I subsided and Guthrie Featherstone rose. I had no particular worries. The middle-of-the-road M.P. was merely a middle-of-the-road cross-examiner.

'Miss Beasley. You say that Colonel Ollard had his little ways,' Guthrie began in a voice like hair oil poured on velvet.

'He did, yes.' Matron faced the old darling with confidence.

'Is Miss Mary Waterhouse one of your nurses?'

'She *was* one of my nurses. Yes.' The name brought a small sign of disapproval from the generalissimo of Sunnyside.

'Did the Colonel take boiled eggs for breakfast?' Featherstone asked what I thought at the time was not much of a question.

'On some days. Otherwise he had bacon and sausage.'

'And did the Colonel once fling his boiled eggs at Nurse Waterhouse and instruct her, and I quote, "To sit on the bloody things and hatch them out"?'

I let out a small guffaw, in which the Judge didn't join. I even began to warm to the memory of Colonel Ollard.

'He . . . may have done,' Matron conceded.

'The Colonel disliked hard-boiled eggs.' Featherstone, bless his timid old heart, seemed to be making a fair deduction.

'He disliked a lot of things, Mr Featherstone. Including young boys who indulged in ballet lessons.' Matron tried to snick a crafty one through the slips, and, of course, fell foul of the Judge immediately.

'Just answer the questions, Miss Beasley. Try not to score points off the other side,' Venables, J., warned her. Again, I got the strong impression that his Lordship hadn't exactly *warmed* to Matey.

'Did he also dislike slices of toast which were more than exactly four inches long?'

'The Colonel liked things just so, yes,' Miss Beasley admitted.

'And did he measure his toast with a slide-rule each morning to make sure it was the correct length?'

'Seems a perfectly reasonable thing to do,' I said to Mr Pontefract, in what I hoped was an audible mutter.

'Did you say something, Mr Rumpole?' The Judge inquired coldly. I heaved myself to my feet.

'I just wondered, my Lord, does the fact that a man measures his toast mean that he's not entitled to dispose of his property exactly as he likes?'

At this, the old sweetheart on the bench decided to do his best to polish up my manners.

'Mr Rumpole,' he said. 'Your turn will come later. Mr Guthrie Featherstone is cross-examining. In the Chancery Division we consider it improper to interrupt a cross-examination, unless there's a good reason to do so.'

Of course I bowed low, and said, '*If* your Lordship pleases. As a rank outsider I am, of course, delighted to get your Lordship's instructions on the mysteries of the Chancery Division.' I supposed old Venables thought that down the Old Bailey we interrupted opponents by winking at the jury and singing sea shanties. It was then my turn to subside and let Featherstone continue.

'Let me ask you something else, Matron. Colonel Ollard had fought, had he not, at the battle of Anzio?'

'That was where he won his Military Cross,' said Miss Beasley, with some understandable pride in the distinction of her late patient.

'Yes, of course. Very commendable.'

That was a tribute, of course, coming from Featherstone. I seemed to remember that he did his military service in the Soldiers' Divorce Division.

Then Featherstone asked another question. 'Matron,' he purred with his usual charm, 'did Colonel Ollard tell you that he had frequently discussed the battle of Anzio with the Prime Minister, the late Sir Winston Churchill?'

'I know that Sir Winston was always interested in Colonel Ollard's view of the war, yes.' Miss Beasley sounded proud, and even the Judge looked impressed.

'And that he had also discussed it with Field-Marshal Lord Montgomery of Alamein?'

'Colonel Ollard called him "Bernard".'

'And with the then Soviet leader, Mr Stalin. Did Colonel Ollard call him "Josef"?' Oh dear, I sighed to myself, things were becoming grim when Featherstone tried to make a funny.

'No. He always called him "Mr Stalin".' Miss Beasley answered primly.

'Very respectful. If I may say so.' Featherstone gave the Judge a chummy little smile and then turned back straight-faced to the witness.

'You know he told Nurse Waterhouse, one morning last October, that he had been talking to Sir Winston, Lord Montgomery and Mr Stalin the evening before. Does that surprise you?' I had the awful feeling that Featherstone had struck gold. There was a sudden silence in Court as Pontefract and I held our breath, waiting for Matron's answer.

When it came, it was a simple, 'No.'

'You say it *doesn't* surprise you, Miss Beasley?' Venables J. leant forward, frowning unpleasantly.

'Not in the least, my Lord.' The answer was positively serene. I wanted to tell the Judge not to interrupt the cross-examination, after all, we didn't do that sort of thing in the Chancery Division. But Featherstone, as he went on, was doing quite well, even without a little help from the Judge.

'Nurse Waterhouse will also say that Colonel Ollard told her that he had been chatting to Alexander the Great, the Emperor Napoleon and the late Duke of Marlborough,' my opponent suggested.

'Well, of course he would, you know.' Miss Beasley smiled back at him.

'He would say that because he was suffering from mental instability?'

'Of course not!' The witness was outraged. 'The Colonel had as much mental stability as you or I, Mr Featherstone.'

'Speak for yourself, Miss Beasley.' Oh, very funny, Featherstone, I thought. What a talent! He ought to go on the Halls.

'Why did you say that the Colonel *would* speak to those gentlemen?' Featherstone asked for clarification.

'Because they were all keenly interested in his subject,' Miss Beasley explained, as though to a rather backward two-year-old.

'Which was?'

'Military matters.'

'Oh, military matters. Yes. Of course.' Featherstone paused, and then asked politely, 'But all the names I have mentioned, Churchill and Montgomery, Marlborough and Napoleon, Stalin and Alexander the Great. They're all *dead*, aren't they, Matron?'

'Yes, indeed. But that wouldn't have worried the Colonel.' She gave the Opposition Leader a patient smile. 'Colonel Ollard was most sympathetic to people who were ill. Being dead wouldn't have put him off at all.'

'But did the Colonel think he *could* talk to those deceased gentlemen?'

'Oh yes. Of course he could.' As Pontefract and I began to see the last will of Colonel Ollard going up in smoke, the Judge said, 'You really believe that, Miss Beasley?'

I must say the answer that Matron gave was not particularly helpful. She merely looked at the Judge with some pity and said, '*You* could talk to the Emperor Napoleon, my Lord. If *you* were a believer.'

'A believer, Miss Beasley?' No doubt a churchwarden and Chairman of the Parish Council, the Judge looked more than a little irked by her reply.

'A believer in communication with the other side.' At least she had the grace to explain.

'And both you and Colonel Ollard were believers?' Featherstone led her gently on, down the primrose path to disaster.

'Oh yes. We had that much in common.'

'Can you communicate with the late Josef Stalin, Miss Beasley?' It was a shot in the dark by Featherstone, but it scored a bull's eye.

'Of course I could,' Miss Beasley said modestly. 'But let's just say I wouldn't care to.'

'Perhaps not. But can you communicate, for instance, with the late Colonel Ollard?'

'Yes indeed.' She had no doubt about that.

'When did you last do so, Miss Beasley?' said the Judge, following his leader, Featherstone, like a bloodhound.

'Yesterday evening, my Lord.'

'Oh dear! Oh, my ears and whiskers!' I groaned to myself as

the psychic Matron blundered on, addressing her remarks to the learned Judge.

'And I may say that the Colonel is very distressed about this case, my Lord. Very distressed indeed. In fact, he thinks it's a disgraceful thing to argue about it when he'd made his will perfectly clear and left it in his uniform box. I wouldn't like to tell you, my Lord, the things that the Colonel had to say about his brother Percy.'

'I think you had better not, Miss Beasley.' Featherstone brought her smoothly to a halt. 'That would be hearsay evidence. We shall have to wait and see whether my learned friend Mr Rumpole calls the deceased gentleman as a witness.'

Oh hilarious, I told myself bitterly. Guthrie Featherstone is being most hilarious. My God, he's working well today!

We, that is, Matron, Mr Pontefract and self, had luncheon in the crypt under the Law Courts, a sepulchral hall, where, it seemed, very old plaice and chips come to die. Miss Beasley's legal team were not in an optimistic mood.

'The Judge doesn't like you all that much I'm afraid, Miss Beasley.' I thought it best to break the news to her gently.

'Never mind, Mr Rumpole. The feeling is entirely mutual.' She looked, all things considered, ridiculously cheerful.

'If you take my advice, Miss Beasley, you should go for a settlement.' Pontefract was trying to talk some sense into her. 'Save what you can from the wreckage. You see, once you had to admit that the late Colonel used to talk to the Emperor Napoleon . . .'

'What's wrong with talking to the Emperor Napoleon?' Miss Beasley frowned. 'He can be quite charming when he puts his mind to it.'

'I don't think the Judge is likely to accept that,' I warned her.

'You'd talk to the Emperor Napoleon, I'm sure, if he came across to you.' Miss Beasley didn't seem to be getting the drift of my argument. I put it more bluntly.

'Mr Pontefract is right. The time has come to chuck in the towel. On the best terms we can manage.'

'You mean, surrender?' She looked at us both, displeased.

'Well, on terms, Miss Beasley.' Mr Pontefract tried to soften the blow, but her answer came like the bugle call which set off the Charge of the Light Brigade.

'Colonel Ollard will never surrender!' she trumpeted. 'Anyway, you haven't cross-examined that wretched Percy Ollard yet. The Colonel says Mr Rumpole's a great cross-examiner!'

'That's very kind of him.' I tried to sound modest.

'He says he'll never forget reading your cross-examination about the bloodstains in the Penge Bungalow Murders. He read every word of it, in the Sunday paper.'

'My dear lady. That was thirty-five years ago. Anyway, I had a jury to play on in that case. I'm at my best with a jury. This is a cold-blooded trial in the Chancery Division, by Judge alone, and that Judge is distinctly unfriendly.'

'The Colonel says, "Mr Rumpole will hit my brother Percy for six." ' She repeated the words as if they were Holy Writ.

'Tell the Colonel,' I asked her, 'that Mr Rumpole isn't at his best, without a jury.'

A trial without a jury is like an operation without anaesthetic, or a luncheon without a glass of wine. 'Shall we drown this old fish, Pontefract, my old darling,' I suggested, 'in a sea of cooking claret?'

What I can't accept about spiritualism is the idea of millions of dead people (there must be standing room only in the Other Side) kept hanging about just waiting to be sent for by some old girl with a Ouija board in a Brighton boarding house, or a couple of table-tappers in Tring, for the sake of some inane conversation about the Blueness of the Infinite. I mean at least when you're dead you'll surely be spared such tedious social occasions. Nevertheless, there was Colonel Ollard apparently at Matey's beck and call, ready and willing to cross the Great Divide and drop in on her at the turn of a card or the shiver of a wine glass. I was expressing some of these thoughts to Hilda in a feverish sort of way that evening as I hugged my dressing-gown round me and downed medicinal claret by the electric fire in Froxbury Court.

'Really, Rumpole,' said She, 'don't be so morbid.'

'I can smell corruption.' I sneezed loudly. 'The angel of death is brushing me with his wings.'

'Rumpole, Dr MacClintock has told you it's only a cold.'

'Dr MacClintock gave me a warning, on the subject of death.' At which there was a ring at the door, and Hilda said, 'Oh good heavens. That's never the front door bell!'

With a good deal of clucking and tutting, Hilda went out to the hall and eventually ushered Miss Rosemary Beasley, who appeared to be carrying some kind of plastic holdall, into the presence of the sick. When she asked me how I was, I told her I was dying.

'Well, don't die yet, Mr Rumpole. You've got our case to win.'

'Don't you think I could conduct it perfectly well from beyond the grave?' I asked Matron.

'Now you're teasing me! Your husband is the most terrible tease,' she told a puzzled Hilda. 'Listen to this, Mr Rumpole. The Colonel says that he has an urgent message for you. He'll deliver it here tonight. So I've brought the board.'

'The what?'

'The planchette, of course.'

To my dismay, Matron then produced, from her black plastic holdall, a small heart-shaped board on castors, which she plonked on to our dining table. There was paper fixed on the board, and Miss Beasley held a pencil poised over it and the board then moved in a curious fashion, causing writing to appear on the paper. It looked illegible to me, but Miss Beasley deciphered some rather cheeky communications from a late and no doubt unlamented Red Indian Chief who finally agreed to fetch Colonel Ollard to the planchette. Tearing himself away from the Emperor Napoleon, the Colonel issued his orders for the day, emerging in Miss Beasley's already somewhat masculine voice as she read the scribbles on the board. 'The Colonel says, "Hullo there, Rumpole," ' Miss Beasley informed us.

'Well, answer him, Rumpole. Be polite!' Hilda appeared enchanted with the whole ludicrous performance.

'Oh, hullo there, Colonel.' I felt an idiot as I said it.

'It's very blue here, Rumpole. And I am very happy,' Miss Beasley came through as the late holder of the Military Cross.

'Oh good.' What else could I say?

'Tomorrow you will cross-examine my brother Percival.'

'Well, I hope to. I'm not feeling . . .' here I sneezed again, 'quite up to snuff.'

'Brace up, Rumpole! No malingering. Tomorrow you will cross-examine my brother in Court.' Miss Beasley relayed Colonel Ollard's instructions.

'Yes, Colonel. Aye, aye, sir.'

'Ask him what we said to each other when he visited me in the nursing home, and he drove me up to the Downs. Ask him what the conversation was when we had cream tea together at the Bide-A-Wee tea-rooms. Go on, Rumpole. Ask Percy that!' Colonel Ollard may have been a very gallant officer and an inspired leader of men. I doubted if he was a real expert in the art of cross-examination.

'Is it a good question?' I asked the deceased, doubtfully.

'Percy won't like it. Just as Jerry didn't like cold steel. Percy will run a mile from that question,' Miss Beasley croaked.

'Colonel, I make it a rule to decide on my own cross-examination.' I wanted to make the position clear, but the answer came back almost in a parade-ground bellow.

'Ask that question, Rumpole. It's an order!'

'I'll . . . I'll consider it.' I suppose it doesn't do to hurt the feelings of the dead.

'Do so! Oh, and see you over here some time.' At which, it seemed, the consultation was over and Colonel Ollard returned to some celestial bowling-green to while away eternity. It was perfectly ridiculous, of course. I knew quite well that the deceased Colonel wasn't manipulating the planchette. But, as for asking his question, I could tell by the Judge's attitude next morning that we had absolutely nothing to lose.

Percival Ollard was not, I thought, a particularly attractive-looking customer. The successful manufacturer of kitchen utensils had run to fat, he had a bristling little ginger moustache and small flickering eyes that seemed to be looking round the Court for ways of escape. Featherstone led him smoothly through his evidence in chief and then I rose to cross-examine. The learned Judge put a damper on my first question.

'I'm really wondering,' he said, 'how much longer this estate is going to be put to the expense of this apparently hopeless litigation.'

'Not long, my Lord,' I said with a confidence I didn't feel, 'after I have cross-examined this witness.' And I turned to the witness-box.

'Mr Percival Ollard. Were you on good terms with your brother, before he went into the nursing home?'

'Extremely good terms. We saw each other regularly, and he always sent my boy, Peter, a postal order for Christmas and birthdays.'

'That was before the Colonel started talking to the dead?' the Judge asked in a way unfriendly to Rumpole.

'Yes, my Lord.' Percy looked gratefully at my Lord.

'Before he became, shall we say, eccentric in the extreme?' the Judge went on.

'Yes, my Lord.'

'Very well.' Venables, J., now seemed to have worn himself out. 'Carry on, if you must, Mr Rumpole.'

'Two weeks after he went into the nursing home, you took him for a drive on the Downs?' Rumpole carried on.

'I did, yes.' Percy's nervousness seemed to have returned, although I couldn't imagine why the memory of tea on the Downs posed any sort of threat to him.

'You were then on good terms?'

'Yes.'

'You shared tea, scones and clotted cream at the Bide-A-Wee café?' It was strange the effect on the witness of this innocent question. He took out a silk handkerchief, wiped his forehead and had to force himself to answer, 'Yes, we did.'

'And talked?'

'We talked, yes.' Percy answered so quietly that the Judge was constrained to tell him to speak up.

'And after that conversation you and your brother never met or spoke to each other again?'

There was a long pause. Had I stumbled, guided by a Dead Hand, on some vital piece of evidence? I couldn't believe it.

'No. We never did.'

'And he made a will cutting out your family, and leaving all his considerable property to my client, Miss Beasley?'

'He made an *alleged* will, Mr Rumpole,' the Judge was at pains to remind me.

I bowed respectfully, and said, 'If that's what you call it in the Chancery Division, yes, my Lord. What I want to ask *you*, Mr Percival Ollard, is simply this – what did you and your brother say to each other at the Bide-A-Wee café?'

Now the pause seemed endless. Percy looked at Featherstone and got no help. He looked at his wife and his ballet-dancing son. He looked vainly at the doors and the windows, and finally his desperate gaze fell on the learned Judge.

'My Lord. Must I answer that question?' he said.

'Mr Rumpole, do you press the question?' His Lordship asked me with distaste.

'My Lord, I do.' For some reason, I was on to a good thing, and I wasn't letting it go.

'Then it is relevant and you must answer it, Mr Ollard.' At least the Judge knew his business.

'My L-L-Lord,' Percival Ollard stammered. He was clearly extremely distressed. So distressed that the Judge had time to look at the clock and relieve the witness's agony for an hour. 'I see the time,' he said. 'You may give us your answer after luncheon, Mr Percival Ollard. Shall we say, two o'clock . . .?'

We all rose obediently to our hind legs, with Rumpole muttering, 'Bloody Chancery Judge. He's let old Percy off the hook.'

Miss Beasley vanished somewhere at lunchtime, and when I had returned from a rather unhappy encounter with the plaice in the crypt, I found Guthrie Featherstone waiting for me outside the Court. He offered me a cigarette, which I refused, and he lit my small cigar with a gold lighter.

'Horace,' he said, 'we've always got on pretty well at the Bar.'

'Have we, Guthrie?'

'My client has come to a rather agonizing decision.'

'You mean he's going to answer my question?'

'It's not that exactly. You see, Horace, we're chucking in the sponge. Our hands are up. We surrender! Matron can have her precious will. We offer no further evidence.'

You could have knocked me down with a Chancery brief, but

I tried to sound nonchalant. 'Oh really, Featherstone,' I said, 'that's very satisfactory.' It was also somewhat incredible. But Guthrie, it became clear, had other matters on his mind.

'I say, Rumpole. A fellow must be certain of his fee. You'll let me have my costs out of the estate, won't you?'

'I suppose so.' I warned him, 'I'd better just check.'

'With your client?'

'Not *only* with her,' I said, 'with the deceased. I mean it's his money, isn't it?' And I left him thinking, no doubt, that old Horace Rumpole had completely lost his marbles.

When Matron came into view I put the proposition to her; I told her that the Percival Ollards would give her all the boodle, only provided that Guthrie, and their other lawyers, got their costs out of the estate. She and the dear departed must have had a convivial lunch together, agreement was reached, and the deal was on. With about as much joy and enthusiasm as King John might have shown when signing Magna Carta, Mr Justice Venables pronounced, in the absence of further argument, for the will of the first of March 1974 benefiting Miss Beasley, and against the earlier will which favoured the Percival Ollards. All parties were allowed their costs out of the estate.

When we came out of Court, Matron seized my hand in her muscular grasp.

'Thanks most awfully, Mr Rumpole,' she said. 'The Colonel knew you'd pull it off and hit them for six.'

'Miss Beasley. May I call you "Matey"?'

'Please.'

'What's the truth of it? What did the brothers say to each other over the scones and Darjeeling?'

There was a pause, and then Miss Beasley said with a small, secret smile, 'How would I know, Mr Rumpole? Only the Colonel and his brother know that.'

However, I was not to be left in total ignorance of the truth of 'In the Estate of Colonel Ollard, deceased'. After we had taken off our robes, Guthrie Featherstone did me the honour of inviting me to crack a bottle of claret at the Sheridan Club, and, as he had given me my first (and my last) Chancery will, I did him the honour of accepting. As we sat in a quiet room, under

97

the portraits of old actors and even older judges, Featherstone said, 'No reason why you shouldn't know, Rumpole. Your client had been Percy's mistress for years.'

'Miss Beasley, Matey, the old dragon of the nursing home, his *mistress*!' I was astonished, and I let my amazement show. 'His *what*?'

'Girlfriend.' Featherstone made it sound even more inappropriate.

'It seems odd, somehow, calling a stout, elderly woman a "girlfriend". Are you trying to tell me, Guthrie, intimacy actually took place?'

'Regularly, apparently. On a Wednesday. Matron's afternoon off. But when Colonel Roderick Ollard went into Sunnyside she dived into bed with *him*, and deserted Percy. The meeting at the tea-room was when the Colonel told his brother all about it and said he meant to leave his money to Rosemary Beasley.'

I was silent. I drank claret. I began to wonder where the planchette came in.

'But why couldn't your client have *told* us that?' I asked my ex-opponent.

'His wife, Rumpole! His wife Marcia! She's a battle-axe and she was kept completely in the dark about Matey. It seems there would have been hell to pay if she'd found out. So we had to settle.'

'Well, well, Featherstone. Matron, the *femme fatale*. I'd never have believed it.'

What did I believe? That the Colonel spoke from the grave? Or that Matron invented all the séances to tell us a truth which would have caused her deep embarrassment to communicate in any other way? As it was, she had told me nothing.

All I knew was that I didn't fancy the idea of the 'other side'. I knew I shouldn't care for long chats with Colonel Ollard and the Emperor Napoleon even if Josef Stalin were to be of the party. Dying, as far as I was concerned, had been postponed indefinitely.

Rumpole and the Rotten Apple

Nothing shocks your Old Bailey Judge more than a bent copper. There the Judge is, his simple world proceeding nicely, with the villains committing enough crimes to keep his Honour in business, and the public-spirited Old Bill out catching them and lobbing them neatly into the dock, and then, horror of horrors, a copper gets on to the wrong side! The Old Bailey universe comes grinding to a halt, and the Judge tends to look on the twisted bobby with the amount of smiling tolerance that Savonarola would have had for a pregnant nun; his only answer would be to kick her out of the convent and into the nick before she starts infecting other members of the Serious Crimes Squad. Of course, the truth is never quite so simple as it appears to an Old Bailey Judge. Coppers and villains spend so much time in each other's company that they often begin to look alike (as dog owners grow to look like their pets). They have the same short-back-and-sides haircut and wear the same navy blue blazers and cavalry twill trousers. King Lear put it in a neat phrase, 'Handy dandy, which is the Justice, which is the thief?'

This was the point at issue in the case of dear old Inspector Dobbs of the Detective Force. I remember leaving Casa Rumpole, our flat in Froxbury Court, Gloucester Road, for a conference with the Inspector one soggy February morning, when I was submitted to a brief interrogation from She Who Must Be Obeyed.

Now it is not, it is certainly not, that I am going deaf. It is just that everyone seems to talk more quietly nowadays, particularly my wife Hilda. I have no doubt that She said something to me on the stairs and the subsequent evidence went to show that her general drift was, 'Will you come straight back this evening, Rumpole?'

Now this may, indeed, be what she said. What I *thought* she said was rather different. From the blurred mumble that reached me over the roar of the traffic and the babble of other people's radios, I thought she said, 'Will you come late back this evening, Rumpole?' To which I replied, with the utmost courtesy, 'I bloody well hope not.' You can imagine my dismay, therefore, when Hilda received my soft answer with a swift intake of breath and retreated back into our matrimonial home as though I had announced a previous engagement with a couple of ladies of the town in an opium den. In a shifting world I felt only one rule was certain, there was no accounting for She.

When I got to my chambers in Equity Court, the clerk's room presented the usual scene of frenzied activity. Henry, my clerk, was making telephone calls. Henry is the devoted servant who is the true master of our Chambers; if he says go, we go, even to the Uxbridge Magistrates' Court. Dianne, his helper, was training as usual for the slow typers' competition, and Uncle Tom, our oldest and most briefless barrister, was practising mashie shots into the waste paper basket. Miss Trant, the Portia of our Chambers and our only lady barrister (now known to some, but not to me, as Phillida Erskine-Brown, having married one of our barristers, Claude Erskine-Brown) was eagerly undoing the tape on her brief in a lengthy 'gang bang' with scarlet finger-nails. Her husband, who now spends a good deal of his time at home drafting affidavits and looking after their baby, was thoughtfully stirring his coffee and Guthrie Featherstone, Q.C., M.P., our Head of Chambers, was picking over his letters in the hope of finding an invitation to play golf with the Lord Chief Justice.

'Inspector Dobbs is in your room, Mr Rumpole, along with Mr Morse from the instructing solicitors.' Henry put down the telephone momentarily to announce my engagements.

'Rumpole! Are you under arrest? Have they caught up with you at last?' Ever since Featherstone was asked to sit as a Commissioner of Assize, or type of part-time Judge, he has shown a regrettable tendency to attempt jokes. All the same I thought I detected, beneath the levity, a certain wishful thinking.

'Not yet, Guthrie, my old darling,' I told him. 'The Inspector comes to me as a client. Like most of the rest of mankind, he's got himself into some sort of trouble with the law.'

'Your letters, Mr Rumpole.' Dianne came up and pressed a number of unwelcome communications into my hand. I took a look at them and threw them into the waste paper basket.

'Little brown envelopes,' I said with horror. 'Communications from Her Majesty's Commissioners of Revenue!'

'All the same, there's no need to throw them away.' Claude Erskine-Brown spoke with disapproval.

'There certainly is, Erskine-Brown. Reading communications from the Revenue only produces palpitations of the heart and quite unnecessary anxiety.'

'You don't deal with the Revenue properly, Rumpole. Philly'll tell you. I've just won a long battle with them on the subject of pin-striped trousers, which I say are absolutely necessary for our work at the Bar. Haven't I, Philly?'

His wife Phillida, appealed to, went on reading her brief. She looked as if she couldn't care less about her husband's pin-striped trousers. Erskine-Brown was our expert on revenue law, good on figures and absolutely hopeless on bloodstains.

'I'm now deducting two pairs of pin-striped trousers a year. It's a perfectly legitimate claim, which has been recognized as such by the Inland Revenue,' the proud father and tax lawyer told me.

'Would you like a cup of coffee up in your room, Mr Rumpole?' Dianne was being remarkably attentive that morning. However, I declined her offer as I knew that Dianne's idea of coffee was a tepid brew tasting faintly of meat extract.

'You might as well have it, Mr Rumpole. You're paying regularly into the coffee money,' Dianne pointed out.

'No time for luxurious living, Dianne. Inspector Dobbs awaits my attention.'

When I went into my room I found dear old Dobbs, a grey-haired, slow-speaking officer sitting stolidly in my client's chair. I had known the Inspector about the Courts for years and we had crossed swords on a number of occasions. I respected him as hard-working and, within his limits, an honest officer. The other man present was Mr Morse, an old solicitor's clerk who had brought me criminal work for longer than I care to remember. He was re-lighting his pipe and my room was filled with the familiar reek of his quite revolting tobacco.

'I never expected to see you in a defending barrister's Chambers, Inspector,' I greeted him. 'Good of Mr Morse to trundle you along.'

'Inspector Dobbs has long been aware, Mr Rumpole, of your talent for getting persons acquitted,' Morse grinned through the smoke-screen.

'I've found your talents frustrating,' Dobbs grumbled. 'Especially when you and I both know the lads are damn well guilty.'

'Really, Inspector! Is it my talent for getting the guilty off you'd like me to exercise in your case?' I couldn't resist it.

'I didn't say that, Mr Rumpole.' Dobbs looked gloomy and I did my best to cheer him up with some gentle reminiscences.

'We met last year, didn't we, after Charlie Pointer's latest warehouse-breaking charge?'

'You had a ridiculous win there, Mr Rumpole.'

'Because you went into the witness-box and swore that he'd said, "It's a fair cop, Mr Dobbs," when you first got him into the nick. Charlie may break into warehouses but he never admits it to the police. He was so incensed at the insult to his intelligence that he was determined to fight.' I'd always wanted to tell old Dobbsy why he lost R. *v.* Pointer.

'And you won!' The Inspector sounded unexpectedly bitter.

'If you hadn't put that little bit of gilt on the gingerbread, it might've been a guilty verdict.'

'Well, I can see we're never going to agree, Mr Rumpole. I told Mr Morse it was going to be hopeless. I'll not waste any more of your time!' He seemed about to struggle up from my easy chair, so I said, as soothingly as possible,

'Agree? Of course we're going to agree.'

'We've never been on the same side in Court.'

'We're on the same side now,' I reminded him.

'Why? What's changed?' The Inspector still seemed to doubt it.

'What's changed, Inspector Dobbs,' I told him, 'is that now *you're* the one in trouble. You've caught a nasty disease and just look at me as the doctor who's here to cure you.'

'What disease is that?'

I found my papers and opened them. Dobbs waited patiently and then I said, 'A little charge of bribery and corruption ... five hundred pounds. Don't worry, though. The most that can happen to you is a spell in an open prison, that's where they send the bent coppers. Cheer up, Dobbs, my old darling. You can exercise your natural talent for hedge clipping and spreading manure.'

My natural high spirits had got the better of me, and I had gone too far at last. Dobbs got up then and grabbed his mac.

'Come along, Mr Morse. I'm not going to sit here and have Mr Rumpole crow over me! He's the chosen representative of the criminal fraternity.' Dobbs made for the door and was out of it, leaving Mr Morse to make his apologies.

'I'm sorry about this, Mr Rumpole.'

'That's quite all right, Mr Morse,' I told him. 'Charlie, Pointer's just the same. He's always extremely difficult when we start working together. He's been trained to be a model client by the time I get him into the witness-box.'

I was sitting brooding on the departure of the Inspector in trouble, when I received a visit from my learned friend Claude Erskine-Brown. He had the grave face and suppressed excitement of a man who has just unearthed a serious scandal.

'Rumpole, in this not undistinguished set of Chambers ...' He started as if opening a ten-week case to the jury.

'You mean this stable of moderate legal hacks?'

'... what do we stand for above all else?' Erskine-Brown ignored the interruption.

'What do we stand for? I would say we provide a place of refuge, for villains in distress.'

'I would say we stand for justice and for honesty! Surely it's up to us, Rumpole, to set an example.'

An example? I wasn't sure I agreed with him. God save us from a state where everyone goes around imitating lawyers.

'That's why it is so particularly distressing when lawlessness is to be found, even in these very Chambers!' Something of grave importance seemed to be distressing poor old Claude. I set about to probe into the mystery.

'What've you done, Erskine-Brown? Unburden yourself to me, Claude. You've been taking home the law reports for solitary reading, or did you indecently assault Mrs Justice Appleby after a long and sultry divorce case?'

'Rumpole. I implore you to be serious for a moment.' His voice sank to a conspiratorial whisper. 'It's Henry.'

'What?' I was handicapped by the habit people have, nowadays, of speaking beyond the level of human audibility, like dog whistles.

'Our clerk, Henry.' Erskine-Brown raised his voice slightly.

'Henry made an improper suggestion to Mrs Justice Appleby?' I was puzzled. We were obviously entering deep waters, but Erskine-Brown brushed the suggestion aside and said, 'Rumpole! Have you any idea what you pay for coffee money? Of course you haven't. Because Henry deducts the coffee money with the rest of our Chambers' expenses and gives us no particulars. But I happened to be in the clerk's room and saw the petty cash book lying on Henry's desk . . .'

'You want to confess an indecent assault upon Henry's petty cash book?' I was still failing to follow the fellow's drift.

'He is charging us two pounds a week each for coffee money!'

'You astonish me, Claude!'

'I have made careful inquiries at my local supermarket. And a large tin of instant coffee . . .'

'That is not instant coffee we drink, Erskine-Brown. Don't flatter the stuff. It's dishwater lightly flavoured with meat extract.'

'Well, a large tin of whatever it is costs no more than £6.50 at the *most*. There are twenty members of Chambers. Henry is getting £40 a week coffee money and making a profit of £33.50. On our coffee!'

'Unbelievable!' I did my best to sound aghast. 'There's only one thing that disturbs me.'

'What's that, Rumpole?'

'Will they have room for a waxwork of our clerk Henry, between Dr Crippen and Herr Hitler in the Chamber of Horrors at Madame Tussaud's?'

I could see that, once again, I had said the wrong thing and given offence. Erskine-Brown got up and prepared to leave in some dudgeon. I seemed to be doing nothing but drive my visitors away that morning.

'Oh really, Rumpole! It's no use talking to you. I should have gone straight to the Head of Chambers.'

As he reached the door, a thought occurred to me. I thought it just might be worth trying to stop Claude creating endless trouble in the clerk's room. 'Just before you go. That's a very elegant new pair of pin-striped bags you're wearing, Erskine-Brown.'

'Nonsense, Rumpole!' My learned friend looked puzzled. 'I haven't had a new pair of pin-striped trousers for years.'

'Haven't you really?' I smiled at him in the friendliest fashion. 'That's what I rather thought!'

I had to turn my thoughts from the vital matter of Erskine-Brown's trousers when Inspector Dobbs, true to the form of Charlie Pointer, the celebrated warehouse breaker, returned in a more docile mood the next day. He was back in the depths of my clients' chair, sitting where some of the most notable villains on his East London patch had sat before him, and I was studying the officer's pained and honest expression through the smoke of Mr Morse's pipe and my own small cigar.

'I'm back here, Mr Rumpole, on the advice of my senior officer.' Left to himself, it was clear, the Inspector would never have darkened the doors of my Chambers in Equity Court again.

'That's remarkably civil of your senior officer, Inspector. Who is he, by the way?'

'Superintendent Glazier. He called at my home special.'

'Inspector Dobbs has been suspended from duty. For over a year,' Mr Morse explained.

'Of course. You've been out of touch with police matters.' I tried to put it as tactfully as I could.

'The Super came to tell me that you were an outstanding brief, Mr Rumpole.'

A 'brief' is just what Charlie Pointer calls me. Once again, I remembered that villains and the Old Bill speak the same language.

'Superintendent Glazier agrees you are outstanding at getting customers off. That being your job of course.'

I must say I was a little surprised. I knew Glazier as a remarkably efficient officer, proud of his conviction rate, and a cautious and unshakeable witness. I would never have guessed that he cherished a warm admiration for the Rumpole talents. However, I felt proper gratitude to the Super for his friendly action and for encouraging Inspector Dobbs to confide his troubles in me, as he was now doing in the measured monotone which he always used when giving evidence.

'I was as surprised as anyone when Charlie Pointer asked to come and see me. He telephoned me at the station. Suggested we had a Chinese together.'

'A Chinese what exactly?' I asked, purely for clarification.

'Meal, of course,' Dobbs explained tolerantly.

'What did you think about that?' It seemed, on the face of it, a strange invitation from a con to a copper. Dobbs gave me a small, reassuring laugh and said, 'I thought he was trying to Doggett a Chinese dinner.'

'Did you say "Doggett", Inspector?' Mr Morse was puzzled. This time I was able to translate.

'Of course he did, Morse. "Doggett's coat and badge". Means "cadge". Thieves' rhyming slang. The language used by Charlie Pointer and Detective Inspector Dobbs. In any event, you agreed to meet Charlie?'

'At the Swinging Bamboo. In the High Street.'

'*Why* did you meet him?'

'I was curious. It was my night off and I was on the lonely side, not being a married man.' I looked at Dobbs; of course, it was a solitary life being a copper, a man with few friends except among the criminals he pursues.

'So the idea of picking over a chop suey with Charlie Pointer appealed to you. You went on your own?'

'I did, yes. Soon it became, well, a regular date we had together.'

'You weren't suspicious?'

'No. Charlie's the old-fashioned type. Sticks to simple warehouse breaking. No violence, an honest sort of tea leaf, in his way.'

'Just as you're an honest sort of copper, in your way. Even though you invented a couple of verbals at Charlie's trial.' I couldn't help myself and this time the Inspector looked only slightly pained. 'Mr Rumpole,' he said, 'do we have to go into that again?'

'I'm sorry. You're quite right. Don't let's dig up old verbals. Go on.'

'As I say, you could've knocked me down with a feather when Charlie offered to be a grass.'

It amazed me too. Charlie Pointer was an old-fashioned type of villain, born before the age of the super-grass, with old-fashioned ideas of honour among thieves. I asked Dobbs if Charlie would have been any use as an informer. 'He's in touch with three or four big firms of shop and warehouse breakers. I thought he might be useful, yes.'

'So what did you do?'

'I consulted my superior officer.'

'Superintendent Glazier?'

'That's right. He told me to carry on at my discretion.'

'Did Charlie give you anything useful?' I wondered.

'Little bits and pieces. Nothing enormous. But when we checked it over, we found it was reliable.'

'And you were prepared to pay him for it?'

'Yes. We owed him five hundred nicker at the time.'

'At the time of the alleged bribery? So *that*'s what you were talking about!' I began, with a feeling of elation, to sniff the faint odour of a defence. I rose from my seat and found and lit another small cigar.

'Of course, Mr Rumpole.' Dobbs sounded vaguely rebuking, as though it should have been obvious to a child.

'That's the defence! You didn't want Charlie to pay you five hundred. You were going to pay *him*.'

'Certainly I was. I'll swear on the book on that. He's a liar who says different.'

Inspector Dobbs looked so solid and convincing when he protested his innocence that I rashly began to assume that we were on a winner. However, one witness was found to contradict the words of the inspector, and to do so, awkwardly enough, in his own words and even with his slow and reassuring voice.

In the good old days when I did the Penge Bungalow Murders, and scored a remarkable success, although I say it myself, alone and without a leader, witnesses were, by and large, human beings. And as human beings, they could be cross-examined, suggestions could be made to them and they were subject to merciful confusion and welcome failures of recollection. Things, I regret to have to say it, have not improved since those distant days, and many of the faults must be laid at the door of automation. Not only have witnesses changed. String quartets, which were once the pride of the tea room, have now been replaced by an abominable form of mechanical music. The toasting fork has given way to an alarming machine that fires singed bread at you like a minute gun. The comforting waitress in black bombazine has become a device that contrives to shoot a warmish and unidentifiable fluid into a plastic cup and over your trousers at the drop of a considerable sum of money. None of these engines is an improvement on the human factor, neither are trials made any easier by the replacement of the living witness with the electronic device. It is hard to cross-examine a machine or to try and shake its recollection.

'Have you seen the additional evidence, Mr Rumpole, in the case of R. *v.* Dobson?'

I confessed I hadn't. Mr Morse and I had had a busy and unpleasant week with an unlawful handling before Judge Bullingham. I staggered away after a day of being chased round the Court by the demented Bull, barely able to raise the glass of Pommeroy's plonk to my parched lips, or read anything more demanding than the *Times* crossword puzzle.

'They've served us with the inspector's little chat with Charlie Pointer in the Chinese restaurant. They've got it word for word.'

'You mean . . .' we were in my favourite wine bar at the time, and I paused to absorb the first glass of the evening, '. . . poor old Dobbsy was bugged?'

'I'm afraid so, Mr Rumpole. Not a lot we can do about it.'

'We can listen to the beastly machine. I mean, don't let's take the word of any sort of transcript.'

Listening to the machine meant a visit to New Scotland Yard where the mechanical witness was in the safe custody of Superintendent Glazier, the officer in charge of the case.

Superintendent Glazier was a tall, rather pale officer with dark hair brushed straight back, wearing a blue suit and a police Rugby Club tie. He greeted Mr Morse and me politely and I took the opportunity of thanking him for recommending my services to the reluctant Inspector.

'I know you're good, Mr Rumpole,' he said, 'and I want Dobbs to have the best. I want him given every chance to put his defence, if he has one. But, if he's crooked, I want him out of my manor and I want him in the nick. I can find a good word to say for all sorts of villains, Mr Rumpole, it's my Christian duty to do so, but I can't stand a bent copper.'

There was a small badge on the officer's lapel, the insignia of the Police Witness to God Society. 'Clean living and high thinking' was the style of Superintendent Glazier.

'This little matter of the additional evidence?'

'Sorry about that, Mr Rumpole. Must have come as a nasty shock to Dobbs that we had that.'

'Tell me, why didn't you put it in at the Magistrates' Court? Was it a little threat you were saving up till the last moment?'

'Let's say, we wanted to spare your feelings, sir.' The Superintendent gave a wintry smile. 'We didn't want to destroy your faith in your client.'

'Oh, I think I can bear to hear the truth about dear old Inspector Dobbsy.'

'A rotten apple, Mr Rumpole! One that could poison the whole barrel if he's not thrown out.' Glazier spoke and I could hear the voice of an officer in Cromwell's army, determined to stamp on corruption and backsliding.

'A rotten apple? He seems to me much more like a swede.'

'A *what*, Mr Rumpole?' The Superintendent frowned.

'Isn't that what you sophisticated officers call the poor old turnip-heads, the simple-minded ploddies who'd look far happier in cycle clips?'

'Simple-minded?' He gave another flicker of a smile. 'I don't think you'd call Dobbs simple-minded, Mr Rumpole. Not when you've heard this tape.'

So the performance we had come to attend began as Superintendent Glazier switched on the little machine. Act One, Scene One. The set, I take it, was the Swinging Bamboo restaurant, the dramatis personae were Detective Inspector

Dobbs and new super-grass Charlie Pointer. The background noises were the crunch of prawn crackers and the gentle simmering of sweet-and-sour pork on the table heaters. On this the curtain rose, or rather, the tape was turned on. Mr Morse and I listened, with growing depression, as Charlie Pointer spoke first.

'You want another payment, Inspector?'

There was a pause, and then the Inspector came through loud and clear. The dialogue went as follows:

DOBBS: No one works for nothing, Charlie.

CHARLIE: What's going to happen if I can't pay?

DOBBS: I've got the whole Squad behind me. And I want to get my fingers on what you promised me. When are you coming through, Charlie?

CHARLIE: How much do you want off me, Mr Dobbs?

DOBBS: Five hundred nicker, Charlie.

CHARLIE: Can I have a few more days to collect the money? I'll sell my old banger.

DOBBS: Next Thursday, Charlie. I want it by then. Next Thursday's pay day.

CHARLIE: Same time and place then, Mr Dobbs.

Glazier clicked off the tape. The performance was over, but we had heard quite enough.

'Still got a lot of faith in your client, have you, Mr Rumpole?'

'Interesting recording that.' I was thinking it over. 'You can hear the clatter of plates and the crackle of crispy noodles throughout. It must have been made in the Chinese restaurant.'

'Of course it was, Mr Rumpole.' Glazier was clearly proud of his evidence. 'Got the transcript of all that, have you?'

I looked at the document Morse produced from the filing system of his overcoat pocket.

'Yes. Dobbs's answers were . . .' I read them out. ' "No one works for nothing, Charlie." "I've got the whole squad behind me. And I want to get my fingers on what you promised me. When are you coming through, Charlie?" "Five hundred nicker, Charlie." And, "Next Thursday, Charlie. Next Thursday's pay day." '

'Those are only Dobbs's answers! You forgot Charlie's

questions.' Superintendent Glazier looked at me as though he were starting to lose his faith in my legal abilities.

'Forgot dear old Charlie the grass's questions, did I?' I did my best to look innocent. 'How particularly stupid of me! Oh well. Come on, Mr Morse. Perhaps it doesn't matter after all.'

When I came home worn out from another day with the Bull, topped up by that somewhat chilling visit to Scotland Yard, I was in a mood to unburden my soul to some sympathetic companion. Imagine my bewilderment when I discovered that She Who Must Be Obeyed had apparently taken a vow of silence and entered a Trappist order. All my attempts to keep up a jolly bubble of conversation fell on very stony ground indeed.

'Had a nice day, have you, Hilda?' was my opening gambit. It got no sort of response.

'Did you buy plenty of Vim to go with the saucepan scourers? Did you treat yourself to a coffee and a couple of ginger nuts upstairs at Pontings and then take a long slow, luxurious turn round the hat department? What did you do this afternoon, Hilda? Put your feet up with the ladies' pages of the *Daily Telegraph*?' All this was greeted by a solemn silence. Perhaps I hadn't made myself heard. I raised the voice a little.

'I said, have a nice day, did you, Hilda?'

'It's all right, Rumpole. You needn't shout. I'm not deaf.' My wife spoke at last. 'Yet.'

'Good. That's marvellous news! I thought I was sending out words like troops to some hopeless battle on the Somme. Knowing they'd never return.'

The vast silence fell again.

'Well, Hilda. Aren't you going to ask me what sort of day *I* had?' She clearly wasn't, so I carried on with the monologue.

'Aren't you going to say, "Had a good day, Rumpole?" Yes, thank you, dear. A very good day. Dear old Inspector Dobbs! Apart from a marked tendency to invent verbal admissions by the villains he felt sure were guilty anyway, I always thought he was rather an honest old copper. Just the sort to send bicycling round the village to clip little boys on the ear-hole when he detected a bad case of scrumping apples. But he's been charged with all sorts of nasty practices. Accepting bribes. Corruption. Perverting the course of justice! And the interesting thing about it is, they've got it all on tape. They've recorded his very incriminating words. Question and Answer. What did you say, dear?'

There was a seemingly endless pause, but at last She gave tongue. 'If you have had such a fascinating day, Rumpole, I really don't know why you bothered to come home at all!'

All things happen if you wait for them long enough, and in due course Inspector Dobbs was called to give an account of himself in Number One Court at the Old Bailey. He stood to attention before Mr Justice Vosper, a cold-hearted Judge who was never particularly fond of rotten apples. Her Majesty, regardless of expense, had secured the service of Mr Martin Colefax, Q.C., to prosecute, and I sat containing myself as best I could whilst that aristocratic voice opened the case to the jury as though, if Dobbs were not convicted, there would be a total breakdown of law and order, rioting in the streets and human sacrifices in the crypt of St Paul's Cathedral.

'Members of the jury,' Colefax spoke with deep disapproval, 'it is fashionable nowadays to "knock" the police. Left-wingers, "do-gooders", protectors of so-called civil liberties . . .'

'Defending barristers such as my learned friend, old Rumpole of the Bailey,' I thought Colefax wanted to add that to his list of villains.

'. . . even some defending barristers.' Martin Colefax said it at last. 'All these people take every opportunity to suggest dishonesty in the police. But you may think, I'm sure you *do* think, members of the jury, that our police are quite the best in the world, and *they* are the sure protectors of our liberties.' Here, I thought the old darling was overdoing it a bit; there might be some hostile reaction. The man with the handlebar moustache top left of the jury-box looked as though he'd just been done for speeding. 'But when one policeman goes wrong. When one copper, as we say, "goes bent" . . .' I wondered if Martin Colefax really did use that sort of language, when chattering to his pals round the Sheridan Club on a Saturday night '. . . that one single bent copper can bring the entire police force into ill-deserved disrepute. That one rotten apple, members of the jury, can infect the whole barrel. He must be weeded out.'

Colefax clearly wasn't a gardener, you don't 'weed out' rotten apples. 'Weeded out,' he repeated. 'And crushed! Detective Inspector Dobbs is a rotten apple, the tape-recordings I have to play you in this case will leave no doubt about that. He was taking bribes from a habitual criminal, a man of the worst possible character, who may yet redeem himself by giving evidence for the Crown in this case . . .' I could hear the sound of distant violins as Colefax concluded, '. . . a man called Charles, or "Charlie" Pointer, whom the Crown will call, after, of course, you have heard the tape-recorded evidence.'

As Colefax concluded his opening speech, I dragged myself to my feet. 'My Lord, while the evidence is being given, I should like Mr Glazier to be outside Court.'

'But he's the officer in charge of the case!' Colefax protested.

'Precisely. I would like him out of Court *because* he's the officer in charge of the case.'

'Oh, very well. Will you leave us, officer?' Mr Justice Vosper conceded with an ill grace. Mr Glazier left the Court, giving me a brief smile to show he didn't blame me for going through the motions, but we all knew the trial could only have one result.

Later, I was cross-examining Charles, or Charlie, Pointer – a cheerful little sparrow of a man who had the decency to look somewhat ashamed as he gave evidence in support of the Old Bill.

'Charlie Pointer. Are you giving evidence for the prosecution?' I asked him, more in sorrow than in anger.

'I'm here to tell the truth, Mr Rumpole,' Charlie said modestly.

'Are you really? Did you tell the truth when you pleaded not guilty to warehouse breaking in 1974?'

'Yes.'

'And yet the jury didn't believe you, and you got convicted?'

'Maybe that's because you were defending me at the time.'

There was general laughter in which the Judge was delighted to join. When he had recovered, His Lordship said, 'You asked for that, didn't you, Mr Rumpole?'

I ignored this rudeness and continued to address my questions to Charlie. 'Inspector Dobbs gave evidence against you then, didn't he?'

'So he did last year, when I got off. You did better for me that time, Mr Rumpole!' Charlie carried on with snappy back-chat and was rewarded by another flurry of laughter.

'You don't like Inspector Dobbs, do you, Charlie?' I asked him.

'I've nothing against the man. Not personally, like.'

'Nothing against him personally?'

'No.'

'In fact you became quite friendly with Inspector Dobbs, didn't you – you rang him and asked him to a Chinese dinner?'

There was a pause. Charlie looked incredulously round the Court and gave an exaggerated gasp of amazement.

'*I* asked him? *I* invited out the Old Bill? You're joking!'

'No, Charlie,' I said seriously. 'Inspector Dobbs's entire career is at stake, and his pension. I'm not joking.'

'Look, Mr Rumpole.' Charlie, it seemed, had decided to take me into his confidence. 'He came to see *me*. He said they'd charge me with the job at Fresh Foods, which I never done.'

'Oh, of course.'

'And he said they had my dabs on the frozen-food store.'

'Did you believe him – about the dabs?'

'About the *what*, Mr Rumpole?' One of Mr Justice Vosper's weaknesses is that he needs simultaneous translation in criminal cases.

'The fingerprints, my Lord,' I explained to the old darling.

'No, I didn't really. But I didn't want to face no trial about it. He said he wouldn't do me if I paid him . . .' Charlie looked accusingly at the grey-haired figure in the dock.

'Paid him five hundred nicker?' I suggested and got an explosion from the learned Judge. 'Mr Rumpole! This is intolerable! There may be members of the jury who are not as familiar as you with criminal argot. Would you kindly translate again.'

'Certainly.' I gave him the retort courteous. 'Five hundred pounds, my Lord.'

'I couldn't pay him straight away,' Charlie suggested. 'So I suggested we meet for a Chinese and talk it over like.'

'You went, wired for sound?' In the pause that followed, the jury started to look interested.

'Yes,' Charlie admitted.

'Who suggested that?'

Charlie looked around the Court as if for help. He saw no officer in charge of the case and finally his eye rested on the Judge. 'My Lord. Do I have to say?'

'Mr Rumpole has asked the question. He may not like the answer,' Mr Justice Vosper told him, so Charlie answered, 'Superintendent Glazier.'

'You see, Mr Rumpole. I did warn you that you might not like the answer.' The Judge looked down on me, pleased with himself.

'On the contrary, my Lord. I like it very much indeed!' I was delighted to disappoint him. Then I turned to Charlie. 'You reported this alleged conversation?'

'This alleged request for a bribe, Mr Rumpole,' the Judge corrected me.

'If your Lordship pleases.' I gave him a brief bow, and then went back to work on Charlie. 'You reported this alleged request for a bribe to my client's superior officer?'

'Yes.'

'So you *are* a grass, aren't you, Charlie Pointer?'

At last I had irritated Mr Justice Vosper beyond endurance. 'Mr Rumpole!' he thundered. 'Are you going to conduct this entire case in what the jury may well find to be a foreign language?'

'You *are* a police informer, aren't you, Charlie?' I asked to make my meaning clear. Charlie cast down his eyes, ashamed.

'On that occasion, I have to admit it, yes.'

'And when you went to Inspector Dobbs, and promised to tell him the name of the firm – I beg your pardon, my Lord, the gang – who did the Fresh Foods job . . .'

'I never!' Charlie sounded genuinely outraged. But I pressed on, 'Oh yes you did, Charlie. And Inspector Dobbs was going to pay you for your information. He promised you five hundred nicker, or, for the benefit of His Lordship, pounds. So that's how the sum of money got to be mentioned in the Chinese restaurant.'

'He was offering to pay *me*?' Charlie pointed to himself, grinning incredulously.

'Exactly!'

'Mr Rumpole.' The Judge appeared to think that it was time he took a hand in the proceedings. 'May I remind you that that suggestion is quite contrary to the evidence of tape-recording the jury have heard.'

'It's inconsistent with this witness's questions, my Lord. It's not in the least inconsistent with my client's answers.' I gave a reply which I hoped was enigmatic and was rewarded by seeing the Judge look totally confused.

'I'm afraid, Mr Rumpole,' he said, 'I no longer follow you.'

'Then perhaps, my Lord, we can have a little demonstration. I would just like to remind the Court of the words of the tape again. May it be played?'

A mechanically minded officer switched on the device. We heard the familiar clatter of the Chinese restaurant, and then the voices.

CHARLIE: You want another payment, Inspector?

DOBBS: No one works for nothing, Charlie.

CHARLIE: What's going to happen if I can't pay?

DOBBS: I've got the whole Squad behind me. And I want to get my fingers on what you promised. When are you coming through, Charlie?

CHARLIE: How much do you want off me, Mr Dobbs?

DOBBS: Five hundred nicker, Charlie.

CHARLIE: Can I have a few more days to collect the money? I'll sell my old banger.

DOBBS: Next Thursday, Charlie. I want it by then. Next Thursday's pay day.

I was painfully aware that the recording was having a depressing effect on the jury: there could not, they must have thought, possibly be stronger evidence of Dobbs's guilt. All the same, I was determined to press on with my little experiment.

'Charlie. We're going to play that tape again with your questions left out. Instead of them, I want you to read the list of questions the usher will hand to you. Will you do that for us?'

I gave the usher a sheet of paper which he took round to the witness-box. Charlie looked at it, gave a small, sporting shrug and said, 'I don't mind.'

'I'm sure you don't. With your new interest in assisting the course of justice. Yes. Shall we begin?' Mr Morse gave the officer the copy of the tape we had prepared with silent gaps instead of Charlie's questions. In these pauses, he read from the list I had handed him. It came out like this:

CHARLIE (*reading*): I'm going to get paid, aren't I, Inspector Dobbs?

DOBBS: No one works for nothing, Charlie.

CHARLIE (*reading*): What's going to happen if the old firm find out I'm a grass?'

DOBBS: I've got the whole Squad behind me. And I want to get my fingers on what you promised. When are you coming through, Charlie?

CHARLIE (*reading*): How much are you paying me for the info, Mr Dobbs?

DOBBS: Five hundred nicker, Charlie.

CHARLIE (*reading*): Can I have a few more days to get the gen on the Fresh Foods job? Then I'll come through with the names.

DOBBS: Next Thursday, Charlie. I want it by then. Next Thursday's pay day.'

The officer switched off the tape. The Court was silent. The jury looked at me, as though I had just lifted my wig and released a pigeon. Even the Judge had the decency to appear thoughtful.

'Very clever, Mr Rumpole,' Charlie conceded.

'Thank you, Charlie.'

'It's just not true. That's all,' Charlie began to bluster. 'That's not how it happened. I'll take my oath.'

'Mr Rumpole.' The Judge saw the consequences of my experiment. 'If what you are suggesting is correct, then someone has been guilty of falsifying this tape.'

'That is so, my Lord.' I was glad of the chance of agreeing with the old darling. 'A falsification to which this witness was clearly a party.'

'And the other party?' His Lordship asked.

'That is something, my Lord, which I hope we may be able to find out, before this trial is over.'

'I'll call Mr Glazier.'

Martin Colefax said this, quite casually, at the end of the prosecution case. The name was called outside and presently the senior officer, still in his blue suit and Rugby Club tie, marched modestly to the witness-box. Glazier lifted the New Testament in an experienced manner, and swore to tell the truth, the whole truth and nothing but the truth. As he did so, I wondered why Colefax had called him 'Mister Glazier'. I mean just '*Mister*' Glazier. Wasn't my learned friend for the prosecution rather underdoing it? Why not give the Super his full title? Why not say proudly: 'I call *Superintendent* Glazier, a most senior and experienced officer, of the Serious Crimes Squad. Step forward, *Superintendent*.' That's what I'd do. So why plain '*Mister*'?

'Mister Glazier, on the fourth of March, when this conversation in the Chinese restaurant took place, were you Inspector Dobbs's senior officer?' Colefax began his examination in chief.

'I was.'

'And as such, would you supervise Dobbs's contacts with police informers?'

'I would expect to do so, yes.'

'And would you have to authorize any proposed payment of five hundred pounds to a police informer?'

'If it was a sum of that size, yes,' Glazier agreed.

'Did Inspector Dobbs ever tell you he meant to use the man Pointer as a police informer?' There was a moment's pause, and Colefax asked again. 'Did he, Mr Glazier?'

'No, my Lord.' The officer turned respectfully to the Judge 'He never did.'

'Or ever ask your permission to pay Pointer five hundred pounds?'

'No, my Lord.' Now Glazier answered without hesitation.

'Or any sum of money whatsoever?'

'No.'

'But Mr Rumpole, our client says he told the Super all about it.' An agitated Mr Morse was whispering into my ear in an excited manner, but I silenced him.

'Sit quiet, Morse, old darling,' I whispered back, 'and let's listen to the damning evidence of *Mr* Glazier.'

'Mr Glazier.' Colefax had done it again. 'At the end of April, did the man Pointer come to you with a complaint against Inspector Dobbs?'

'Yes, he did.'

'What was the nature of that complaint?'

'Just a moment. Do you object to that question, Mr Rumpole?' The Judge looked at me as though he was expecting an attempt to stifle the witness.

'Oh no, my Lord,' I told him cheerfully. 'I'd like to hear the full extent of the case that can be fabricated against my client.'

'Mr Rumpole.' Vosper, J., was not pleased. Whether or not it is fabricated is entirely a matter for the jury!'

'Exactly, my Lord!' I looked at the twelve old darlings in the jury-box with the deepest respect, and said as meaningfully as I could, 'and for no one else in this Court.'

'What was Pointer's complaint?' Colefax went back to work with the witness.

'He said that Inspector Dobbs had demanded money from him and threatened to charge him with participating in the Fresh Foods robbery if he didn't pay up.'

'So what course did you take?'

'I provided Pointer with a pocket tape-recorder and asked him to keep an appointment with Dobbs in a Chinese restaurant, my Lord.' At this Vosper, J., nodded his understanding, and made a note.

'And, as a result of that instruction, was this conversation recorded?' Colefax asked.

'*Part* of this conversation was recorded.'

'Thank you, Mr Glazier.' Colefax sat down and the Judge looked in my direction.

'Mr Rumpole. I imagine you have questions for this officer?'

'Just a few, my Lord.'

'Then I've no doubt the jury will be better equipped to understand your case after a little *rest*. Ten thirty tomorrow morning then, members of the jury.'

His Lordship rose, we stood and bowed him out with more or less respect, and then I gave my orders to the faithful Morse.

'Mr Morse. I'll have to tear you away from your tomato plants. I want you to call on my friend Fred Timson, head of the Clan Timson, biggest family of south London villains, valued clients of mine. Oh, and send someone up to see the waiters in the Swinging Bamboo, we might unearth something. Your man needn't speak Chinese, but he should be prepared to invest in a mound of sweet-and-sour lobster.'

'What do I ask Fred Timson?'

'Ask him to tell us all he knows about Charlie Pointer, and everything he's heard about *Mr* Glazier. Now Dobbs, my old darling.' The Inspector had been released from the dock and set at liberty for the night. 'Why does your Super dislike you so?' The Inspector scratched his head and mused a little.

'I can only think,' he said at last. 'Well, I did once make a complaint. It's ironic really, what I complained about . . .' This was exactly what I'd wanted to hear. I interrupted him in some excitement. 'Why didn't you say so to me before? Never mind, Dobbsy. It's not too late to tell me all about it . . .'

That evening, in front of the electric fire in Casa Rumpole, I did my best to engage my better half in conversation. 'Not a bad day, Hilda.' Silence. 'Quite an effective little trick with a tape-recorder. I think the ladies and gentlemen of the jury enjoyed it.' More silence. 'You know what we always say in Court? Listen to the questions. The questions are so much more important than the answers.' Still more silence. 'My questions, Hilda. Are more important than your answers!' Still more silence. 'Just as well, seeing that you haven't got any answers to provide.' A prolonged pause, after which I said. 'What's the matter? Are you about to enter a nunnery? Have you taken a vow to ever hold your peace? Oh please, don't even bother to tell me.'

I found it hard to sleep and was up early the next morning. By seven thirty I was having breakfast with old Morse in Rex's café opposite the Old Bailey. As he puffed his smouldering pipe tobacco over my bacon and fried slice, he gave me news which caused me to rise to cross-examine my client's superior officer with a good deal of interest and some anticipation of pleasure to come.

'*Mister* Glazier.'

'Yes, *Mister* Rumpole?' The witness looked at me, unperturbed.

'When did you first know that Charlie Pointer was a grass?'

'When he came to me and told me that your client had asked for a bribe, Mr Rumpole.' Glazier was a cool customer and I would have to be careful.

'Did that surprise you?'

'Surprise me that your client was a rotten apple? I *was* surprised, sir. And extremely upset.' The jury looked at Dobbs; it was a look of great suspicion.

'Oh, I'm so sorry. No, I meant did it surprise you that Charlie should be prepared to act as a police informer, for the first time in an honourable career as a warehouse breaker?'

'Did you say "honourable", Mr Rumpole?' Mr Justice Vosper asked in a carefully calculated tone of surprise.

'Yes, my Lord. Charlie Pointer was breaking his own code of honour when he decided to grass. That's why I suggested he didn't do so voluntarily.' I did my best to explain my meaning to His Lordship, who merely sighed and said, 'I should be interested to know just what you *are* suggesting.'

'Certainly, my Lord.' I called Glazier to provide an explanation and asked him, 'You thought Charlie was involved in the Fresh Foods job, didn't you?'

'Shall we say he was under suspicion.'

'Did you tell him his fingerprints were on the store-room door at Fresh Foods?'

'I think I may have done.' Glazier admitted that a little less readily.

'So you interviewed him, did you? Long before he told you that Inspector Dobbs was asking for a bribe?'

There was a long pause; then Glazier saw that the Judge was looking at him, waiting for an answer. He gave one at last.

'I may have done.'

'Yes, you may have done. And told him he might be involved in a serious charge?'

'Is that what Pointer has said?' Glazier looked a little confused and I blessed the day we had the officer in charge out of Court.

'Don't you worry about what Pointer has said. You just try to tell us the truth, Superintendent. Oh, I'm sorry . . .'

'Why are you apologizing, Mr Rumpole?' the Judge asked, and I smiled at Mister Glazier with some sympathy. 'It's no longer *Superintendent*, is it? You've been demoted.' Martin Colefax had the grace to look slightly guilty then, and the jury were clearly interested.

'I have been . . . re-ranked. Yes.'

'After a disciplinary hearing?'

'My Lord, has that got anything to do with this case? . . .' Glazier tried appealing to the Judge, but I interrupted him.

'I suggest it has everything to do with this case. There was a complaint, wasn't there, that you had failed to investigate? Was it a little matter of an officer receiving bribes? Your superiors took the view that you had been culpably negligent.'

'There was a complaint.' The witness agreed cautiously.

'And the prosecution have tried to conceal your demotion by referring to you in Court as plain "Mister", and not disclosing your new rank?'

'My Lord, I really must protest.' The elegant Colefax shimmered to his feet, but I motioned him   subside.

'Oh, don't bother,' I said. 'The jury know the truth about that now. Just as they will soon learn the *whole* truth about this case!'

'Mr Rumpole.' The Judge felt, perhaps, that he was losing his grasp of the proceedings. 'If he was once negligent in investigating bribery, this officer has surely made up for it by the thoroughness with which he has had your client investigated.'

'Or was my client investigated so thoroughly, *Mister* Glazier,' I ignored the Judge and asked the witness, 'because he *wasn't* taking bribes?'

'I don't know what you mean, Mr Rumpole.' Glazier played for safety.

'Do you not? Let me make it clear to you. My client, Inspector Dobbs, was a "swede", wasn't he?'

'You are saying your client's not English?' Poor old Vosper. He had the greatest difficulty in keeping up with the dialogue.

'I'm sorry. I'll interpret again, for the benefit of your Lordship. A "swede" is an old-fashioned policeman, a "turnip-head", a "vegetable", one who is honest according to his lights, and never takes bribes. Have you heard that description used by less scrupulous officers?' I asked Glazier.

'I have heard it. Yes.'

'But the "swede" was getting suspicious. Old Dobbsy was starting to smell a rat. Was it Inspector Dobbs who made the first complaint against you? Don't bother to lie, Mr Glazier, I can call for the record . . .'

'I'm not at all sure if this is relevant.' Colefax was stirring again, but I interrupted him by almost shouting at the witness, '*Will* you answer?'

'I think it was. Yes.' The words came out of Glazier like pulled teeth.

'You *think* it was! So Dobbsy had to be shut up. You put pressure on Charlie Pointer! You threatened to do him for the Fresh Foods job, which was one of those he *hadn't* done. You lied and told him you had his fingerprints on the frozen-food store, and got him to help you frame Inspector Dobbs. Oh, by the way, does the word "frame" require translation for your Lordship?'

'No thank you, Mr Rumpole. I understand it perfectly well.' At last the Judge appeared to be cooperating. I helped him to understand the rest of the case.

'Pointer offered Inspector Dobbs information and took him to the Chinese restaurant where he led him into some answers you could slot into the other tape you made later. It was careful of you to make that second tape in the same restaurant, so you could get the right background noises.'

'It's not true! I never went to that restaurant with Charlie – with Pointer. I swear that on my oath!'

It was when he talked about his oath that I knew the witness was lying, and I told him so. 'You *are* rather a careless officer, aren't you, Mr Glazier? You see, I shall be calling a Mr Wah Li Po, who remembers Charlie eating in the Swinging Bamboo with certain solid gentlemen in plain clothes, among them your good self, on a number of occasions. Perhaps Mr Wah would just step into Court, so that we can make quite sure he identifies you later.'

The next day I returned from the Old Bailey in good spirits. After a quick and refreshing glass at Pommeroy's Wine Bar I wandered into Chambers and joined our Head, Guthrie Featherstone, Mr and Mrs Claude Erskine-Brown, Uncle Tom and various barristers for one of those meetings in which we decide high and important matters of Chambers policy. As I entered the room, Guthrie noticed my cheerful appearance and asked if I'd had another triumph at the Bailey.

'A *bit* of a triumph, I suppose, Featherstone.' Well, there was no point in being modest about it. 'You see, they were looking for a rotten apple. They found the right one in the end. Ex-Superintendent Glazier'll end up in an open prison, spreading muck and slipping out to the pub on Saturdays.'

'It's the question of a rotten apple which I have to raise at this Chambers meeting,' Erskine-Brown weighed in. 'It's also a question of morality in Chambers.'

'Claude Erskine-Brown has a problem about the coffee made in the clerk's room,' Featherstone explained.

'And I have a problem about trousers,' I told the meeting.

'What on earth do you mean, Rumpole?' Our Head of Chambers wanted to be put in the picture.

'Pin-striped trousers, barristers, for the use of. What would you say if I, if anyone, charged the Commissioners of Inland Revenue for the purchase of two brand new pairs of pin-striped trousers a year, and went on sporting the same faded old bags that had been run up for us on our call to the Bar.'

'I'd say that would clearly amount to deception, and making a false return.' Featherstone pronounced judgement severely.

'I suppose we all have to live with a certain amount of deception,' I said thoughtfully. 'Gingering up the verbals or the coffee money. It can go too far though, like false tape-recordings, or profiting from non-existent trousers.'

'Horace. I'm not sure I follow.' Featherstone looked left behind.

'Never mind. Let's go on with the Chambers meeting.

Claude did you want to raise the question of coffee money?'
There was a long pause before Claude Erskine-Brown had the
decency and good sense to answer:

'No. I don't think so. On second thoughts ... I don't think
so.'

I took a bottle of claret home to share with Hilda. I even
bought her a handful of ruinously expensive chrysanths at the
Tube station, but She still wasn't communicative, even when
I told her about my excellent win in the case of R. *v*. Dobson.

'The worst part of it all was, Hilda, that Glazier recommended
me as a barrister to poor old Dobbsy. He must've thought that I'd
got such a dislike for the police, having attacked them so often,
that I wouldn't defend a copper properly. Doesn't he know my
religious faith? A client is a client, no matter how disreputable
and unattractive his profession. You understand that, Hilda,
don't you?' Silence. 'Hilda. Would you mind telling me. *What's
eating you?*'

'Oh, very well.' She Who Must Be Obeyed spoke out at last.
'It was your answer to my question.'

'When?'

'A month ago. You were off to a conference with that policeman.'

'Inspector Dobbs?'

'Yes. You were leaving to see him. And I asked you, "Will
you come straight back this evening, Rumpole?" And you
said ...'

'What did I say?'

'You said, "I bloody well hope not."'

I began to see a light at the end of the tunnel. Normal re-
lations might at last be resumed with She.

'Nonsense. I said that when you asked me if I'd be late back.'

'But ...'

'I didn't hear any other question.'

'Rumpole. Are you sure?'

'Sure? Of course I'm sure. It's the questions that are important, you see Hilda. Never the answers.'

Rumpole and the Expert Witness

> Canst thou not minister to a mind diseased,
> Pluck from the memory a rooted sorrow,
> Raze out the written troubles of the brain,
> And with some sweet oblivious antidote
> Cleanse the stuffed bosom of that perilous stuff
> Which weighs upon the heart . . .

Certainly not young Dr Ned Dacre, the popular G.P. of Hunter's Hill, that delightful little dormitory town in Surrey, where nothing is heard but the whirr of the kitchen mixers running up Provençal specialities from the Sunday supplements and the purr of the Hi Fis playing baroque music to go with the Buck's Fizz.

Ned Dacre lived in a world removed from my usual clients, the Old Bailey villains whose most common disease is a criminal conviction. He had a beautiful wife, two cars, two fair-haired children called Simon and Sara at rather nice schools, an au pair girl, an Old English sheepdog, a swimming pool, a car port and a machine for recording television programmes so that he didn't have to keep watching television. His father, Dr Henry Dacre, had settled in Hunter's Hill just after the war and had built up an excellent practice. When his son grew up and qualified he was taken into the partnership and father and son were the two most popular doctors for many miles around, the inhabitants being almost equally divided as to whether, in times of sickness, they preferred the attentions of 'Dr Harry' or 'Dr Ned'. With all these advantages it seemed that Ned Dacre had all that the heart of man could desire, except that he had an unhappy wife. One night, after they had enjoyed a quiet supper together at home, Dr Ned's wife Sally became extremely ill. As she appeared to lose consciousness, he heard her say,

'I loved you Ned . . . I really did.'

These were her last words, for although her husband rang the casualty department of the local hospital, and an ambulance was quickly dispatched, the beautiful Mrs Sally Dacre never spoke again, and died before she was taken out of the house.

I learned, as did the world, about the death of Sally Dacre and its unfortunate consequences from *The Times*. I was seated at breakfast in the matrimonial home at Froxbury Court in the Gloucester Road, looking forward without a great deal of excitement to a fairly ordinary day practising the law, ingesting Darjeeling tea, toast and Oxford marmalade, when the news item caught my eye and I gave a discreet whistle of surprise. My wife, Hilda, who was reading her correspondence (one letter on mauve paper from an old schoolfriend) wanted her share of the news.

'What's the news in *The Times*, Rumpole? Has war started?'

'A Dr Dacre has been arrested in Hunter's Hill, Surrey. He's charged with murdering his wife.'

Hilda didn't seem to find the intelligence immediately gripping. In fact she waved her correspondence at me.

'There's a letter from Dodo. You know, my friend Dodo, Rumpole?'

'The one who keeps the tea-shop in Devon?' I had a vague recollection of an unfriendly female in tweed who seemed to imagine that I tyrannized somewhat over She Who Must Be Obeyed.

'She's always asking me to pop down and stay.'

'Why don't you?' I muttered hopefully, and then returned to the Home News. ' "Dr Dacre . . .? Dacre!" The name's distinctly familiar.'

'Dodo never cared for you, Rumpole,' Hilda said firmly.

'The feeling's mutual. Isn't she the one who wears amber beads and smells of scones?' I repeated the name, hoping to stir some hidden memory, 'Harry Dacre.'

'Dodo's been suffering from depression,' Hilda rambled on. 'Of course, she never married.'

'Then I can't think what she's got to be depressed about!' I couldn't resist saying it, perhaps not quite audibly from behind the cover of *The Times*. 'Dr Harry Dacre!' I suddenly remembered. 'He gave evidence in my greatest triumph, the Penge Bungalow Murders! He'd seen my client's bruises. Don't you remember?'

'Dodo writes that she's taking a new sort of pill for her depression. They're helping her, but she mustn't eat cheese.'

'Poor old Dodo,' I said, 'deprived of cheese.' I read the story in the paper again. 'It couldn't be him. This is Dr "Ned" Dacre. Oh well, it's just another nice little murder that's never going to come my way. "Cause of death, cerebral haemorrhage", that's the evidence in the Magistrates' Court, "sustained in an alleged attack . . ." '

As I read, Hilda was casting a critical eye over my appearance.

'You're never going to Chambers like that, are you, Rumpole?'

'Like what, Hilda?' I was wondering what sort of a savage attack by a local doctor could explain his wife's cerebral haemorrhage.

'Well, your stud's showing and you've got marmalade on your waistcoat, and do you *have* to have that old silk handkerchief half falling out of your top pocket?'

'That was the silk handkerchief I used to blow my nose on three times, tearfully, in my final speech in the double murder in the Deptford Old People's Home. It has a certain sentimental value. Will you leave me alone, Hilda?' She was dabbing at my waistcoat with a corner of a table napkin she had soaked in the hot water jug.

'I just want you to look your best, Rumpole.'

'You mean, in case I get run over?'

'And I'll put that old hanky in the wash.' She snatched the venerable bandana out of my breast pocket. 'You'd be much better off with a few nice, clean tissues.'

'You know what that fellow Dacre's been accused of, Hilda?' I thought I might as well remind her. 'Murdering his wife.'

As I had no pressing engagement until two thirty, when I was due for a rather dull touch of defrauding the Customs and Excise at the Uxbridge Magistrates' Court, I loitered on my way to the Tube station, walked up through the Temple gardens smoking a small cigar, and went into the clerk's room to complain to Henry of the run-of-the-mill nature of my legal diet.

'No nice murders on the menu, are there?' When I asked him this, Henry smiled in a secretive sort of way and said,

'I'm not sure, sir.'

'You're not *sure*?'

'There's a Dr Henry Dacre phoned to come and see you urgently, sir. It seems his son's in a bit of trouble. He's come with Mr Cossett, solicitor of Hunter's Hill. I've put them in your room, Mr Rumpole.'

Old Dr Dacre in my room! I began to sniff the memory of ancient battles and a never-to-be-forgotten victory. When I opened my door, I was greeted by a healthy-looking country solicitor, and a greying version of a witness whose evidence marked a turning point in the Penge Bungalow affair. Dr Harry Dacre held out his hand and said,

'Mr Rumpole. It's been a long time, sir.'

How long, was it, perhaps a legal lifetime, since I did R. *v.* Samuel Poulteny, better known as the Penge Bungalow Murders, which altered the course of legal history by proving that Horace Rumpole could win a capital case, alone and without a leader? Young Dr Harry Dacre, then a G.P. at Penge, gave valuable evidence for the defence, and young Rumpole made the most of it. I motioned the good doctor to my client's chair and invited Mr Cossett, the instructing solicitor, to take a seat.

'Well now, Doctor,' I said, 'what can I do for you?'

'You may have read about my son's little trouble?' The old doctor spoke of the charge of wife murder as though it were a touch of the flu which might be cured by a couple of aspirin and a day in bed.

'Yes. Was it a stormy sort of marriage?' I asked him.

The doctor shook his head.

'Sally was an extraordinarily pretty girl. Terribly spoilt, of course. Ned gave her everything she wanted.'

I wondered if that included a cerebral haemorrhage, and then told myself to keep my mouth shut and listen quietly.

'She had her problems, of course,' Dr Dacre went on. 'Nervous trouble. Well. Half the women in Hunter's Hill have got a touch of the nervy. All these labour-saving devices in the kitchen, gives them too much time to think.'

Not a pioneer of women's lib., I thought, old Dr Harry. And I asked him, 'Was she taking anything for her nerves?'

'Sally was scared of pills,' the doctor shook his head. 'Afraid she might get hooked, although she didn't mind taking the odd drink too many.'

'Do you think she needed medical treatment?'

'Ned and I discussed it. He thought of a course of treatment but Sally wouldn't cooperate. So he, well, I suppose he just put up with her.' Dr Harry seemed to think that no one would have found his daughter-in-law particularly easy to live with.

'And on, as the prosecutors say, the night in question?' I decided it was time to get down to the facts.

'Mr Rumpole! That's why we need you,' Dr Harry said flatteringly enough. 'I know from past experience. You're the man who can destroy the pathologist's evidence! I'll never forget the Penge Bungalow case, and the way you pulverized that expert witness for the Crown.'

I wouldn't have minded a lengthy reminiscence of that memorable cross-examination, but I felt we should get on with the work in hand.

'Just remind me of the medical evidence. We don't disagree with the Crown about the cause of death?'

'Cerebral haemorrhage? No doubt about that. But it's the other findings that are the difficulty.'

'Which are?'

'Multiple bruising on the body, particularly the legs, back and buttocks, and the wound on the head where the deceased girl fell and knocked the edge of the coffee table.'

'Which caused the haemorrhage to the brain?' I frowned. The evidence of bruising was hardly encouraging.

'No doubt about it,' Dr Harry assured me. 'The trouble is the pathologist says the bruising was inflicted *before* death; the implication being that my son beat his wife up.'

'Is that likely?' It sounded rather unlike the home life of a young professional couple in Hunter's Hill.

'I told you Sally was a spoilt and highly strung girl, Mr Rumpole.' Dr Harry shrugged. 'Her father was old Peter Gaveston of Gaveston Electronics. She always had everything she wanted. Of course she and Ned quarrelled. Don't all married couples?'

Not all married couples, of course, include She Who Must Be Obeyed, but I had reason to believe that the good doctor was right in his diagnosis.

'But Ned would never beat his wife up like that,' Ned's father assured me. 'Not beat her up to kill her.'

It sounded as if I would have to do battle with another pathologist, and I was anxious to find out who my opponent would be.

'Tell me, who's the Miracle of the Morgues, the Prosecution Prince of the Post Mortems? Who's the great brain on the other side?'

'It's a local pathologist. Does all the work in this part of the country.'

'Would I have heard of him?' I asked casually.

'It's not a "him". It's a Dr Pamela Gorle. And the irony is, Ned knows her extremely well. They were at Barts together, before he met Sally, of course. He brought her home for the weekend once or twice, and I almost thought they might make a go of it.'

'You mean, get married?'

'Yes.' Dr Harry seemed to think that the lady with the formaldehyde might have been a better bet than Sally.

By this time I was beginning to feel some sympathy for Dr Ned. It's enough to be put on trial for murder without having your ex-girlfriend examine your deceased wife's body, and provide what turns out to be the only real evidence for the prosecution.

'I just don't understand! I simply don't understand it.'

Friendly young Dr Ned sat in the unfriendly surroundings of the prison interview room. He looked concerned but curiously detached, as though he had just hit on a mysterious tropical disease which had no known cure.

'Doctor,' I said, 'did you and your wife Sally get on moderately well together?'

'We had our quarrels, of course. Like all married couples.'

It was the second time I had heard that. But, I thought, all married couples don't end up with one dead and the other one in the nick awaiting trial on a charge of wilful murder.

I looked at Dr Ned. He was better-looking than his father had been at his age; but Dr Harry, as I remembered his appearance in the Penge Bungalow Murders trial, had seemed the stronger character and more determined. As I looked at the charming, but rather weak younger doctor (after all, he hadn't had to struggle to build up a practice, but had picked up his father's well-warmed stethoscope and married an extremely wealthy young woman) I found it hard to imagine him brutally beating his wife and so killing her. Of course I might have been mistaken; the most savage murder I was ever mixed up in was the axeing of a huge Regimental Sergeant-Major by a five-foot-nothing Sunday school teacher from East Finchley.

'Your father told me that Mrs Sally Dacre was depressed from time to time. Was she depressed about anything in particular?'

'No. In fact I always thought Sally had everything she wanted.'

'But did she suffer from depression?'

'I think so. Yes.'

'And took nothing for it?'

'She didn't approve of pills. She'd heard too many stories about people getting hooked. Doctors and their wives.'

'So she took nothing?' I wanted to get the facts established.

'My father was her doctor. I thought that was more professional. I'm not sure if he prescribed her anything, but I don't think he did. There was nothing found in the stomach.'

He said it casually and seemed only politely concerned. I don't know why I felt a sudden chill at discussing the contents of his dead wife's stomach with the doctor.

'No pills,' I agreed with him. 'The medical evidence tells us that.'

'Dr Pamela Gorle's report,' Dr Ned went on, still quite dispassionately. I fished out the document in question.

'Yes. It talks of the remains of a meal, and a good deal of alcohol in the blood.'

'We had a bottle of Chianti. And a soufflé. We were alone that night. We ate our supper in front of the television.'

'Your wife cooked?' I asked, not that there was any question of the food being anything but harmless.

'Oh no.' Dr Ned smiled at me. 'I may not be an absolutely brilliant doctor, but my soufflés are nothing short of miraculous.'

'Did you quarrel that evening?' I asked him. 'I mean, like all married couples?'

'Not at all. We had a discussion about where we'd go for our holiday, and settled on Crete. Sally had never been there, and I had only once. Before we met, actually.'

Had that been, I wondered, a romantic packaged fortnight with the pathologist for the Crown? Mine not to reason who with, so I kept him at the job of telling me the story of that last night with his wife.

'And then?'

'Then Sally complained of a headache. I thought it was perhaps due to watching the television for too long, so I switched it off. She was standing up to get herself a brandy.'

'And?'

'She stumbled and fell forwards.'

'Face *forwards*? Are you sure of that?'

'Yes, I'm certain. It was then that her forehead hit the corner of the coffee table.'

'And caused the cerebral haemorrhage?'

Dr Ned paused, frowning slightly. He seemed to be giving the matter his detached and entirely professional opinion. At last, he said cautiously,

'I can only think so.'

'Doctor, your friend, the pathologist . . .'

'Hardly my *friend* any longer.' Dr Ned smiled again, ruefully this time, as though he appreciated the irony of having an old colleague and fiancée giving evidence against him on a charge of wilful murder.

'No,' I agreed with him. 'She isn't your friend, is she? She says she found extensive bruising on your wife's back, her buttocks and the back of her legs.'

'That's what I can't understand.' My client looked genuinely puzzled.

'You're quite sure she didn't fall backwards?' I asked after a careful silence. Dr Ned and his wife were quite alone. Who would quarrel with the description of her falling backwards and bruising herself? I had given him his chance. A professional villain, any member of the Timson family for instance, would have taken that hint and agreed with me. But not Dr Ned.

'No, I told you. She fell forwards.' He was either being totally honest or wilfully obtuse.

'And you can't account for the alleged bruises on her back?'

'No.' That was all he had to say about it. But then he frowned, in some embarrassment, and said,

'There is one thing perhaps I ought to tell you.'

'About your wife?'

'No. About Dr Pamela Gorle.' Again, he hesitated. 'We were at Barts together, you know.'

'And went to Crete together once, on a packaged holiday.'

'How did you know that?' He looked at me, puzzled. It was an inspired guess, so I didn't answer his question. As I am a perpetual optimist, I asked, 'Do you think the Crown's expert witness might be a little helpful to us in the witness-box?'

'Not at all. In fact, I'm afraid she'll do everything she can to get me convicted.'

As I have said, I am an incorrigible optimist, and for the first time in my conference with Dr Ned I began to sniff the faint, far-away odour of a defence.

'Pamela was an extraordinarily possessive girl,' the doctor told me. 'She was always unreasonably and abnormally jealous.'

'When you married Sally?'

'When I met Sally. I suppose, well, after that holiday in Crete Pam thought we might get married. Then I didn't ring her and I began to get the most awful letters and phone calls from her. She was threatening . . .'

'Threatening what?'

'It was all very vague. To tell my father, or my patients, or the G.M.C., that she was pregnant.'

'Would any of those august bodies have cared?'

'Not in the least. It wasn't true anyway. Then she seemed to calm down for a while, but I still got letters – on my wedding anniversary and on some date which Pamela seemed to think was important.'

'Perhaps the day your affair started, or ended?'

'Probably. I really can't remember. She'd got her job with the Home Office, retained as a pathologist for this part of the county. I hoped she might settle down and get married, and forget.'

'She never did? Get married, I mean?'

'Or forget. I had a dreadful letter from her about a month ago. She said I'd ruined her life by marrying a hopeless drunk, and that she'd tell Sally we were still meeting unless . . .'

'Yes?' I prompted him, he seemed reluctant to go on.

'Well. Unless we still met. And continued our affair.'

'Did your wife see the letter?'

'No. I always get up early and opened the post.'

'You've kept the letter, of course?'

'No. I tore it up at once.'

If only people had the sense to realize that they might be facing a murder trial at any moment, they might keep important documents.

'And what did the letter say?'

'That she'd find some way of ruining my life, however long it took her.'

Hell, I supposed, hath no fury like a lady pathologist scorned. But Dr Pamela Gorle's personal interest in the Dacre murder seemed to provide the only faint hope of a cure for Dr Ned's somewhat desperate situation. I didn't know if a murder case had ever been won by attacking the medical evidence on the grounds of a romantic bias, but I supposed there had to be a first time for everything.

Everything about the Dacre murder trial was thoroughly pleasant. The old, red brick, local Georgian courtroom, an object of beauty among the supermarkets and boutiques and the wine bar and television and radio stores of the little Surrey town, was so damned pleasant that you expected nice girls with Roedean accents to pass round the Court serving coffee and rock cakes whenever there was a lull in the proceedings. The jury looked as though they had dropped in for a rather gentle session of 'Gardeners' Question Time', and Owen Munroe, Q.C., was a pleasant prosecutor who seemed thoroughly distressed at having to press such a nasty charge as wilful murder against the nice young doctor who sat in the dock wearing his well-pressed suit and old Barts tie.

Worst of all, Nick McManus was a tremendously pleasant judge. He was out to be thoroughly fair and show every courtesy to the defence, ploys which frequently lead to a conviction. It is amazing how many villains owe their freedom to the fact that some old sweetheart on the Bench seemed to be determined to get the jury to pot them.

We went quickly, and without argument, through the formal evidence of photographs, fingerprints and the finding of the body, and then my learned friend announced that he intended to call the pathologist.

'Will that be convenient to you, Mr Rumpole?' The Judge, as I have said, was a perfect gent.

'Certainly, my Lord. That will be quite convenient.' I made myself perfectly pleasant in return.

'I wish to make quite sure, Mr Rumpole, that you have every opportunity to prepare yourself to cross-examine the expert witness.'

You see what I mean? Old McManus was making sure I would have no alibi if I didn't succeed in cracking Dr Pamela. I'd've been far better off with someone like the mad Judge Bullingham, charging head-on at the defence. In this very pleasant trial, Rumpole would have no excuses. However, there was no help for it, so I bowed and said,

'I'm quite prepared, my Lord. Thank you.'

'Very well. Mr Munroe, as you are about to call the pathologist . . .'

'Yes, my Lord.' My opponent was on his feet.

'I suppose the jury will *have* to look at the photographs of the dead lady?'

'Yes, my Lord. It is Bundle No. 4.'

Pictures of a good-looking young woman, naked, bruised, battered and laid on a mortuary slab, are always harrowing and never helpful to the defence. McManus, J., introduced them to the jury quietly, but effectively.

'Members of the jury,' said the Judge. 'I'm afraid you will find these photographs extremely distressing. It is necessary for you to see them so you may understand the medical evidence fully, but I'm sure counsel will take the matter as shortly as possible. These things are never pleasant.'

Death isn't pleasant, nor is murder. In the nicest possible way, the Judge was pointing out the horrific nature of the crime of which Dr Ned was charged. It was something you just didn't do in that part of Surrey.

'I swear by Almighty God that the evidence I shall give shall be the truth, the whole truth and nothing but the truth.'

I was aroused from my thoughts by the sound of the pathologist taking her Bible oath. Owen Munroe hitched up his gown, sorted out his papers and started his examination in chief.

'Dr Pamela Gorle?' he asked.

'Yes.'

'Did you examine the body of the late Sally Dacre, the deceased in this case?'

'I did. Yes.'

'Just tell us what you found.'

'I found a well-nourished, healthy woman of thirty-five years of age who had died from a cerebral haemorrhage. There was evidence of a recent meal.' The demure pathologist had a voice ever gentle and low, an excellent thing in a woman, but a bit of a drawback in the witness-box. I had to strain my ears to follow her drift. And unlike the well-nourished and healthy deceased, Dr Pamela was pale and even uninteresting to look at. Her hair was thin and mousy, she wore a black suit and National Health spectacles behind which her eyes glowed with some obsession. I couldn't be sure whether it was love of her gloomy work or hatred of Dr Ned.

'You say that you found widespread bruising on the deceased's back and buttocks. What was that consistent with?'

'I thought it was consistent with a violent attack from behind. I thought Mrs Dacre had probably been struck and kicked by ... well, it appeared that she was alone that evening with her husband.'

'I object!' I had risen to protest, but the perfect gent on the Bench was ahead of me.

'Yes, Mr Rumpole. And you are perfectly right to do so. Dr Gorle, it is not for you to say *who* beat this lady and kicked her. That is entirely a matter for the jury. That is why Mr Rumpole has quite rightly objected.'

I wished his Lordship would stop being so lethally pleasant. 'But I understand,' the Judge continued, 'that your evidence is that she was kicked and beaten – by *someone*.' McManus, J., made it clear that Sally Dacre had been attacked brutally, and the jury could have the undoubted pleasure of saying who did it.

'Yes, my Lord.'

'Kicked and beaten!' His Lordship repeated the words for good measure, and after he'd written them down and underlined them with his red pencil, Munroe wound up his examination in chief.

'The immediate cause of death was?'

'A cerebral haemorrhage, as I said!'

'Could you form any opinion as to how that came about?' Munroe asked.

'Just a moment.' McManus, J., gave me one of his charming smiles from the Bench. 'Have you any objection to her opinion, Mr Rumpole?'

'My Lord, I wouldn't seek to prevent this witness saying anything she wishes in her effort to implicate my client in his wife's tragic death.'

McManus, J., looked slightly puzzled at that, and seemed to wonder if it was an entirely gentlemanly remark. However, he only said, 'Very well. Do please answer the question, Dr Gorle.'

'My opinion, my Lord, is that the deceased had received a blow to the head in the course of the attack.'

'The attack you have already described?'

'That is so, my Lord.'

'Thank you, Dr Gorle,' said Owen Munroe, and sat down with a quietly satisfied air and left the witness to me.

I stood up, horribly conscious that the next quarter of an hour would decide the future of my client. Would Dr Ned Dacre go back to his pleasant house and practice, or was he fated to vanish into some distant prison only to emerge, pale and unemployable, after ten or more long years? If I couldn't break down the medical evidence our case was hopeless. I stood in the silent Court, shuffling the photographs and the doctor's notes, wondering whether to lead up to my charge of bias gently laying what traps I could on the way, or go in with all my guns blazing. I seemed to stand for a long time undecided, with moist hands and a curious feeling of dread at the responsibility I had undertaken in the pit of my stomach, and then I made a decision. I would start with my best point.

'Dr Gorle. Just help me. You knew Dr Ned Dacre well, didn't you?'

The first question had been asked. We'd very soon find out if it were the right one.

'We were at Barts together.' Dr Gorle showed no sign of having been hit amidships.

'And went out together, as the saying is?' I said sweetly.

'Occasionally, yes.'

' "Going out" as so often nowadays meaning "staying in" together?' I used a slightly louder voice, and was gratified to see that the witness looked distinctly narked.

'What do you mean?'

'Yes. I think you should make that a little clearer, Mr Rumpole,' the Judge intervened, in the pleasantest possible way.

'You and Dr Ned Dacre went on holiday to Crete together, didn't you? Before he was married.'

There was a distinct pause, and the doctor looked down at the rail of the witness-box as she admitted it.

'Yes. We did.'

The dear old 'Gardeners' Question Time' fans on the jury looked suddenly interested, as if I had revealed a new and deadly form of potato blight. I pressed on.

'Did you become, what expression would you like me to use, his girlfriend, paramour, mistress?'

'We shared a bed together, yes.' Now the pathologist looked up at me, defiant.

'Presumably not for the purpose of revising your anatomy notes together?' I got a small chuckle from the jury which increased the witness's irritation.

'He was my lover. If that's how you want to put it.'

'Thank you, Dr Gorle. I'm sure the members of the jury understand. And I would also like the jury to understand that you became extremely angry when Dr Ned Dacre got married.' There was another long pause, but the answer she came up with was moderately helpful.

'I was disappointed, yes.'

'Angry and jealous of the lady whose dead body you examined?' I suggested.

'I suppose I was naturally upset that Ned Dacre had married someone else.'

'So upset that you wrote him a letter, only a week or so before this tragedy, in which you told him you wanted to hurt him as much as you possibly could?' Now the jury were entirely hooked. I saw Munroe staring at me, no doubt wondering if I could produce the letter. The witness may have decided that I could, anyway she didn't risk an outright denial.

'I may have done.'

'You may have done!' I tried the effect of a passage of fortissimo incredulity. 'But by then Dr Ned Dacre had been married for eight years and his wife had borne him two children. And yet you were still harbouring this terrible grudge?'

She answered quickly this time, and with a great intensity.

'There are some things you don't forget, Mr Rumpole.'

'And some things you don't forgive, Dr Gorle? Has your feeling of jealousy and hatred for my client in any way coloured your evidence against him?'

Of course I expected her to deny this. During the course of cross-examination you may angle for useful admissions, hints and half-truths which can come with the cunning cast of a seemingly innocent question. But the time always comes when you must confront the witness with a clear suggestion, a final formality of assertion and denial, when the subtleties are over. I was surprised, therefore, when the lady from the morgues found it difficult to answer the question in its simplest form. There was a prolonged silence.

'Has it, Dr Gorle?' I pressed her gently for an answer.

Only Dr Gorle knew if she was biased. If she'd denied the suggestion hotly no one could have contradicted her. Instead of doing so, she finally came out with,

'I don't *think* so.' And she said it so unconvincingly that I saw the jury's disapproval. It was the first game to Rumpole, and the witness seemed to have lost her confidence when I moved on to deal with the medical evidence. Fortunately a long career as an Old Bailey hack has given me a working knowledge of the habits of dead bodies.

'Dr Gorle. After death a body becomes subject to a condition called "hypostasis"?'

'That is so. Yes.'

'The blood drains to the lowest area when circulation ceases?'

'Yes.'

'So that if the body has been lying on its back, the blood would naturally drain to the buttocks and the backs of the legs?'

'That's perfectly right,' she answered, now without hesitation.

'Did you say, Mr Rumpole's right about that?' The Judge was making a note of the cross-examination.

'Yes, my Lord.'

'Yes. Thank you, Doctor.' I paused to frame the next question carefully. 'And the draining of the blood causes discoloration of the skin of a dead body which can *look like bruising*?' I began to get an eerie feeling that it was all going too well, when the pale lady doctor admitted, again most helpfully,

'It can look exactly like bruising, yes.'

'Therefore it is difficult to tell simply by the colour of the skin if a patch is caused by "hypostasis" or bruising? It can be very misleading?'

'Yes. It can be.'

'So you must insert a knife under the skin to see what has caused the discoloration, must you not?'

'That is the standard test, yes.'

'If some blood flows, it is "hypostasis", but if the blood under the skin has coagulated and does *not* flow, it is probably a bruise?'

'What do you have to say about that, Dr Gorle?' the Judge asked the witness, and she came back with a glowing tribute to the amateur pathologist in the wig.

'I would say, my Lord, that Mr Rumpole would be well equipped to lecture on forensic medicine.'

'That test was carried out in a case called the Penge Bungalow Murders, Dr Gorle.' I disclosed the source of almost all my information, and added a flattering, 'No doubt before you were born.' I had never got on so well with a hostile witness.

'I'm afraid it was.'

'So what happened when you inserted a knife into the

coloured portions?' I had asked the question in a manner which was almost sickeningly polite, but Dr Pamela looked greatly shaken. Finally, in a voice of contrition she admitted,

'I didn't.'

'What?'

'I didn't carry out that particular test.'

'You didn't?' I tried to sound encouragingly neutral to hide my incredulity.

'No.'

'Can you tell us *why* not?' The Judge now sounded more like an advocate than the calm, detached Mr Justice Rumpole.

'I'm afraid that I must have jumped to the conclusion that they were bruises and I didn't trouble to carry out any further test, my Lord.'

'You *jumped* to the conclusion?' There was no doubt about it. The courteous McManus was deeply shocked.

'Yes.' Dr Pamela looked paler, and her voice was trembling on the edge of inaudibility.

'You know, Dr Gorle, the jury aren't going to be asked to convict Dr Dacre by "jumping to conclusions".' I blessed the old darling on the Bench when he said that, and began to see a distinct hope of returning my client to piles and prescriptions in the not-too-distant future.

'My Lord is, of course, perfectly right,' I told the witness. 'The case against Dr Ned Dacre has to be proved beyond reasonable doubt, so that the jury are *sure*. Can I take it that you're not sure there were any bruises at all?'

There was a pause and then out came the most beautiful answer.

'Not as you put it now. No. I'm not sure.'

Again I had the strange feeling that it was too easy. I felt like a toreador poised for a life-and-death struggle, seeing instead the ring doors open to admit a rather gentle and obedient cow.

'I'm not *sure* there were any bruises,' His Lordship repeated to himself as he wrote it down in his note.

'And so you're not sure Mrs Dacre was attacked by anyone?' It was a question I would normally have avoided. With this witness, it seemed, I could dare anything.

'I can't be sure. No.'

And again, the Judge wrote it down.

'So she may simply have stumbled, hit her head against the coffee table, and died of a cerebral haemorrhage?'

'It might have happened in that way. Yes.' Dr Gorle was giving it to me with jam on it.

'Stumbled because she had had too much to drink?'

The cooperative witness turned to the Judge.

'Her blood alcohol level was considerably above the breathalyser limit, yes, my Lord.'

'And you knew this family?'

'I knew about them. Yes.'

'And was it not one of your complaints that, in marrying Sally, Dr Ned had married a drunk?'

'I did say that in my letter.'

'The sort of girl who might drink too much wine, stumble against a chromium coffee table, hit her head and receive a cerebral haemorrhage, *by accident*?' It was the full frontal question, but I felt no embarrassment now in asking it. The Judge was also keen on getting an answer and he said,

'Well, Dr Gorle?'

'I must admit it might've happened that way. Yes.'

It was all over then, bar the odd bit of shouting. I said, 'Thank you very much, Dr Pamela Gorle.' And meant it. It was game, set and match to Rumpole. We had a bit of legal argument between counsel and then I was intoxicated by the delightful sensation of winning. The pleasant Judge told the jury that, in view of the concessions made by the expert witness, there really was no evidence on which they could possible convict the good doctor, and directed them to stop the case and pronounce those two words which are always music to Rumpole's ears, 'Not guilty'. We all went out in to the corridor and loyal patients came to shake Ned's hand and congratulate him as politely as if he'd just won first prize for growing the longest leek.

'Mr Rumpole. I knew you'd come up trumps, sir. I shall never forget this, never!' Old Dr Harry was pumping my hand, slapping my shoulder, and I thought I saw tears in his eyes. But then I looked across the crowd, at a door through which the expert witness, the Crown's pathologist, Dr Pamela Gorle had just appeared. She was smiling at Dr Ned and, unless I was very much mistaken, he was smiling back. Was it only a smile, or did I detect the tremble of a wink? I left his father and went up to the young doctor. He smiled his undying gratitude.

'Mr Rumpole. Dad was right. You're the best!' Dr Ned was kind enough to say.

'Nonsense. It was easy.' I looked at him and said, 'Too easy.'

'Why do you say that?' Dr Ned looked genuinely puzzled.

I didn't answer him. Instead, I asked a question.

'I was meaning to ask you this before, Doctor. I don't suppose it matters now, but I'd like to know the answer, for my own satisfaction. What sort of soufflé was it you cooked for your wife that evening?' He might have lied, but I don't suppose he thought there was any point in it. Instead he answered as if he enjoyed telling the truth.

'Cheese.'

I was at breakfast with She Who Must Be Obeyed a few days later, after I had managed to spring the charming young doctor, and my wife was brandishing another mauve letter from her friend Dorothy or 'Dodo', the nervous tea-shop owner from the West Country.

'Another letter from Dodo! She's really feeling much better. So much more calm!'

'She's been taking these new pills, didn't you say?'

'Yes, I think that's what it must be.'

I remembered about a drug Dr Ned was discussing with his father for possible use on his nervous wife. Was it the same drug that was keeping Dodo off cheese?

'Then Dodo will be feeling better. So long as she doesn't eat cheese. If she eats cheese when she's on some sort of tranquillizer she's likely to go the way of the doctor's beautiful wife, and end up with a haemorrhage of the brain.'

I had a letter too. An invitation to a cocktail party in Hunter's Hill. Dr Ned Dacre, it seemed, felt that he had something to celebrate.

'Mr Rumpole! I'm so glad you could come.' Dr Ned greeted me enthusiastically.

I looked round the pleasant room, at the pleasant faces of grateful patients and the two thoroughly nice children handing round canapés. I noticed the Queen of the Morgues, Dr Pamela Gorle, dressed up to the nines, and then I looked at the nice young doctor who was now pouring me out a generous Buck's Fizz made, regardless of the expense, with the best Krug. I spoke to him quietly.

'You got off, of course. They can't try you again for the same murder. That was the arrangement, wasn't it?'

'What "arrangement"?' The young doctor was still smiling in a welcoming sort of way.

'Oh, the arrangement between you and the Crown pathologist, of course. The plan that she'd make some rather silly suggestions about bruises and admit she was wrong. Of course, she lied about the contents of the stomach. You're a very careful young man, Dr Ned. Now they can never try you for what you really did.'

'You're joking!' But I saw that he had stopped smiling.

'I was never more serious in my life.'

'What did I really do?' We seemed to be alone. A little whispering oasis of doubt and suspicion in the middle of the happy, chattering cocktail party. I told him what he'd done.

'You opened a few of those new tranquillizer capsules and poured them into your wife's Chianti. The cheese in the soufflé reacted in just the way you'd planned. All you had to do was make sure she hit her head on the table.'

We stood in silence. The children came up and we refused canapés. Then Dr Ned opened an alabaster box and lit a cigarette with a gold lighter.

'What're you going to do about it?' I could see that he was smiling again.

'Nothing I can do now. You know that,' I told him. 'Except to tell you that I know. I'm not quite the idiot you and Dr Pamela took me for. As least you know that, Dr Ned.'

He was a murderer. Divorce would have given him freedom but not his rich wife's money; so he became a simple, old-fashioned murderer. And what was almost worse, he had used me as part of his crime. Worst of all, he had done his best to spoil the golden memory of the Penge Bungalow Murders for me.

'Quiet everyone! I think Ned's got something to say!' Old Dr Harry Dacre was banging on a table with his glass. In due course quiet settled on the party and young Dr Ned made his announcement.

'I just wanted to say. Now all our friends are here. Under one roof. That of course no one can ever replace Sally. For me and the children. But with Simon and Sara's approval . . .' He smiled at his charming children. 'There's going to be another doctor in the Dacre family. Pamela's agreed to become my wife.'

In the ensuing clapping, kisses, congratulations and mixing of more Buck's Fizz, Rumpole left the party.

I hear it was a thoroughly nice wedding. I looked hard at the photograph in the paper and tried to detect, in that open and smiling young doctor's face, a sign of guilt.

> '. . . that perilous stuff
> Which weighs upon the heart.'

I saw none.

Rumpole and the Spirit of Christmas

I realized that Christmas was upon us when I saw a sprig of holly over the list of prisoners hung on the wall of the cells under the Old Bailey.

I pulled out a new box of small cigars and found its opening obstructed by a tinselled band on which a scarlet-faced Santa was seen hurrying a sleigh full of carcinoma-packed goodies to the Rejoicing World. I lit one as the lethargic screw, with a complexion the colour of faded Bronco, regretfully left his doorstep sandwich and mug of sweet tea to unlock the gate.

'Good morning, Mr Rumpole. Come to visit a customer?'

'Happy Christmas, officer,' I said as cheerfully as possible. 'Is Mr Timson at home?'

'Well, I don't believe he's slipped down to his little place in the country.'

Such were the pleasantries that were exchanged between us legal hacks and discontented screws; jokes that no doubt have changed little since the turnkeys locked the door at Newgate to let in a pessimistic advocate, or the cells under the Coliseum were opened to admit the unwelcome news of the Imperial thumbs-down.

'My Mum wants me home for Christmas.'

'Which Christmas?' It would have been an unreasonable remark and I refrained from it. Instead, I said, 'All things are possible.'

As I sat in the interviewing room, an Old Bailey hack of some considerable experience, looking through my brief and inadvertently using my waistcoat as an ashtray, I hoped I wasn't on another loser. I had had a run of bad luck during that autumn season, and young Edward Timson was part of that huge south London family whose criminal activities provided such welcome grist to the Rumpole mill. The charge in the seventeen-year-old Eddie's case was nothing less than wilful murder.

'We're in with a chance though, Mr Rumpole, ain't we?'

Like all his family, young Timson was a confirmed optimist. And yet, of course, the merest outsider in the Grand National, the hundred-to-one shot, is in with a chance, and nothing is more like going round the course at Aintree than living through a murder trial. In this particular case, a fanatical prosecutor named Wrigglesworth, known to me as the Mad Monk, was to represent Beechers and Mr Justice Vosper, a bright but wintry-hearted Judge who always felt it his duty to lead for the prosecution, was to play the part of a particularly menacing fence at the Canal Turn.

'A chance. Well, yes, of course you've got a chance, if they can't establish common purpose, and no one knows which of you bright lads had the weapon.'

No doubt the time had come for a brief glance at the prosecution case, not an entirely cheering prospect. Eddie, also known as 'Turpin' Timson, lived in a kind of decaying barracks, a sort of high-rise Lubianka, known as Keir Hardie Court, somewhere in south London, together with his parents, his various brothers and his thirteen-year-old sister, Noreen. This particular branch of the Timson family lived on the thirteenth floor. Below them, on the twelfth, lived the large clan of the O'Dowds. The war between the Timsons and the O'Dowds began, it seems, with the casting of the Nativity play at the local comprehensive school.

Christmas comes earlier each year and the school show was planned about September. When Bridget O'Dowd was chosen to play the lead in the face of strong competition from Noreen Timson, an incident occurred comparable in historical importance to the assassination of an obscure Austrian archduke at Sarajevo. Noreen Timson announced, in the playground, that Bridget O'Dowd was a spotty little tart quite unsuited to play any role of which the most notable characteristic was virginity.

Hearing this, Bridget O'Dowd kicked Noreen Timson behind the anthracite bunkers. Within a few days war was declared between the Timson and O'Dowd children, and a present of lit fireworks was posted through the O'Dowd front door. On what is known as the 'night in question', reinforcements of O'Dowds and Timsons arrived in old bangers from a number of south London addresses and battle was joined on the stone staircase, a bleak terrain of peeling walls scrawled with graffiti, blowing empty Coca-Cola tins and torn newspapers. The weapons seemed to have been articles in general domestic use such as bread knives, carving knives, broom handles and a heavy screw-driver.

At the end of the day it appeared that the upstairs flat had repelled the invaders, and Kevin O'Dowd lay on the stairs. Having been stabbed with a slender and pointed blade he was in a condition to become known as the 'deceased' in the case of the Queen against Edward Timson. I made an application for bail for my client which was refused, but a speedy trial was ordered.

So even as Bridget O'Dowd was giving her Virgin Mary at the comprehensive, the rest of the family was waiting to give evidence against Eddie Timson in that home of British drama, Number One Court at the Old Bailey.

'I never had no cutter, Mr Rumpole. Straight up, I never had one,' the defendant told me in the cells. He was an appealing-looking lad with soft brown eyes, who had already won the heart of the highly susceptible lady who wrote his social inquiry report. ('Although the charge is a serious one this is a young man who might respond well to a period of probation.' I could imagine the steely contempt in Mr Justice Vosper's eye when he read that.)

'Well, tell me, Edward. Who had?'

'I never seen no cutters on no one, honest I didn't. We wasn't none of us tooled up, Mr Rumpole.'

'Come on, Eddie. Someone must have been. They say even young Noreen was brandishing a potato peeler.'

'Not me, honest.'

'What about your sword?'

There was one part of the prosecution evidence that I found particularly distasteful. It was agreed that on the previous Sun-day morning, Eddie 'Turpin' Timson had appeared on the

149

stairs of Keir Hardie Court and flourished what appeared to be an antique cavalry sabre at the assembled O'Dowds, who were just popping out to Mass.

'Me sword I bought up the Portobello? I didn't have that there, honest.'

'The prosecution can't introduce evidence about the sword. It was an entirely different occasion.' Mr Barnard, my instructing solicitor who fancied himself as an infallible lawyer, spoke with a confidence which I couldn't feel. He, after all, wouldn't have to stand up on his hind legs and argue the legal toss with Mr Justice Vosper.

'It rather depends on who's prosecuting us. I mean, if it's some fairly reasonable fellow . . .'

'I think,' Mr Barnard reminded me, shattering my faint optimism and ensuring that we were all in for a very rough Christmas indeed, 'I think it's Mr Wrigglesworth. Will he try to introduce the sword?'

I looked at 'Turpin' Timson with a kind of pity. 'If it is the Mad Monk, he undoubtedly will.'

When I went into Court, Basil Wrigglesworth was standing with his shoulders hunched up round his large, red ears, his gown dropped to his elbows, his bony wrists protruding from the sleeves of his frayed jacket, his wig pushed back and his huge hands joined on his lectern in what seemed to be an attitude of devoted prayer. A lump of cotton wool clung to his chin where he had cut himself shaving. Although well into his sixties he preserved a look of boyish clumsiness. He appeared, as he always did when about to prosecute on a charge carrying a major punishment, radiantly happy.

'Ah, Rumpole,' he said, lifting his eyes from the police verbals as though they were his breviary. 'Are you defending *as usual*?'

'Yes, Wrigglesworth. And you're prosecuting *as usual*?' It wasn't much of a riposte but it was all I could think of at the time.

'Of course, I don't defend. One doesn't like to call witnesses who may not be telling the truth.'

'You must have a few unhappy moments then, calling certain members of the Constabulary.'

'I can honestly tell you, Rumpole,' his curiously innocent blue eyes looked at me with a sort of pain, as though I had questioned the doctrine of the immaculate conception, 'I have never called a dishonest policeman.'

'Yours must be a singularly simple faith, Wrigglesworth.'

'As for the Detective Inspector in this case,' counsel for the prosecution went on, 'I've known Wainwright for years. In fact, this is his last trial before he retires. He could no more invent a verbal against a defendant than fly.'

Any more on that tack, I thought, and we should soon be debating how many angels could dance on the point of a pin.

'Look here, Wrigglesworth. That evidence about my client having a sword: it's quite irrelevant. I'm sure you'd agree.'

'Why is it irrelevant?' Wrigglesworth frowned.

'Because the murder clearly wasn't done with an antique cavalry sabre. It was done with a small, thin blade.'

'If he's a man who carries weapons, why isn't that relevant?'

'A man? Why do you call him a man? He's a child. A boy of seventeen!'

'Man enough to commit a serious crime.'

'*If* he did.'

'If he didn't, he'd hardly be in the dock.'

'That's the difference between us, Wrigglesworth,' I told him. 'I believe in the presumption of innocence. You believe in original sin. Look here, old darling.' I tried to give the Mad Monk a smile of friendship and became conscious of the fact that it looked, no doubt, like an ingratiating sneer. 'Give us a chance. You won't introduce the evidence of the sword, will you?'

'Why ever not?'

'Well,' I told him, 'the Timsons are an industrious family of criminals. They work hard, they never go on strike. If it weren't for people like the Timsons, you and I would be out of a job.'

'They sound in great need of prosecution and punishment. Why shouldn't I tell the jury about your client's sword? Can you give me one good reason?'

'Yes,' I said, as convincingly as possible.

'What is it?' He peered at me, I thought, unfairly.

'Well, after all,' I said, doing my best, 'it is Christmas.'

It would be idle to pretend that the first day in Court went well, although Wrigglesworth restrained himself from mentioning the sword in his opening speech, and told me that he was considering whether or not to call evidence about it the next day. I cross-examined a few members of the clan O'Dowd on the presence of lethal articles in the hands of the attacking force. The evidence about this varied and weapons came and went in the hands of the inhabitants of number twelve as the witnesses were blown hither and thither in the winds of Rumpole's cross-examination. An interested observer from one of the other flats spoke of having seen a machete.

'Could that terrible weapon have been in the hands of Mr Kevin O'Dowd, the deceased in this case?'

'I don't think so.'

'But can you rule out the possibility?'

'No, I can't rule it out,' the witness admitted, to my temporary delight.

'You can never rule out the possibility of anything in this world, Mr Rumpole. But he doesn't think so. You have your answer.'

Mr Justice Vosper, in a voice like a splintering iceberg, gave me this unwelcome Christmas present. The case wasn't going well but at least, by the end of the first day, the Mad Monk had kept out all mention of the sword. The next day he was to call young Bridget O'Dowd, fresh from her triumph in the Nativity play.

'I say, Rumpole. I'd be *so* grateful for a little help.'

I was in Pommeroy's Wine Bar, drowning the sorrows of the day in my usual bottle of the cheapest Château Fleet Street (made from grapes which, judging from the bouquet, might have been not so much trodden as kicked to death by sturdy peasants in gum boots) when I looked up to see Wrigglesworth, dressed in an old mackintosh, doing business with Jack Pommeroy at the sales counter. When I crossed to him, he was not buying the jumbo-sized bottle of ginger beer which I imagined might be his celebratory Christmas tipple, but a tempting and respectably aged bottle of Château Pichon Longueville.

'What can I do for you, Wrigglesworth?'

'Well, as you know, Rumpole, I live in Croydon.'

'Happiness is given to few of us on this earth,' I said piously.

'And the Anglican Sisters of St Agnes, Croydon, are anxious to buy a present for their Bishop,' Wrigglesworth explained. 'A dozen bottles for Christmas. They've asked my advice, Rumpole. I know so little of wine. You wouldn't care to try this for me? I mean, if you're not especially busy.'

'I should be hurrying home to dinner.' My wife, Hilda (She Who Must Be Obeyed), was laying on rissoles and frozen peas, washed down by my last bottle of Pommeroy's extremely ordinary. 'However, as it's Christmas, I don't mind helping you out, Wrigglesworth.'

The Mad Monk was clearly quite unused to wine. As we sampled the claret together, I saw the chance of getting him to commit himself on the vital question of the evidence of the sword, as well as absorbing an unusually decent bottle. After the Pichon Longueville I was kind enough to help him by sampling a Boyd-Cantenac and then I said, 'Excellent, this. But of course the Bishop might be a Burgundy man. The nuns might care to invest in a decent Mâcon.'

'Shall we try a bottle?' Wrigglesworth suggested. 'I'd be grateful for your advice.'

'I'll do my best to help you, my old darling. And while we're on the subject, that ridiculous bit of evidence about young Timson and the sword . . .'

'I remember you saying I shouldn't bring that out because it's Christmas.'

'Exactly.' Jack Pommeroy had uncorked the Mâcon and it was mingling with the claret to produce a feeling of peace and goodwill towards men. Wrigglesworth frowned, as though trying to absorb an obscure point of theology.

'I don't quite see the relevance of Christmas to the question of your man Timson threatening his neighbours with a sword . . .'

'Surely, Wrigglesworth,' I knew my prosecutor well, 'you're of a religious disposition?' The Mad Monk was the product of some bleak northern Catholic boarding school. He lived alone, and no doubt wore a hair shirt under his black waistcoat and was vowed to celibacy. The fact that he had his nose deep into a glass of Burgundy at the moment was due to the benign influence of Rumpole.

'I'm a Christian, yes.'

'Then practise a little Christian tolerance.'

'Tolerance towards evil?'

'Evil?' I asked. 'What do you mean, evil?'

'Couldn't that be your trouble, Rumpole? That you really don't recognize evil when you see it.'

'I suppose,' I said, 'evil might be locking up a seventeen-year-old during Her Majesty's pleasure, when Her Majesty may very probably forget all about him, banging him up with a couple of hard and violent cases and their own chamber-pots for twenty-two hours a day, so he won't come out till he's a real, genuine, middle-aged murderer . . .'

'I did hear the Reverend Mother say,' Wrigglesworth was gazing vacantly at the empty Mâcon bottle, 'that the Bishop likes his glass of port.'

'Then in the spirit of Christmas tolerance I'll help you to sample some of Pommeroy's Light and Tawny.'

A little later, Wrigglesworth held up his port glass in a reverent sort of fashion.

'You're suggesting, are you, that I should make some special concession in this case because it's Christmas time?'

'Look here, old darling.' I absorbed half my glass, relishing the gentle fruitiness and the slight tang of wood. 'If you spent your whole life in that high-rise hell-hole called Keir Hardie Court, if you had no fat prosecutions to occupy your attention and no prospect of any job at all, if you had no sort of occupation except war with the O'Dowds . . .'

'My own flat isn't particularly comfortable. I don't know a great deal about *your* home life, Rumpole, but you don't seem to be in a tearing hurry to experience it.'

'Touché, Wrigglesworth, my old darling.' I ordered us a couple of refills of Pommeroy's port to further postpone the encounter with She Who Must Be Obeyed and her rissoles.

'But we don't have to fight to the death on the staircase,' Wrigglesworth pointed out.

'We don't have to fight at all, Wrigglesworth.'

'As your client did.'

'As my client *may* have done. Remember the presumption of innocence.'

'This is rather funny, this is.' The prosecutor pulled back his lips to reveal strong, yellowish teeth and laughed appreciatively. 'You know why your man Timson is called "Turpin"?'

'No.' I drank port uneasily, fearing an unwelcome revelation.

'Because he's always fighting with that sword of his. He's called after Dick Turpin, you see, who's always duelling on the television. Do you watch the television, Rumpole?'

'Hardly at all.'

'I watch a great deal of the television, as I'm alone rather a lot.' Wrigglesworth referred to the box as though it were a sort of penance, like fasting or flagellation. 'Detective Inspector Wainwright told me about your client. Rather amusing, I thought it was. He's retiring this Christmas.'

'My client?'

'No. D.I. Wainwright. Do you think we should settle on this port for the Bishop? Or would you like to try a glass of something else?'

'Christmas,' I told Wrigglesworth severely as we sampled the Cockburn, 'is not just a material, pagan celebration. It's not just an occasion for absorbing superior vintages, old darling. It must be a time when you try to do good, spiritual good to our enemies.'

'To your client, you mean?'

'And to me.'

'To you, Rumpole?'

'For God's sake, Wrigglesworth!' I was conscious of the fact that my appeal was growing desperate. 'I've had six losers in a row down the Old Bailey. Can't I be included in any Christmas spirit that's going around?'

'You mean, at Christmas especially it is more blessed to give than to receive?'

'I mean exactly that.' I was glad that he seemed, at last, to be following my drift.

'And you think I might give this case to someone, like a Christmas present?'

'If you care to put it that way, yes.'

'I do not care to put it in *exactly* that way.' He turned his pale blue eyes on me with what I thought was genuine sympathy. 'But I shall try and do the case of R. *v.* Timson in the way most appropriate to the greatest feast of the Christian year. It is a time, I quite agree, for the giving of presents.'

When they finally threw us out of Pommeroy's, and after we had considered the possibility of buying the Bishop brandy in the Cock Tavern, and even beer in the Devereux, I let my instinct, like an aged horse, carry me on to the Underground and home to Gloucester Road, and there discovered the rissoles, like some traces of a vanished civilization, fossilized in the oven. She Who Must Be Obeyed was already in bed, feigning sleep. When I climbed in beside her she opened a hostile eye.

'You're drunk, Rumpole!' she said. 'What on earth have you been doing?'

'I've been having a legal discussion,' I told her, 'on the subject of the admissibility of certain evidence. Vital, from my client's point of view. And, just for a change, Hilda, I think I've won.'

'Well, you'd better try and get some sleep.' And she added with a sort of satisfaction, 'I'm sure you'll be feeling quite terrible in the morning.'

As with all the grimmer predictions of She Who Must Be Obeyed this one turned out to be true. I sat in Court the next day with the wig feeling like a lead weight on the brain, and the stiff collar sawing the neck like a blunt execution. My mouth tasted of matured birdcage and from a long way off I heard Wrigglesworth say to Bridget O'Dowd, who stood looking particularly saintly and virginal in the witness-box, 'About a week before this did you see the defendant, Edward Timson, on your staircase flourishing any sort of weapon?'

It is no exaggeration to say that I felt deeply shocked and considerably betrayed. After his promise to me, Wrigglesworth had turned his back on the spirit of the great Christmas festival. He came not to bring peace but a sword.

I clambered with some difficulty to my feet. After my forensic efforts of the evening before, I was scarcely in the mood for a legal argument. Mr Justice Vosper looked up in surprise and greeted me in his usual chilly fashion.

'Yes, Mr Rumpole. Do you object to this evidence?'

Of course I object, I wanted to say. It's inhuman, unnecessary, unmerciful and likely to lead to my losing another case. Also, it's clearly contrary to a solemn and binding contract entered into after a number of glasses of the Bishop's putative port. All I seemed to manage was a strangled, 'Yes.'

'I suppose Mr Wrigglesworth would say,' Vosper, J., was, as ever, anxious to supply any argument that might not yet have occurred to the prosecution, 'that it is evidence of "system".'

'System?' I heard my voice faintly and from a long way off. 'It may be, I suppose. But the Court has a discretion to omit evidence which may be irrelevant and purely prejudicial.'

'I feel sure Mr Wrigglesworth has considered the matter most carefully and that he would not lead this evidence unless he considered it entirely relevant.'

I looked at the Mad Monk on the seat beside me. He was smiling at me with a mixture of hearty cheerfulness and supreme pity, as though I were sinking rapidly and he had come to administer supreme unction. I made a few ill-chosen remarks to the Court, but I was in no condition, that morning, to enter into a complicated legal argument on the admissibility of evidence.

It wasn't long before Bridget O'Dowd had told a deeply disapproving jury all about Eddie 'Turpin' Timson's sword. 'A man,' the Judge said later in his summing up about young Edward, 'clearly prepared to attack with cold steel whenever it suited him.'

When the trial was over, I called in for refreshment at my favourite watering hole and there, to my surprise, was my opponent Wrigglesworth, sharing an expensive-looking bottle with Detective Inspector Wainwright, the officer in charge of the case. I stood at the bar, absorbing a consoling glass of Pommeroy's ordinary, when the D.I. came up to the bar for cigarettes. He gave me a friendly and maddeningly sympathetic smile.

'Sorry about that, sir. Still, win a few, lose a few. Isn't that it?'

'In my case lately, it's been win a few, lose a lot!'

'You couldn't have this one, sir. You see, Mr Wriggles-worth had promised it to me.'

'He had *what*?'

'Well, I'm retiring, as you know. And Mr Wrigglesworth pro-mised me faithfully that my last case would be a win. He pro-mised me that, in a manner of speaking, as a Christmas present. Great man is our Mr Wrigglesworth, sir, for the spirit of Christmas.'

I looked across at the Mad Monk and a terrible suspicion entered my head. What was all that about a present for the Bishop? I searched my memory and I could find no trace of our having, in fact, bought wine for any sort of cleric. And was Wrigglesworth as inexperienced as he would have had me be-lieve in the art of selecting claret?

As I watched him pour and sniff a glass from his superior bottle, and hold it critically to the light, a horrible suspicion crossed my mind. Had the whole evening's events been nothing but a deception, a sinister attempt to nobble Rumpole, to pre-sent him with such a stupendous hangover that he would stumble in his legal argument? Was it all in aid of D.I. Wain-wright's Christmas present?

I looked at Wrigglesworth, and it would be no exaggeration to say the mind boggled. He was, of course, perfectly right about me. I just didn't recognize evil when I saw it.

Rumpole and the Boat People

'You'll have to do it, Rumpole. You'll be a different man.'

I considered the possibilities. I was far from satisfied, naturally, with the man I was, but I had grown, over the years, used
to his ways. I knew his taste in claret, his rate of consumption
of small cigars, and I had grown to have some respect for his
mastery of the art of cross-examination. Difficult, almost im-
possible, as he was to live with on occasions, I thought we
could manage to rub along together for our few remaining
years.

'A different man, did you say?'

Dr MacClintock, the slow-speaking, Edinburgh-bred quack
to whom my wife, Hilda, turns in times of sickness, took a
generous gulp of the sherry she always pours him when he visits
our mansion flat. (It's lucky that all his N.H.S. patients aren't
so generous or the sick of Gloucester Road would be tended by
a reeling medico, yellow about the gills and sloshed on amontil-
lado.) Then he said,

'If you follow my simple instructions, Rumpole, you'll become a different man entirely.'

Being Horace Rumpole in his sixties, still slogging round the
Old Bailey with sore feet, a modest daily hangover and an aching
back was certainly no great shakes, but who else could I be? I
considered the possibilities of becoming Guthrie Featherstone,
Q.C., M.P., our learned Head of Chambers, or Claude Erskine-
Brown, or Uncle Tom, or even Dr MacClintock, and retreated
rapidly into the familiar flesh.

'All you have to do, old man, is lose two or three stone,' the
doctor told me.

' "Old man"? ' I looked closely at the sherry-swilling saw-
bones and saw no chicken.

'Just two or three stone, Rumpole. That's all you have to

lose.' Hilda was warming to her latest theme, that there was too much Rumpole.

'It's a very simple diet, perfectly simple. I've got it printed here.' Dr MacClintock produced a card with the deftness of a conjurer. The trick was known as the vanishing Rumpole, and the rapid materialization of a thinner and more eager barrister.

'No fat, of course.' The doctor repeated the oath on the card. 'Because it makes *you* fat. No meat, too rich in protein. No bread or potatoes, too many calories. No pastries, puddings, sweetmeats or sugar. No biscuits. No salt on the food. Steer clear of cheese. I don't recommend fruit to my patients because of its acid qualities. Eggs are perfectly all right if hard-boiled. Not too many though, or you won't do your business.'

'My business in the courts?' I didn't follow.

'No. Your business in the lavatory.'

'Didn't you say,' Hilda put in encouragingly, 'that Rumpole could eat spinach?'

'Oh yes. As much spinach as he likes. And brown rice for roughage. Now you could manage a diet like that, couldn't you, Rumpole? Otherwise I can't be responsible for your heart.'

'I suppose I might manage it for a while.' The Rumpole ticker, I knew, had come to resent the pressure put on it during a number of hard-fought battles in front of the mad Judge Bullingham down the Bailey. 'Of course, it'd have to be washed down by a good deal of claret. Château-bottled. I could afford that with all this saving on pastries and puddings.'

'Oh, good heavens!' The quack held his sherry glass out for a refill. 'No alcohol!'

'You're asking me to give up claret?'

'No alcohol of any sort!'

'Certainly not, Rumpole.' Hilda was determined.

'But you might as well ask me to give up breathing.'

'It'll come quite easily to you, after a couple of days.'

'I suppose when you've been dead a couple of days you find it quite easy to give up breathing.'

'It's you that mentioned death, Rumpole.' The doctor smiled at me tolerantly. 'I haven't said a word about it. Now why not get your wife to take you away for a holiday? You could spare a couple of weeks at the seaside, surely? It's always easier to give things up when you're on holiday.'

Brown rice, spinach and a holiday were not an appetizing combination, but Hilda seemed delighted at the prospect.

'We could go down to Shenstone, Doctor. I've always wanted to go to Shenstone-on-Sea. My old friend Jackie Bateman, you know I've told you, Rumpole, Jackie Hopkins as was, we were at school together, runs a little business at Shenstone with her husband. Jackie's always writing begging me to come down to Shenstone. Apparently it's a dear little place and extremely quiet.'

'My partner, Dr Entwhistle keeps his boat at Shenstone.' Dr MacClintock seemed to think this fact might lend some glamour to the hole. 'It's quite a place for the boating community.'

'I don't boat,' I said gloomily.

'Better not, Rumpole,' the doctor was actually laughing. 'Better not take out a small dinghy. You might sink it! Shenstone sounds just the place for you to get a bit of rest. Pick a small hotel. A *temperance* hotel. That's all you'll be needing.'

That night, Hilda booked us in to the Fairview Private Hotel in Shenstone-on-Sea, and wrote off to Mrs Bateman, the former Miss Jackie Hopkins, announcing the glad tidings. I viewed the approaching visit with some dismay, tempered by the knowledge that it did seem to be becoming a minor Everest expedition for me to mount the shortest staircase. My bones ached, my head seemed stuffed with cotton wool and buttons were flying off me like bullets at the smallest unexpected move. Perhaps desperate measures were called for and a holiday *would* do me good. We set out for Shenstone armed with umbrellas, mackintoshes, heavy pullovers and, in my case, the *Complete Sherlock Holmes Stories*, Marjoribanks's *Life of Sir Edward Marshall Hall* and *The Oxford Book of English Verse* (I make it a rule not to read anything I haven't read before, except for *The Times* and briefs). We launched ourselves into the unknown as, up to the time of our departure, Mrs Jackie Bateman hadn't been heard from.

Shenstone-on-Sea, in the county of Norfolk, was to be seen, like most English pleasure resorts, through a fine haze of perpetual rain. However, the main feature of Shenstone-on-Sea was undoubtedly the wind. It blew straight at you from the Ural mountains, crossing some very icy steppes, parky portions of Poland, draughty country round Dortmund and the flats of Holland, on the way. In this cruel climate the inhabitants gathered, stowing spinnakers and splicing ropes with bluish fingers, the wind blowing out their oilskins tight as a trumpeter's cheeks and almost doffing their bobble hats. For Shenstone-on-Sea was, as my Scottish medical man had said, quite the place for the boat community.

Apart from watching the daily armada of small boats set out, there was little or nothing to do at Shenstone. Hilda and I sat in the residents' lounge at the Fairview Hotel, and I read or did the crossword while she knitted or wrote postcards to other old schoolfriends and we listened to the rain driven across the windows by the prevailing wind. On our arrival we telephoned Jackie Bateman and got no reply. Then we called on her at the address Hilda had, which turned out to be a shop on the harbour called Father Neptune's Boutique, a place for the sale of bobble hats, seamen's sweaters, yellow gum boots, tea mugs with the words 'Galley Slave' written on them and such-like nautical equipment. The Batemans, according to Hilda, owned this business and had a flat above the shop. We called, as I have said, but found the place silent and locked up, and got no answer when we rattled the door handle.

Hilda wrote a note for her elusive schoolfriend, and put it through the door. We were standing looking helplessly at the silent shop, when someone spoke to us.

'She's moved. Gone away.'

A tallish, thin person clad in a Balaclava helmet and a belted mackintosh, and sporting a large pair of field-glasses, came by pushing a gaunt bicycle.

'Mrs Bateman's not here?' Hilda seemed slow to absorb the information.

'I tell you. She moved away. After it happened. Well. They reckoned she couldn't abide the place after that.'

'After what?' Hilda hadn't heard from Jackie Bateman since, she now remembered, the previous Christmas, and seemed not have been kept *au courant* with the major developments in her friend's life.

'Why, after the accident. When her husband got drowned. Hadn't you heard?'

'No, we hadn't. Oh dear.' Hilda looked surprised and shocked. 'What a terrible thing.'

The tall man pushed his bicycle away from us and we were left staring through the rain at the harbour where the frail boats were again putting out full of those, it now seemed, in considerable peril on the sea.

That night I was pecking away at a minute quantity of fish, almost entirely surrounded by spinach, in our private hotel, and moodily sipping water (an excellent fluid no doubt, most useful for filling radiators and washing socks, but of absolutely no value as a drink) when Hilda said,

'She was devoted to him, you know.'

'Devoted to whom?'

'To Barney. To her husband Barney Bateman. Jackie was. She always said he was such a wonderful man, and a terrific sailor with a really good sense of humour. Of course, he had your problem, Rumpole.'

'What's that? Judge Bullingham?'

'Don't be silly! Of course, I never met Barney, but Jackie told me he was a big man.'

'You mean fat?'

'That's what I think she meant. Jackie was always afraid he was going to get too heavy for dinghy racing. And he simply refused to go on a diet!'

'Sensible fellow.'

'How can you say he was sensible, Rumpole? Don't you remember, poor Jackie's husband's dead.'

Did Mr Bateman's weight become so gross that he simply sank with all hands? As I gave the lining of my stomach the unusual shock of a cascade of cold water, I decided not to ask the question, but to try at the earliest opportunity to get a little free time from She Who Must Be Obeyed.

My chance came the next day when Hilda said that she had a cold coming on, and I would have to take the morning walk alone. I sympathized with Hilda (although I supposed that the natural state of an inhabitant of Shenstone must be a streaming nose and a raised temperature) and left carefully in the direction of the cliffs, as a direct route towards licensed premises would have raised a questioning cry from the window of the residents' lounge.

I struggled up a path in a mist of rain and came, a little way out of town, upon the thin man with the Balaclava helmet. He was staring through his powerful field-glasses out to sea. I gave him a moderately depressed 'good morning', but he was too engrossed in watching something far out on the grey water to return my greeting. Then I took the next turn, down to the harbour and the Crab and Lobster, a large, old-fashioned pub with a welcoming appearance.

It was clearly the warmest place in Shenstone and the place was crowded. In very little time the landlord had supplied me with a life-restoring bottle of St Émilion and a couple of ham rolls, and I sat among the boat people in a cheerful fug, away from the knife-edged wind and the whining children in life-jackets, among the polished brass and dangling lobster pots, looking at the signed photographs of regatta winners, all dedicated to 'Sam', whom I took to be the landlord. In pride of place among these pictures was one of a windswept but resolutely smiling couple in oilskins, proudly clutching a silver trophy with "love from Jackie and Barney, to Sam and all the crowd at the Lobster" scrawled across it. The man seemed considerably and cheerfully overweight, and the colour print showed his flaming red hair and bushy beard. Jackie, Hilda's schoolfriend, also looked extremely cheerful. She had clear blue eyes, short hair which must have been fair but was now going grey, and the sort of skin which showed its long exposure to force-nine gales. Such, I thought, were the women who flew round the world in primitive planes, crossed deserts or rode over No Man's Land on a bicycle. I bought Sam, the landlord, a large whisky and water, and in no time at all we were talking about the Batemans, a conversation in which a number of the regulars at the Crab and Lobster, also supplied with their favourite tipples, seemed anxious to join.

'One thing I could never understand about Jackie,' Sam said. 'I mean, she lost a wonderful personality like Barney Bateman, and they thought the world of each other. Never a cross word between the two of them!'

'And Barney was a man who always had a drink and a story for everyone. Never fumbled or rang the wife when it came to his round.' A red-faced man in an anorak whom the others called Buster told me. 'As I say, I can't understand why after being married to Barney, the winner of the Shenstone regatta five years running, she ended up with a four-letter man like Freddy Jason! Hope he's not a friend of yours, is he?'

'Jason.' The name was entirely new to me.

'Jackie married him just six months after Barney died. We couldn't believe it.' A voluminous blonde bulging out of a pair of jeans and a fisherman's jersey shouted, 'Of course, I've never actually met Mr Jason. He's moved her up to Cricklewood.'

'Dreadful house,' said Buster. 'Absolutely miles from the sea.'

'Well, it is Cricklewood.' The blonde lady seemed prepared to excuse the house.

'Like I told you, Dora. I went there once when I was up in London. On business.'

'What business, Buster? Dirty weekend?' the seafaring woman addressed as Dora screamed, and after laughter from the boat people, Buster continued.

'Never you mind, Dora! Anyway, I looked up Freddy Jason in the book and rang Cricklewood. Finally Jackie came on the phone. Well, you remember what Jackie *used* to be like? "Come on over, Buster; stew's in the oven. We'll have a couple of bottles of rum and a sing-up round the piano." Not a bit of it. "Ever so sorry, dear. Freddy's not been all that well. We're not seeing visitors."'

'Can you imagine that coming from Jackie Bateman? "We're not seeing visitors!"' Dora bawled at me, as though I would be bound to know. She was clearly used to conversation far out to sea, during gale-force winds.

'What you're saying is, there was a bit of a contrast between the two husbands?' I was beginning to get the sense of the meeting. 'At least she didn't repeat the same mistake; that's what most people do.'

'Barney wasn't a mistake,' Dora hailed me. 'Barney was a terrific yachtsman. And a perfect gent.'

I didn't repeat all this information to She Who Must Be Obeyed. To do so would only have invited a searching and awkward cross-examination about where I had heard it. But when we were back in London and recovering from our seaside holiday, Hilda told me she had had an unexpected telephone call from Jackie Bateman, Hopkins as was, Jason, as she had now discovered she had become. Apparently the boat woman had got our note by some means, and she wanted to bring her new husband to tea on Sunday to get 'a few legal tips' from Rumpole of the Bailey.

Hilda spent a great deal of Saturday with her baking tins in celebration of this unusual visit, and produced a good many rock cakes, jam tarts and a large chocolate sponge.

'Not for you, Rumpole,' she said in a threatening fashion. 'Remember, *you're* on a diet.'

In due course, Jackie turned up looking exactly like her photograph, bringing with her a thin and rather dowdy middle-aged man introduced as Freddy, who could not have been a greater contrast to the previous yachtsman and gent. Jason was dark, mouse-coloured and not red-haired; his one contribution to the conversation was to tell us that going out in any sort of boat made him seasick, and we discovered that he was a retired chartered accountant, whose hobby was doing chess problems. When Hilda pressed rock cakes and chocolate sponge on him, he waved her confections aside.

'What's the matter?' I asked him gloomily. 'Not on a diet too, are you?'

'Freddy never has to go on a diet,' his wife said with some sort of mysterious pride. 'He's one of nature's thin people.'

'That's right,' Freddy Jason told us. 'I simply never never put on weight.' All the same, I noticed that he didn't do any sort of justice to Hilda's baking, and he took his tea neat, without milk or sugar.

After some general chat we came on to the legal motive for the party.

'It's awfully boring, but naturally Barney was insured, and

166

the insurance company paid out. That's how we were able to get married and buy the house. But now it seems that Chad Bateman, that's Barney's brother in New Zealand, has raised some sort of question about the estate. Look, can I leave you the letters? You see, we really don't know any lawyers we can trust.'

I had to say that I had only done one will case (in which I had been instructed from beyond the grave by a deceased military man) and that my speciality was violent death and classification of blood. However, I was prepared to get the opinion of Claude Erskine-Brown, the civil lawyer in our Chambers (civil lawyers are concerned with money, criminal practitioners with questions of life and death), and I would give Mrs Jason, whose clear-eyed and sensible look of perfect trust I found appealing, the benefit of his deliberations in due course.

Before I had time to keep my promise, however, something happened of a dramatic nature. Hilda's old schoolfriend Jackie was arrested, as we heard the next week on the television news, on a charge of the wilful murder of her late husband, Barney Bateman.

We heard no more of Jackie Jason, Bateman, Hopkins and her troubles for a considerable period. And then, one morning, as I was walking into my Chambers in a state of some depression brought about by having mislaid about a stone of Rumpole in the course of my prolonged fast, my clerk Henry uttered words which were music to my ears.

'There's a new case for you, Mr Rumpole. A murder, from a new firm of solicitors.'

It was good news indeed. A new firm of solicitors meant a new source of work, claret and small cigars, and of all the dishes that figure on the Criminal Menu, murder is still the main course, or *pièce de résistance*.

'It's an interesting case, Mr Tonkin was telling me.' Henry handed me the bulky set of papers.

'Tonkin?'

'Of Teleman, Tonkin and Bird. That's the new firm from Norfolk. He says the odd thing about this murder is, they never found the body.'

'No corpse?' Without a corpse the thing should not, I thought, present much difficulty, although like all cases it would probably be easier without a client also. I looked down at the brief in my hands and saw the title on it 'R. *v.* Jason'.

In due course, I read the papers and issued out into Fleet Street to find a taxi prepared to take me to Holloway prison for an interview with Jackie Jason and Mr Tonkin. Waiting on the curb, I was accosted by a tall figure wearing a bowler hat and an overcoat with a velvet collar, none other than our learned Head of Chambers, Guthrie Featherstone Q.C., M.P.

'Hullo there, Horace!'

'Sorry, Guthrie. I'm just off to Holloway. Got a rather jolly murder.'

'I know.'

'Henry told you, did he? Strange thing, when I married She Who Must Be Obeyed, I never thought she'd be much help in providing me with work. But she's turned up trumps! She had the good luck to go to an excellent school where one of her form mates grew up to be charged with an extremely interesting . . . '

'I know.' Guthrie repeated himself. 'Jackie Jason.'

'*How* do you know?' Was Featherstone, I wondered, a spare-time boat person? His reply quite wiped off my grin of triumph and added, I thought, new difficulties to our defence.

'Because I'm leading you, of course. It'll be a pleasure to have you sitting behind me again, Horace. Ah, there's a cab. Holloway prison, please.'

Because I never took silk and was not rewarded by the Lord Chancellor with a long wig and a pair of ceremonial knee breeches I am compelled, in certain cases, to sit behind some Queen's Counsel and, although I am old enough to be Featherstone's father, I must be his 'junior', and sit behind the Q.C., M.P. and listen, with what patience I can muster, to him asking the wrong questions. In the Shenstone-on-Sea murder, it would hardly be a pleasure. No doubt with his talent for agreeing with the Judge, Guthrie Featherstone could manage to lose even a corpseless case, in the nicest possible way.

'The evidence against us is pretty strong,' Featherstone said, as we sat together in the taxi bound for the ladies' nick. 'Two heads are better than one in a matter like this, Horace.'

'I didn't find that,' I told him, 'when I won the Penge Bungalow Murders, entirely on my own.'

'Penge Bungalow? Oh, I think you told me. That was one of your old cases, wasn't it? Well, people couldn't afford leading counsel in those days. It was before legal aid.'

So, Q.C.s have become one of the advantages of our new affluence, I was about to say, like fish fingers and piped music in Pommeroy's Wine Bar. However, I thought better of it and we reached the castellated turreted entrance to Holloway prison in silence.

I may be, indeed I am, extremely old fashioned. No doubt an army of feminists are prepared to march for women to have equal rights to long-term imprisonment, but I dislike the sight of ladies in the cooler. For a start, Holloway is a far less jovial place than Brixton. The lady screws look more masculine and malignant than gentleman screws, and female hands never seem made for slopping out.

When we got to the Holloway interview room, my new solicitor Tonkin rose to greet us. He was an upright, military-looking man with a ginger moustache and an M.C.C. tie.

'Mr Featherstone. Mr Rumpole. Good of you to come, gentlemen. This is the client.'

Jackie Jason was looking as tanned and healthy as if she'd just stepped off a boat on a sunny day into the Crab and Lobster. She smiled at me from a corner of the room and said, 'I'm so glad I could find you a legal problem more in your line, Horace.'

I looked at her with gratitude. No doubt it was Jackie who had had the wisdom to choose Rumpole for the defence, and her solicitor Tonkin who had been weak-minded enough to choose Featherstone as a leader.

'I think it would help if you were just to tell us your story in your own way,' Featherstone kicked off the conference. I was sure that it would help him; no doubt he'd been far too busy with his parliamentary duties to read the brief.

'Well, Barney and I,' Jackie started.

'That was the late Mr Barney Bateman?' Featherstone asked laboriously.

'Yes. We used to live at Shenstone-on-Sea. Well, we were boat people.'

'Mrs Jason doesn't mean far-eastern refugees,' I explained to my leader. 'She means those who take to the water in yellow oilskins and sailing dinghies, with toddlers in inflated life-jackets, and usually call out the lifeboat to answer their cries of distress.'

'Barney and I never had toddlers,' Jackie said firmly.

'Horace, if I could put the questions?' Featherstone tried to assert his leadership.

'And we were pretty experienced sailors.'

'Yes,' I said thoughtfully, 'of course you were. And yet your husband died in a yachting accident.'

'Just remind me . . . ' Featherstone continued to grope for the facts.

'We went out very early that day. We wanted to sail the regatta course without anyone watching.'

'You and your late . . . husband?' Featherstone was examining the witness.

'Barney and I.'

'You were on good terms?'

'Always. He was a marvellous man, Barney. Anyone'd tell you, anyone in the crowd in the Crab and Lobster at Shenstone. We were the best of pals.'

Dear old pals, jolly old pals. Everyone in the Crab and Lobster agreed with that. And yet one pal fell out of the boat and his body was never recovered.

'You say there was a sudden gust of wind?' Featherstone was making a nodding acquaintance with his brief.

'Yes,' Jackie told him. 'It came out of nowhere. Well, it will in that bit of sea. Barney was on his feet and the boom must have hit his head. It was all so unexpected. The boat went over and there I was in the drink.'

'And your husband?'

'Stunned, I suppose. By the boom, you see. I looked for him for ten minutes, swimming, and then, well, I clung to the boat. I couldn't get her righted, not on my own I couldn't. I waited almost half an hour like that and then the harbour motor boat came out. They'd got a phone call. Someone must have seen us.

I was lucky, really. There aren't many people around in Shenstone at six o'clock in the morning.'

'But if you and your husband were on perfectly good terms . . . ' Featherstone was frowning, puzzled, when Mr Tonkin gave him some unhelpful clarification.

'That's not really the point, is it, Mr Featherstone? It's the policy with the Colossus Mercantile that made them bring this prosecution.' He was referring to the subject of the correspondence that Jackie Jason had given me when she was still at liberty, so I knew a little about the Colossus policy. Featherstone looked blank. If he hadn't been a politician he would have said, 'All-night sitting last night. I never got round to reading the brief.' As it was, he said,

'Do just remind me . . . '

'Mrs Jason insured her first husband's life with the Colossus Mercantile just two weeks before the accident,' Tonkin explained. 'Before these inquiries got going she had remarried and collected the money.'

'How much was it? Just remind me,' Featherstone asked.

Mr Tonkin gave us the motive which had undoubtedly led to the prosecution of the yachtswoman.

'Just about two hundred thousand pounds.'

'You know I'm going to Norfolk today,' I reminded Hilda at breakfast some weeks later. 'It's Jackie's trial.'

'You will get her off, won't you, Rumpole? She's relying on you, you know.' Hilda said it as if the case presented no particular problem.

'I might get her off. I don't know about my friend.'

'You didn't tell me you were taking a friend with you.' Hilda looked at me with sudden suspicion

'Didn't I? I'm taking Guthrie Featherstone. It's a secret romance. We've been passionately in love for years, Guthrie and I.'

'Rumpole, I don't know why you deliberately say things you know will annoy me. Also, it's not in the least degree funny!'

'I thought it was a *little* funny.'

'This is a letter from Lucy Loman.' This time Hilda showed me a pale green envelope.

'Is it really? I thought it was your pools.'

'Do stop being silly, Rumpole! I was at school with "Lanky" Loman!' As I wondered if there were anyone that Hilda *hadn't* been at school with, she went on, 'She tells me her daughter Tessa has just divorced a bankrupt garage proprietor with a foul temper and a taste for whisky.'

'Sounds a reasonable thing to do.'

'The problem is that Tessa has remarried.'

'Has she indeed?'

'Yes. A bankrupt ex-launderette owner with a much worse temper and a taste for gin.'

'So there's been no real change?'

'No. People don't change, do they?'

I was beginning to find She Who Must Be Obeyed unusually depressing that morning, when she went on thoughtfully,

'When they change partners, they always go for the same again, only slightly worse.'

Was there some similar, but even more ferocious version of She waiting to entrap me the second time around? The thought was too terrible to contemplate. I prepared to take self and brief off to Liverpool Street. On my way out, I said,

'Well, if you're going to change husbands while I'm gone . . .'

'Please don't be silly, Rumpole. I've had to tell you that once already. I'm quite prepared to make do with you, provided you're a good deal thinner.'

Make do for the rest of our natural lives, I thought. Matrimony and murder both carry a mandatory life sentence.

In the train from Liverpool Street Featherstone looked at me in a docile and trusting manner, as though he were depending on his learned junior to get him and his client out of trouble.

'I suppose you've read the birdwatcher's evidence?' he started gloomily.

'Mr "Nosey-Parker" Spong? Saw the whole thing through a pair of strong opera-glasses? Yes, I've read it.'

'Odd he never went to the police straight away.'

'The whole timetable's odd. The police and the insurance company accept her story of an accident. Colossus Mercantile pays out, she collects her two hundred thousand, calls herself a widow, marries Mr Jason, a retired accountant, buys a small house in Cricklewood and then . . .'

'The long-lost brother turns up from New Zealand.'

'Mr Chad Bateman. Hungry for his brother's estate which our client won't get if she's a murderess. So he disputes the insurance payment and starts inquiries. Advertises for the long-lost birdwatcher and puts together a case.'

'Puts together far too good a case for my liking.'

A silence fell between us, and somewhere in East Anglia I said, 'Featherstone?'

'Yes, Horace?'

'I get the feeling sometimes that you don't like me very much.'

'Now, whatever could have given you that idea?' My learned leader looked pained.

'We don't see eye to eye always on the running of Chambers. I find your cross-examination feeble and your politics anaemic and I don't mind saying so. I do ask you, however, to win this case. If you don't I may be in for a very rough time indeed from She Who Must Be Obeyed. She doesn't like having her old school chums convicted of murder.'

'You've got to help me, Horace.' The man looked positively desperate, so I gave my learned leader the benefit of a full account of my conversation with the habitués of the Crab and Lobster on the day I broke into my diet. When I had finished, Featherstone didn't look any more cheerful.

'Does that tell us anything?'

'Oh yes. Three things to be precise.'

'What on earth?'

'That the Batemans never had a cross word. That Jackie's second husband doesn't like visitors and that Barney Bateman won the regatta five times.'

'I don't see how that helps.'

'You're right. It doesn't help at all.'

'Now who's being depressing, Horace?'

'I know,' I told him perfectly frankly. 'I find the whole business very depressing indeed.'

In due course, I found myself sitting in the ancient, panelled Norfolk courtroom, in a place of importance behind my undecided leader, with a jury of solid East Anglian citizens and old Piers Craxton, a reasonably polite Judge, sent to try us. Our opponent was a jovial local silk named Gerald Gaunt who, being for the prosecution and with a strongish case, looked a great deal less gloomy than the nervous artificial silk in front of me. The witness-box was occupied by a figure familiar to me from my visit to Shenstone, the birdwatcher whom I had last seen surveying the North Sea with a pair of strong field-glasses. Without his Balaclava helmet, he looked older and slightly less dotty than when I had first seen him.

'Your name is Henry Arthur Spong?' Gaunt asked the ornithologist in the witness-box.

'Yes it is.'

'Do you remember being out very early one morning in July two years ago?'

'Tell him not to bloody well lead!' I whispered in a vain attempt to keep my learned leader on his toes.

'Ssh, Rumpole. I don't like to interrupt. It creates a bad impression.' Featherstone sounded deeply embarrassed.

'Creates a damn sight worse impression to let him lead the witness.'

'I remember it clearly. It was quite light at six a.m. and the date was July the sixth.' Mr Spong intruded on our private dialogue.

'How can he remember that?' I whispered to Guthrie Featherstone, and Mr Spong supplied the answer.

'I wrote a note in my diary. I saw a number of kittiwake and gannets and I thought I saw a Mediterranean shearwater. I have all that noted down in my birdwatcher's diary. I was looking out to sea through a pair of powerful field-glasses.'

'Did you happen to spot a boat?' Gaunt asked and I prodded Featherstone again.

'Don't let him lead!'

'Please, Rumpole! Leave it to me.'

'Mr Spong. Out of deference to my learned friend's learned junior, I will frame the question in a non-leading form.' Gerald Gaunt raised a titter in Court. 'Did you see anything unusual?'

'Yes.' Spong clearly knew what he was being asked about. 'I saw a boat.'

'Surprise, surprise!' I whispered to Featherstone, who tried not to hear me.

'I noticed it because . . .'

'Yes. Tell us why you noticed it.' Gaunt encouraged the birdwatcher.

'There were two people standing up in it. One, I thought, was a man. He had a red beard. The other was a woman.'

'What did they appear to be doing?'

'I would say, struggling together. I couldn't see all that clearly.'

'And then?'

'Then the man seemed to fall from the side of the boat.' Gaunt, as any good barrister would, allowed a substantial pause for that to sink in, and then he asked,

'Tell me, Mr Spong. Was there any wind at the time?'

'No wind at all. No. It had been gusty a little earlier, but at the time the man fell from the boat it was perfectly calm.' It wasn't a helpful answer, being clean contrary to our client's instructions.

'And after he fell?'

'The woman waited for about five minutes.'

'She didn't dive in after him?'

'No.'

I saw the Judge make a note and the jury looked at the woman in the dock with no particular sympathy.

'What did she do then?'

'She deliberately upset the boat.'

During Gaunt's next and even longer pause, not only the Judge but the reporters were writing hard and the jury looked even less friendly.

'What do you mean by that, exactly?'

'She stood on the side and then swung herself out, pulling on the side ropes. She seemed to me to capsize the boat deliberately.'

'And after it had capsized?'

'She went into the water, of course. Then I saw her clinging to the boat.'

'What did you do?'

'Well, I thought she might be in some danger, so I bicycled off to telephone the police.'

'To the harbour?'

'Yes. The harbour office was locked up. It was so early you see. It took me some time to wake anyone in the cottages.'

'Thank you, Mr Spong.'

Gaunt sat down, clearly delighted with his witness and Guthrie Featherstone rose to cross-examine. Tall and distinguished, at least he managed to *look* like a barrister.

'Mr Spong,' he started, in his smoothest voice. 'You knocked up a Mr Newbold in one of the cottages?'

'Yes, I did. I banged on the door, and he put his head out of the window.'

'What did you tell him?'

'I asked him to phone the police and tell them that there was a woman in trouble with a boat.'

'You didn't tell him anything else you'd seen?'

'No, I didn't.'

'And having told Mr Newbold that a woman was in trouble with a boat, you got on your bicycle and rode away?'

'Yes. That is correct.'

Not a bad exchange, for Featherstone. I whispered my instructions to him.

'Leave it there.'

'What?' Guthrie whispered back, turning his head away from the witness.

'Don't give him a chance to explain! Comment on it later, to the jury.'

The trouble with leaders is that they won't take their learned junior's advice. Featherstone couldn't resist trying to gild the lily.

'Why didn't you tell Mr Newbold or the police the whole story? About the struggle in the boat and so on?'

'Well, sir. I thought I saw a Mediterranean shearwater, which would be extremely interesting so far out of its territory. I got on my bike to follow its flight, but when I spotted it later from the cliffs, it was a great shearwater, which is interesting enough.'

I sighed with resignation. From a dedicated birdwatcher, the answer was totally convincing.

'Mr Spong. Did you think sighting shearwaters was more important than a possible murder?' Featherstone asked with care-fully simulated anger and incredulity.

'Yes, of course I did.'

Of course he did. The jury could recognize a man dedicated to his single interest in life.

'In fact, you only came forward when Mr Chad Bateman arrived from New Zealand and advertised for you?'

'That is correct.'

'How much did he get paid?' I whispered the question ferociously to my leader's back.

'Did you get paid for your information?' At least Featherstone obeyed orders, sometimes.

'I was given no money.'

'Thank you, Mr Spong.' My leader folded his silk gown about him and prepared to subside, but I stimulated him into a final question.

'Don't sit down! Ask him what he got apart from money,' I whispered, and my leader uncoiled himself. After a pause which made it look as though he'd thought of the question himself he said,

'Just one thing. Did you get rewarded in any other way?'

'I was offered a holiday in New Zealand,' Spong admitted.

'By the deceased's brother?'

'Yes.'

'Do you intend to take it?'

'Oh yes.' And Spong turned to the jury with a look of radiant honesty. 'There are some extremely interesting birds in New Zealand. But I must make this clear. It hasn't made the slightest difference to my telling the truth in this Court.'

I looked at the jury. I knew one thing beyond reasonable doubt. They believed the birdwatcher.

'Yes, thank you, Mr Spong.' Featherstone was finally able to sit down and turn to me for some whispered reassurance.

'It was a disaster, old darling,' I told him, but admitted, 'not entirely your fault.'

Later, Featherstone had another opportunity to practise the art of cross-examination on the police officer in charge of the case.

'Inspector Salter. The body of Barney Bateman was never

recovered?' he asked. Well, at least it was a safe question, the answer to which was not in dispute.

'No, sir.' The Inspector, who looked as though he enjoyed fishing from his own small boat, had no trouble in agreeing.

'Is that not an unusual factor, in this somewhat unusual case?' Featherstone soldiered on, more or less harmlessly.

'Not really, sir.'

'Why do you say that?'

'There are particularly strong currents off Shenstone, sir. We have warnings put up to swimmers. Unfortunately, there have been many drowning accidents where bodies have never been recovered.'

'Did you say "accidents", Inspector?'

'Oh Featherstone, my old sweetheart. Don't try to be too brilliant,' I whispered, I hoped inaudibly. 'Just plod, Featherstone. It suits your style far better.'

'We have had bodies lost in accidents, yes, sir,' Inspector Salter answered carefully. 'I'm by no means suggesting that *this* was an accident. In fact, the view of the police is that it was deliberate.'

The Judge interrupted mercifully to spare Featherstone embarrassment.

'Yes. Thank you, Inspector Salter. I'm sure we all understand what the police are suggesting here.'

'If your Lordship pleases.' There was another rustle of silk as Featherstone sat. I had warned him. He should plod, just plod, and never attempt brilliance.

During the luncheon break we went to see our client in the cells.

'Mrs Jason. I'm sure it's a nerve-racking business, giving evidence on a charge of murder.' Featherstone was doing his best to prepare our client for the ordeal to come. But Jackie gave him a far too cheerful smile.

'I've been in cross-Channel races with Barney. And round Land's End in a force-nine gale which took away our mast in the pitch dark. I don't see that Mr Gaunt's questions are going to frighten me.'

'There's just one thing.' I thought I ought to insert a word of warning. 'I think the jury are going to believe the birdwatcher. It would be nice if we didn't have to quarrel with too much of his evidence.'

'What do you mean, it would be nice?' Jackie looked at me impatiently. 'That man Spong was talking absolute nonsense.'

'Well, for instance, he said that you were standing up in the boat together? Now, what could you have been doing – other than fighting, of course?'

'I don't know.' Jackie frowned. 'What could we have been doing?'

'Well, perhaps,' I made a suggestion, 'kissing each other good-bye?'

'That's ridiculous! Why on earth did you say that? Anyway,' she looked at Featherstone, 'who'll be asking me the questions in Court?'

'I shall, Mrs Jason,' he reassured her, 'as your leading counsel. Mr Rumpole won't be asking you any questions at all.'

Our client looked as if the news came to her as a considerable relief. Featherstone's questions would be like a gentle following breeze, and Rumpole's awkward voice would not ˙ heard. However, I had to warn her, and said,

'Gerald Gaunt's going to ask you some questions for the prosecution as well. You should be prepared for that, otherwise they're going to strike you like a force-nine gale amidships.'

'Don't worry, Mrs Jason.' Featherstone poured his well-oiled voice on the choppy waters of our conference. 'I'm sure you'll be more than a match for the prosecuting counsel. Now, let's go through your proof again, shall we?'

In the course of time, Featherstone steered Jackie through her examination in chief, more or less smoothly. At least he managed to avoid the hidden rocks and shallows, but more by ignoring their existence and hoping for the best than by expert navigation. Finally, he had to sit down and leave her unprotected and without an anchor, to the mercy of such winds as might be drummed up by the cross-examination of our learned friend, Mr Gerald Gaunt, Q.C., who rose, and started off with a gentle courtesy whicl was deceptive.

'Mrs Jason. Your husband was a swimmer?'

'Barney could swim, yes. The point was,' Jackie answered confidently, 'we were too far out to swim ashore.'

'Oh, I quite agree,' Gaunt smiled at her. 'And he always said, didn't he, that it was far safer to cling to the wreckage and wait to be picked up than attempt a long and exhausting swim against the current?'

'Any experienced sailor would tell you that.' Jackie spoke to him as to a novice yachtsman.

'And that's exactly what *you* did?'

'Yes,' Jackie admitted.

'Why didn't your husband?'

'As I told you. He must have been stunned by the boom as we went about.'

Gaunt nodded and then produced a document from his pile of papers.

'I have here the account which you gave to the insurance company at the time. You said "the accident took place between the eighth and ninth marker buoys of the regatta course".'

'Yes.'

'Halfway between?'

'About that.'

'With the wind from the quarter it was on that morning, you could have sailed between those two points without going about at all, could you not?'

The healthy-looking woman in the witness-box seemed somewhat taken aback by his expertise. After a small hesitation she said,

'Perhaps we could.'

'Then why didn't you?' Gaunt was no longer smiling.

'Perhaps we're not all as clever as you, Mr Gaunt. Perhaps Barney made a mistake.'

'Made a mistake?' Gaunt looked extravagantly puzzled. 'On a course where he'd raced and won five times?'

Jackie Jason was proving to be the worst kind of witness. She was over-emphatic, touchy and had treated the question as an insult. I could see the jury starting to lose faith in her defence.

'Anyway, you've never been out from Shenstone on the regatta course.' She raised her voice, making matters a good deal worse. 'I don't know what you know about it, Mr Gaunt!'

'Mrs Jason!' the Judge warned her. 'Just confine yourself to answering the questions. Mr Gaunt is merely doing his duty with his usual ability.'

'Mrs Jason.' Gaunt was quiet and courteous again. 'Did you tell your husband you'd taken out this large life insurance?'

The jury were looking hard at my client, as she did her best to avoid the question.

'I didn't tell him the exact amount. I ran our business affairs.'

'Which were in a terrible mess, weren't they?'

'Not terrible, no.' She answered cautiously, and our opponent fished out another devastating document.

'I have here the certified accounts for the shop Father Neptune's Boutique which you ran in Shenstone. Had a petition in bankruptcy been filed by one of your suppliers?'

'You seem to know all about it.' Again, the answer sounded angry and defensive.

'Oh yes, I do.' Gaunt assured her, cheerfully. 'And were the mortgage repayments considerably overdue on your cottage at Shenstone-on-Sea?'

'We only needed a bit of luck to pay off our debts.'

'And the "bit of luck" was your husband's death, wasn't it?'

It was a cruel question, but I knew her answer chilled the hearts of the jury. It came coldly, and after a long pause.

'I suppose it came at the right moment, from the business point of view.'

'I thought that she stood up to that reasonably well.'

Featherstone and I were removing the fancy dress in the local robing room and he turned to me, once again, for a reassurance that I failed to give.

'It was a disaster,' I said. 'Can't wait to chat. I'm off to London.'

'London?' Featherstone looked perplexed. 'We could have had dinner together and discussed my final speech.'

'Before your final speech, we ought to discuss whom we're going to call as a witness.'

'Witness? Have we got a witness?'

But I was on my way to the door.

'See you here in the morning. We'll talk about our witness.'

i left my puzzled leader and caught an Inter City train. I sat munching an illicit tea-cake as a railway guard, pretending to be an air hostess, came over the intercom, and announced that we were due on the ground at Liverpool Street approximately twenty minutes late, and apologized for the delay. (I waited to be told to fasten my seat belt because of a spot of turbulence around Bishop's Stortford.) What I was doing was strictly unprofessional. We legal hacks are not supposed to chatter to witnesses in criminal matters, and Featherstone would have been deeply pained if he had known where I was going. And yet I was on a quest for the truth and justice for Jackie, although she, also, would not have thought my journey really necessary. We arrived at Liverpool Street station after half an hour's delay (Please collect all your hand baggage and thank you for flying British Rail), and I persuaded a taxi to take me to Cricklewood.

When we stopped at the anonymous suburban house, I was glad to see a light on in a downstairs room. Freddy Jason came to the door when I rang the electric chime. He was wearing an old sweater and a pair of bedroom slippers. He led me into a room where a television set was booming, and I noticed a tray decorated with the remains of a pork pie, French bread and cheese, and a couple of bottles of Guinness.

'Aren't you afraid,' I asked him, 'of putting on weight?'

'I told you. I don't.' He clicked the television set into silence.

'How long can you keep it up, I wonder?'

'Keep what up?'

'Being a thin person.'

He looked at me, the skinny, mousy ex-accountant and said, with real anxiety,

'How's the trial going? Jackie won't let me near the place. Is it going well?' He had a dry, impersonal voice like the click of a computer adding up an overdraft.

'It's going down the drain.'

He sat down then. He seemed exhausted.

'I warned her,' he said. 'I was afraid of that. What can I do?'

'Do? Come and give evidence for her!'

'I don't know.' Jason looked at me helplessly. 'What can I say? I didn't get to know Jackie until after Barney's accident. I don't think I'd be much help in the witness-box, do you?'

'It depends,' I said, 'on what you mean by help.'

'Well. Does Jackie want me to come?'

'Jackie doesn't know I'm asking you.'

'Well, then. I can't help.'

'Listen,' I said. 'Do you want your wife to do a life sentence in Holloway? *For a murder she didn't commit?*'

He looked deeply unhappy. A thin man who had become, however unwillingly, involved in a fat man's death.

'No,' he said. 'I don't want that.'

'Then you'd better come back on the Inter City to Norfolk. You might as well finish off your supper. I mean, you don't have to worry, do you? About your weight.'

When I got to the Court the next morning I found Featherstone and Mr Tonkin anxiously pacing the hall. I gave them what comfort I could.

'Cheer up, old darlings. Things may not be as bad as you think. Her husband's here. He'll have to give evidence.'

'Freddy Jason?' Tonkin frowned.

'What on earth can *he* do for us?' Featherstone asked.

'Well, he certainly can't make things any worse. He can say he didn't get to know Jackie until after the accident. At least we can scotch the idea that she pushed Barney out to marry another man.'

'I suppose he could say that.' Mr Tonkin sounded doubtful. 'You think we need this evidence, Mr Rumpole?'

'Oh yes. I'm sure we need it.' I turned to my leader. 'Featherstone. I have a certain experience in this profession. I did win the Penge Bungalow Murders alone and without a leader.'

'So you're fond of telling me.'

'In any case, the junior is accorded the privilege of calling at least one witness in a serious case, with the permission of his learned leader, of course.'

'*You* want to call Jason?' In fact, Featherstone sounded extremely grateful. If the witness turned out a disaster, at least I should get the blame.

'Would you leave him to me?' I asked politely.

'All right, Rumpole. You call him. If you think it'll do the slightest good. At least you won't be whispering instructions to me the whole time.'

When the Court had reassembled, and the Judge had been settled down on his seat, found his place in his notebook, been given a sharp, new pencil and put on his glasses, he looked at my leader encouragingly and said,

'Yes, Mr Featherstone.'

'My Lord,' Featherstone said with a good deal of detachment, 'my learned junior, Mr Rumpole, will call the next witness.'

'Yes, Mr Rumpole?' His Lordship switched his attention to my humble self.

For the first and last time in the Shenstone-on-Sea murder trial, I staggered to my feet. The calm woman in the dock gave me a little smile of welcome.

'Yes, my Lord,' I said. 'I will call the next witness. Call Frederick Jason.'

'No!' Jackie was no longer smiling. As the usher went out to fetch her husband I whispered to Tonkin to keep our client quiet and tell her that the evidence I was about to call was vital to her case. In fact, it was one of those rare defences which depended on nothing less than the truth.

Tonkin was busy whispering to the lady in the dock when her pale and nervous second husband was brought into the Court and climbed into the witness-box. He took the oath very quietly.

'I swear to God that the evidence I shall give shall be the truth, the whole truth and nothing but the truth.'

It was then that I asked the question which I had been waiting to put throughout the trial.

'Is your name Barney Bateman?'

The reactions were varied. The Judge looked shocked. Showing some tolerance towards an ageing junior who was undoubtedly past it, he said,

'Haven't you made a mistake, Mr Rumpole?'

Featherstone felt it was his turn to whisper disapproving instructions and said,

'*Jason*, Rumpole. His name's Jason.'

My client remained silent. I asked the question again.

'I repeat. Is your name Barney Bateman?' Then the witness

looked, for the first time, at the prisoner with a sort of apology. She seemed, suddenly, much older and too tired to protest. I reflected that there is a strange thing about taking the oath, it sometimes makes people tell the truth. Anyway, we had at least found the corpse in the Shenstone murder. It was now speaking, with increasing liveliness, to the learned Judge.

'My Lord,' the witness said, 'you can't go on trying Jackie for murder. I'm still alive, you see.' He smiled then, and I got a hint of the old Barney Bateman. 'Still alive and living in Cricklewood.'

It took another couple of days, of course, for the whole story to be told and for the good citizens of East Anglia to find Jackie Bateman (as she always was) not guilty of the murder with which she had been charged. Featherstone and I were eventually released and sat opposite each other in the British Rail tea car. My leader looked at me with a contented smile.

'Well, Horace,' he said. 'I think that can be notched up among my successes.'

'Oh yes, Guthrie,' I agreed. 'Many congratulations.'

'Thanks. Of course one depends a good deal on one's learned junior. Two heads are better than one, Horace. That's what I always say.'

'Three heads. Don't forget Hilda's.'

'Your wife's, Horace?'

'You can't fool She Who Must Be Obeyed,' I said. 'She told me that people don't change, they keep on marrying the same husband. Jackie Bateman did exactly that.'

It was quite a touching story, really. I was right about what they were doing when the birdwatcher spotted them. Not fighting, of course, but kissing each other goodbye. It was only to be a temporary parting. Barney was to swim ashore, to some quiet little bit of beach. Then he shaved off his beard, went on a diet, dyed his hair and waited for his loving wife to collect the boodle. The murder trial was a nasty gust of wind, but she thought she'd sail through it. He knew she wasn't going to. So he *had* to tell the truth.

'They'll charge her with the insurance swindle,' my leader reminded me.

'Oh, I'm afraid they will,' I said, biting into another tea-cake. 'I think I'll do that case, Featherstone, if you don't mind – alone and without a leader.'

That night, still grateful to Hilda, I took her out for a celebration dinner at my favourite restaurant in the Strand. She looked at me, somewhat aghast as I placed my order.

'Potted shrimps, I think. With plenty of hot toast. Oh, and steak and kidney pud, potatoes, swedes and Brussels sprouts. After that, we might consider the sweet trolley and I'll have the wine list, please.'

'Rumpole! You *mustn't* eat all that,' said She Who Must Be Obeyed.

'Oh yes I must. You're married to Rumpole, you know. Not some skinny ex-chartered accountant. You're stuck with him and so am I. We can't alter him, can we? Jackie's case proved that. You can't just change people entirely to suit your own convenience.'